THE LAKES OF
SOUTHERN HOLLOW

Also by Steve Yates

The Legend of the Albino Farm: A Novel

Morkan's Quarry: A Novel

Sandy and Wayne: A Novella

Some Kinds of Love: Stories

The Teeth of the Souls: A Novel

THE LAKES OF
SOUTHERN HOLLOW

A novel

Steve Yates

Lake Dallas, Texas

FIRST EDITION

This is a work of fiction, and is not intended to resemble
anyone living or dead.

Requests for permission to reprint or reuse material
from this work should be sent to:

Permissions
Madville Publishing
PO Box 358
Lake Dallas, TX 75065

Cover Design: Jacqueline Davis
Cover Photographer: Steven Spencer
Cover Model: Lexi Miles

ISBN: 978-1-956440-91-1 paperback,
978-1-956440-92-8 ebook

Library of Congress Control Number: 2023952601

This book is for my wife, Tammy, and especially
for my nephew, Will Plunkett IV,
who introduced me to Tyndall,
and as always **OAMDG**.

~ ~ ~

The jogger exits Southern Hollow Subdivision and pounds the trail into Sequiota Park. He's nailing his best pace, and in his earbuds the Australian voice of Reverend Jack Sprague assures him: *When you declare your purpose, by your faith you obligate the Almighty and instantly claim your blessings. Yes or yes?*

He's stopped before he can answer. A foot and calf, glistening slick, juts from the mob of mulberry twigs in front of him. Skin color gray, like a sunless Ozarks rain, that's fentanyl. On the calf, a tattoo of a muscled arm and finger points up the leg. It's needled in a style like a carnival banner—OZARKS written above the tat's forearm; MUSIC written below.

He removes an earbud and listens. No one in front of him. No one behind coming from Southern Hollow. So little traffic on Lone Pine Road, just the mysterious grunts of machinery deep in the Old Morkan Quarry. He can jog away right now.

An abscess craters her thigh. So thin her legs. When has she last craved food in all her dope sickness? Sandy hair, darkened with oil and dew. But the face, round cheekbones, freckles. *Any obstacle to your rich success comes from Satan, the Architect of All Obstacles to Your Wealthy Reward! Yes or yes?* Blue lips. Wide eyes, irises like sapphires, pupils so small, he has to lean in on hands and knees to ascertain them.

Recognition kicks him like a Charlie horse in the groin. This is that singer. Behind the Creekside Pub, she had lofted notes like an angel casting doves. Just weeks ago. And he drunkenly offered her $500 for a blowjob.

Charity is not a Moral Duty. YA GO BE! You Are God's Own Best Expression.

Voices approach from Southern Hollow, runners, women, breathy in conversation.

1

Scrambling, he finds his Blastik and turns the Reverend off. He rips the Velcro that straps his cell to his arm, dials 911, then kneels much closer to turn her wrists. Cold. Pocked. Collapsed veins. No way to tell if she was vaccinated or still contagious.

The runners quiet, slowing to a halt. His morning, his whole month is shot. There's no way he can skip the hospital's quarantine.

"Hey," one of the women says. "Isn't that, like, the Poor Voodoos girl?"

"Oh, my God, from that video," her running partner says. "Wait. She's too tall."

One of the women unstraps a cell phone from her toned arm. "Video does that. They can make you anything now. Tiny, thin, ripped." She begins to film, but he waves this off.

"Respect, please?" he says. "I'm a doctor. Police and paramedics are on the line."

He shows the women joggers his phone and tells them that he found the poor junkie dead. No ID, no vaxx card. They must not approach. But not to worry. He's a doctor, he says again. They need to back off to a safe distance. He has everything under control.

1

Casey Strong steps to the mic and sweeps the neck of her bass at her two pals, Tyndall and Devon, drawing a heart around them at their table out in the crowd. Casey has her mother's sandy hair, piles of it, and she's neglected it, so it's looking like a golden retriever's fur, brassy, dry and rowdy. She has a round face, freckles that Tyndall can see even in the stage lighting. Casey is tiny, shortest in their class and often mistaken for a grade school kid. For Tyndall, Casey Strong affirms that God made us all strangely and wonderfully—there's nothing exceptional about Casey until she opens her mouth and sings. Once that happens, everyone agrees she's bound for something way bigger than Southern Hollow, way bigger than Springfield. Could be Casey, the next Ozark Mountain Daredevil-sized smash hit; or could be Casey, engineer of some legendary trainwreck.

But to Tyndall, that's all vanity of vanities, old people noise. For her, it has ever been, always will be just the three of them—Tyndall to save the lives; Devon to save the planet; Casey to save the music. At their table right up front, Tyndall grips Devon's hand as though he's the one about to escape the L5 of the Ozarks. Casey, Tyndall, and Devon, Southern Hollow kids, Glendale High Falcons, they've torn each other's hair and lied about each other's wounds since kindergarten. It's a Thursday night in September 2019, their senior year. Anything, the worst or the best, seems possible. And Casey's band, New Wave Vultures, packs them in on teen night at the Cedar Shake, a club above a law firm right on the square.

Casey winks at some pierced chub dressed in black who's lowering the mic for her.

"She has stagehands now?" Tyndall leans into Devon not just to be heard over the buzzing crowd, but to get his arm pressed into her chest. His denim shirt releases warm grease against her fingers. Tyndall wants to wear his denim shirt and nothing else, and stride down stone hallways in his parents' house with golden ribbons of light off First Lake swimming the walls. She wants to walk right into his arms, into a binding, deep touch.

New Wave Vultures play no originals so far, only rearranged oldies—Squeeze, The Jam, Echo and the Bunnymen. Some of it is older even than their parents' music, yeah, but Casey, she changes everything. They launch into this Go-Go's song with synthesizers and drums. The rush comes the instant Casey starts her hook on the bass. Then she vaults the lyrics while still playing, really driving the whole train. It's girl power dialed to eleven seeing her perform this. That voice, its volume and depth, is better than the original. Devon swoons, and Tyndall may as well be made of vape smoke. Here Tyndall's the one taking all the risks. She's the one who downed three Quietarol because it's the only pill she's ever found that allows her to tolerate all this commotion.

In the club lights, Devon's face—square jaw, blond, straight hair—glows like a beatitude. She would give anything to be the ecstasy stoking his bliss. That medical fact takes her breath away. Why is she meant to feel like this about someone she can't have all to herself? An achy chemistry binds her to him. It's like a wicked compound glowing from some phial she's spilled at the hospital, a stain weighing down her scrubs, soaking through her skin, permeating her system just from the touch of him. Spice victims on gurneys roll their eyes and squirm while the trash they've smoked crushes their veins and starves their hearts. That's her with Devon in her bloodstream.

New Wave Vultures have the Cedar Shake grooving.

Tyndall leans closer to him. "Dance with me," she insists. "Right now." He doesn't budge.

"Wait," he shouts over the music. She jerks his hand so hard there's a pop. He glares at her. "After this next part. Okay?"

At the bridge, the stage lights drop to a circle around Casey, and her voice reaches way up, pleading. Even Tyndall feels hushed and consoled as if Casey really were some darling angel. The groove resumes, and Devon surges to the dance floor but loses her hand. In a bolt she hops in front of him and lodges her back against him. He is the only boy ever to understand: When they dance, he must stand behind her and wrap his arms around her tightly and mash her forearms against her stomach. They sway, skipping every other beat. Tonight, flooded with the contentment that the Quietarol forces through her, she pushes it and wraps his arms snug to her stomach, and grips him, though his forearms feel like emery boards rubbing against her abdomen. Kids from other schools side-eye them—*They dance backwards! Like zombies! Weirdos!*—but the Glendale kids know. That's just Tyndall. And that's Devon. Grew up together. Southern Hollow. They live on First Lake, the one that's gray and gooey and all creepy with brain-eating amoeba.

In a pause between songs, Tyndall swings his hand in hers. She loves holding hands—she held her brother Ben's hand all the time in those weeks before he died—but looking even Devon in the eye let alone kissing him... that would take a whole bottle of Quietarol. She's so hungry right now on just three capsules, she could eat a bakery.

Something jolts the crowd, such a stir that Devon tenses. Tyndall drops out of the moment and into emergency-room mode. How many times has she imagined this tension and then the gunfire erupting like Aurora or Parkland?

From the back strides Patrick Turin, and he's dressed like some cowboy vampire. He's applauding, eyes glazed.

Tyndall grabs Devon's face and dares to get eye to eye

with him. "Don't you fight him. No one wins fighting Patrick Turin."

Casey and the Vultures huddle around the drummer. The guitar player casts a vicious stare at Patrick Turin, once a bandmate. Turin is still applauding, but slowly. A wake opens around him.

"Why does he clap like that?" Tyndall asks loud enough for others to hear.

Devon brushes her ear with his lips, and she swerves away. He holds up a finger, their signal for her to focus. "He's an asshole," Devon says.

"'Heaven'," Casey announces, sticking her tongue out at Turin, who used to sing this song. She hooks the bass on a stand and straps on her acoustic. She says into the mic: "We're gonna slow this down. Saddle up, kiddies! It's a country song!"

What comes out of her next, someone should be recording this on something way better than a cell phone. It is hard to imagine. The whole place stills, and Casey is no longer any girl they ever knew. She's no longer the girl who jeered with them at numbing safety drills, who slept on Devon's shoulder in Ms. Lines' biology, who taught Tyndall piano scales. Even Turin is spellbound. If anyone is dancing, it's close, slow dancing, and it's only the truest of loves.

Tyndall mashes her forehead against Devon's collarbone, adrenaline flushing from her in a cold chill. She can't melt down, not here, not now. No one is going to get shot. *Breathe.* No rain of automatic rifle fire. *Breathe.* The world will not end here tonight at the Cedar Shake. No death-plea video on TikTok. *Breathe.* No one is going to die. She holds her finger up to Devon, but he's already looking right at her. He is the best neurotypical she will ever meet, so adept, so adaptable. She whirls and wrenches his arms around her. "Dance," she commands. "Listen to Casey. Hold me way tighter."

2

Like most kids in Southern Hollow, Devon knew of Patrick Turin before he ever met him—Patrick Turin, the kid so violent a military school expelled him; the kid so dreaded, people in the neighborhood used both his first and last name. The Turins, Italians and rumored still to be Catholic, kept their yard mowed and edged and always paid their dues at Southern Hollow Swim Club, where every Saturday the mother and father oiled their bodies and roasted in the summer sun. Patrick Turin needed to be distinguished from them, like a named winter storm.

Devon was twelve and running around First Lake with the Correy kids when they saw a taller boy wearing a bandana tied over his head. He was fishing at the spillway on First Lake, a bucket beside him. The taller boy reached in the bucket, then hurled a fish in an arc over the spillway. Curving as it tumbled, the bluegill landed with a scratchy smack and then skidded, stiff, stunned, and dying down the trickling, algae-browned concrete. One of the Correy kids pulled out her phone and started filming.

Devon approached with his fists clenched. "What the hell?"

Already the taller boy had littered the spillway with corpses, shattered silver scales, trails of blood red. Patrick Turin gave Devon a dull glance, then plucked another bluegill from his white bucket. "Fly. Be Free!" he hollered and heaved the fish upward.

Devon rushed him, planting a shoulder in his gut. They rolled in a flailing ball down the shoreline and into First Lake. Screaming, the Correy girls scrambled, one to call their father, the other to keep filming the fracas with her phone. Luckily a pickup truck stopped on Southern Hollow Boulevard, and two off-duty firemen leapt out. The firemen saved Devon from being drowned only by knocking the Turin kid out cold. At the emergency room, one of the firemen presented a broken wrist and hand, the other a broken rib and a ruptured kidney. Turin's father, a fat, balding lawyer with an unlit cigar stuck in his mouth, appeared at the hospital. Once he learned there was cell phone video, he did and said amazing things. Medical bills evaporated. The firemen each got new pickup trucks. Thereafter Devon's father had Giacomo Turin by his side in endless hearings about First Lake's deterioration. And Patrick Turin roamed free.

Repeating grades and falling behind, Patrick Turin might never have touched their circle again. But to everyone's surprise, he tried out for a high school musical when Casey was a junior. The two of them harmonized on a number that shivered the auditions. Though he refused to read music, if you played or sang a song for him once, Patrick Turin could sing it back in an alluring, rugged baritone and never miss a note. Given almost any melody, he improvised its harmonies without instruction. He won the lead for *Oklahoma*.

He came late to rehearsals with black-ringed, scorched eyes, with stitches once, always reeking of cigarettes. None of the students expected Patrick Turin to show on opening night. But he strode on stage in chaps and a white shirt and leather vest, red bandanna at his neck, and they killed every number. That night after the premiere, he was suspended for beating the tar out of his understudy and the kids who played Jud and Aunt Eller. He never darkened the theatre room again.

His first band, Three Bags Full, used Mitch on drums and Dwayne on guitar, so two of Casey's New Wave Vultures. The night after Three Bags Full headlined at a hipster brew pub downtown, Patrick Turin decked his father and ran away from home. That winter he turned up in Nashville, cut a solo album on vinyl, and was featured mainstage at Telluride. In a YouTube video, just him banging a strange acoustic guitar like something from a Django Reinhart photograph, he sings his song about Sofia, Bulgaria, and a castle, and vampire rag dolls raining down from mountain clouds. Sixteen million views. Now he shows up at the Thursday night show at the Cedar Shake and stares at Casey and broods alone, the vampire cowboy slouched at his corner table, flipping a bird at anyone who approaches.

3

Backstage after the Thursday show, Patrick Turin enters their narrow dressing room. Most of the equipment is stowed, and New Wave Vultures are waiting on the manager of the Cedar Shake to come lie about the take at the door. A yeasty smell from the brewery in the adjoining building makes the dingy dressing room even closer and grosser. Who knows what this room used to be? In part of it, even Casey has to duck. There's hardly any privacy to the dressing space, which is back behind low pipes and amounts to just a ragged crimson and gold stage curtain dropped between two folding partitions.

Patrick Turin hooks a finger in the curtain's tear and wags the fabric. Dwayne and Mitch step up to him and cross their arms on their chests. "As if," Turin snaps.

"Who let you back here?" Mitch is way too small for this. But he's a Cataldo, from the Northside. He's like some squirt from *Jersey Boys* with his black hair, pale skin, brown eyes, and his cardigans.

Patrick Turin looks only at Casey, who chews her thumbnail and returns his stare. This curly red hair of his, and his height and ginger skin—he looks more Irish than Italian. Why are the most handsome people sometimes the most reckless? But then to Casey it has never seemed fair how looks are doled out. Think of Tyndall, who has a gorgeous, strong body, biceps, triceps, and hair like honey, amazing when she washes and dries it. But more often she'll look like some kid from a church bus crash who's been found in the woods after a week, dazed, no makeup. Jesus already burns her for a sunbeam.

"What do you want?" Casey asks, and spits skin on the floor.

"You," Turin answers.

"We're a band," Casey says. "And you're not in it." And talent. It's not any fair how that's granted either. Dwayne told her that as soon as Patrick Turin figured out how to play guitar right-handed, the thug taught himself how to play left handed to "challenge himself." And he did so while pedaling a bike down Jefferson Street in traffic. "You should leave."

"Your voice deserves a lot more than old cover songs."

"That's the longest complete sentence you've ever drooled," Mitch says. Dwayne drops his hands to his sides and stands like a hockey player ready to go.

Patrick Turin hardens, and to Casey and the boys his face becomes a snarling mask, just like in his YouTube video for his one big song, "Sofia Castle." "I write songs," he says. "Full of sorrow and waste in abandoned places."

"Deep. Real deep," Mitch sneers.

"You'll never make it out of Springfield with these choades."

Maybe she shouldn't say this. But when your dad is a cop, and is murdered by tweakers when you're thirteen, you've been thrown a grief hammer. Wield it and live, or get smashed. "Patrick Turin, you ain't seen sorrow till you seen a police widow try to climb in her dead husband's coffin." That usually shuts everyone right up.

"There's exactly why I want you. Authentic loss. My songs need your voice. Ditch these turds."

Casey stops for a moment, and the narrow dressing room tilts as if she's trapped in a chute going down. Recovering, she looks at Dwayne, then nudges her chin at the door.

"Okay, Felonious." Dwayne bumps Turin's chest. Mitch takes up his wing. "Out."

Smiling, Patrick Turin backs away watching Casey until he reaches the door. Once he's gone, Dwayne shakes, and Mitch paces.

"I hate that guy," Mitch says, throwing his hands in the air. His neck and cheeks go red in bolts. "I wish I were fricking ten feet tall and three hundred pounds!"

Casey strokes Dwayne's arm. "Settle down and write a song about it, Mitch. You did great. He's gone, right?"

There's a knock and the manager of the Cedar Shake comes in, cash in his hand. "Holy hell! That was Patrick Turin, right? Y'all know him? Is he playing anywhere?"

4

Tyndall meets Devon at The Friary, a derelict gazebo on Welsh's Hill above First Lake. "Are you going to be too tired?" she asks. Early Saturday morning, he volunteered at the Conservation Commission and then worked the afternoon for his Dad's company, Merritt Organics. Now in the twilight, she can't tell a thing about how he really feels, with that Merritt Organics ballcap spoiling his blond hair and hiding his eyes. WE SMOKE WEEDS is embroidered along the side of the cap—no help there.

"Nah, it's fine. Happy to help. So... this is therapy? Like... how?"

If she tells him how, then she is shepherding, and Dr. Durian, her psych, says that's almost as bad as dominating the conversation with yourself, yourself, yourself.

"That plumber who came Friday for the septic tank, I told him about my progress, and he said that Dr. Durian is one of 'The People Behind Everything.' Have you ever heard that? Who would those people be? How many people would that take?"

He's still for such a long time, it makes her heart swell. Any other neurotypical guy would spout off and demean her fears. He listens and watches. He watches her.

"I thought plumbers were behind everything." He brushes off a bench for her, but that's a waste, so much moss. He remembered the towel and puts it down so she can sit.

Moonlight makes the purple water flash. He removes his hat and hooks it to a belt loop. He's careful, fit, not itty bitty

13

like Casey, but close. She could lift him over her head probably. She fights the urge. "Inappropriate," she can hear Dr. Durian warn.

"So." He pops his hands on his knees, twice. "How do we do this?"

She grits her teeth. How can she not shepherd? "Talk about the lake!"

Long pause. "Kidding, right?"

"I am Tyndall Hastings. You know I don't kid. Ever." This is failure. That was about herself. She's going to fail. She straightens her arms and clenches her fists.

He nods. She can feel him watching her though she cannot look him in the eyes.

"You asked for it. First Lake's a spring lake. No stream flowing in, but one flowing out," he begins. "Bronson and Gauldy, your Dad, and that old pissant Fisher wouldn't let City Utilities run sewer lines. Septic tanks leak. Plumbers have to come when they back up. So no matter how hard or what we try…" He trails off when he is tired, but she needs to keep him going. These are socio-normative victory points, Dr. Durian says. She's supposed to keep a timer on how long she allows someone to talk about whatever they want to yap about, but she figures a timer, even on her phone, that's awkward. Father calls Dr. Durian a Godless, West Coast elite nutjob. And now, worse, he's also one of The People Behind Everything.

"A spring isn't a stream?" she asks and dares to move closer. His hair smells bitter as husked black walnuts when his head has been under a ball cap all day.

"More? Okay. Well, the spring is groundwater with force under it, but no surface water added to it. It can pass through contaminants underground. A stream, though, is moving groundwater exposed, with surface water, the runoff adding to it. A lake's not a pool of trapped water rained in from above. It's a moment when groundwater is exposed."

"Like a wound?" she asks. "Veins under your skin only

look blue, not because your blood is going back to the heart deoxygenated. But because of how dark the blood is and how light plays on the skin. When you expose blood in a wound, the oxygen accepts the electrons in the hemoglobin's iron. It's like a fire, and turns the blood red. The iron is on fire." There, Dr. Durian. Was that about Tyndall Hastings or Devon Merritt? Or was it about Tyndall Merritt with Devon Hastings? Her heart churns. She's winning.

His eyes travel the bruise of the lake, and in them there are sparks of the silver moonlight and the orange of the gaslights from big houses on the opposite shore. "Tyndall. You take everything too far."

That scorches like fire down her veins, right through her heart, burning everywhere. The insides of her arms ache with it. Why him, Lord? He doesn't ever go to church. Her parents think his father is a tree-humping madman. She's volunteered the whole day at Saint Martin's Hospital, hours beyond her ILE Shadowing. She's witnessed all kinds of excitement today—an emergency appendectomy, the last breaths of an abandoned, ancient woman who wouldn't let go of her hand. That's her Saturday. She doesn't have to take this from him. Yet every second of him choosing to be with her thrills her, even when he hurts her.

It's very hard to understand whether a neurotypical means to harm you or just happens to damage you out of an inability to focus. There are almost no good reasons to change a subject before the heart of that topic has been fully vivisected. But, Tyndall has learned, pain marks a valid signal to put down a suture. "Do you still love Casey Strong?"

His shoulders slump. Big question, and he lets it swirl around in the air. "Do you think she's even going to be here in a year?" he asks. "If she makes it big?"

Casey making it and leaving them behind, that could be real. Casey's people have lived in Southern Hollow since Casey's grandfather stalked and arrested Ether Eddie in the 1980s. Tyndall knows how rare it is for three kids to have lived in one neighborhood for so long. Maybe that only ever happens here in the Ozarks anymore? Still, ten percent of kids at Glendale High are designated homeless, though her parents insist that's Fake News. Casey leaving them, that isn't just Dark Devon. Casey Strong could blow up famous any minute.

Dodging the Casey subject, Devon tells her that each lake has a specific retention time, a measure of how long it takes a single drop of water to enter then exit. It takes 191 years for a drop of water to enter and exit Lake Superior. In parts of Table Rock Lake, it might take just one or two days. So, Tyndall thinks, growing weary of all his water stuff, it takes seventeen years for Casey Strong to enter and pass through the Lakes of Southern Hollow. Tyndall held that woman's hand today, a ninety-year-old who had fallen down a ravine on her farm out in the hills. No one in the world came to help her die. Beneath her cold, slack skin, Tyndall could feel bones like warm stones. "Devon. See how you are like me? Sometimes you know so much, you don't understand what's in front of you."

He pulls away from her, turns to the lake.

Why hide from this? Can he not feel the Lord crashing over the water like thunder to demand they be together? She will win. Her faith tells the Lord she cannot fail. She runs a hand up his thigh and holds it there until he turns his beautiful face back to her.

5

Casey asks to go to church Sunday with Tyndall. She knows this excites Tyndall's parents, Marion and Nora, because maybe Jesus will finally call Casey Strong and save the poor girl. It also means she and Tyndall can go to lunch on Marion's credit card, unchaperoned in the afterglow of this near conversion. Tyndall warns her this is not Oak Creek but a different church, a satellite of Reverend Jack Sprague's Worldwide Victory Faith Triumphant.

In the car, everything starts as scripted. There's never, thank God, any mention of Ben, Tyndall's brother, dead of a heroin overdose. "Died after a long illness," the obituary read. There is, though, the "Your father was such a good man" moment from Marion. That's her cue. A story you're supposed to tell is like a song that everyone knows, and yet everyone needs. Casey recounts how her Dad, Officer Strong, and her grandfather Detective Voss recovered Marion's stolen Lincoln with the family portraits still in the trunk. Nora cries quietly, her index finger poked into a tissue to make a tidy ghost. Early morning sun glows in this huge Lincoln Town Car. Everything shimmers powder blue. Casey smiles at Tyndall, who looks gorgeous, except her face and eyes are as dead as an abandoned mannequin's. An old Led Zeppelin tune starts in Casey's head, a lonely pedal steel and the bit about parents forbidding kids to play with each other. The open tuning, the bright twelve strings lift her heart and roll through her like a rising roadway over green hills.

Tyndall has washed, dried, and brushed her hair, and it tumbles in gold down her shoulders. When she is not in scrubs for her ILE Shadowing at Saint Martin's, she wears dark blue jeans without any tears or dings and always a cable-knit sweater with the sleeves rolled up in two donuts whether it's hot or cold—navy, black, gray, brown, then cream—in undeviating rotation. Marion and Nora appear so prim, Marion with his silver hair, like thick whorls of frosting, and Nora looking like one of those athletic hostesses on morning TV. The music in Casey's head and the lemon sun off the boxy and battered houses along Bennett Avenue and this charming family converge warmly in her heart. Casey could accept Jesus Christ right here riding in this Lincoln. She could claim Jesus as her Lord and Savior if family were like this—Big Old Dad, Strong Mom, Goofy Geek Sister, all gliding along like a pedal steel's slide on power wound strings. For just a bit, she wants to cry with Nora, hold hands and cry a good, long time together. In the light she notices, for the first time, some of Nora's hairs have turned gray. She reaches across the backseat and rests her fingertips on Tyndall's knuckles. Tyndall, clueless, pushes back with her fist.

This new megachurch that Marion and Nora now attend used to be frequented by the parents of Springfield's most famous actor. Its campus is cleaner, its hallways are brighter, its bathrooms more spectacular, and its sanctuary more brassy and cush than any classroom or auditorium at old cinder block and linoleum Glendale High. A Bible study before everybody meets for worship forces all the high school-age girls into a separate classroom from the boys. The teacher, a lady as fit as an Olympian with biceps and quads shown off in a dress that's too summery, makes a big deal about giving Casey a King James Bible. Suddenly all the girls crowd around and touch Casey's shoulders and back and pray over her. It's really intense but pleasant, like huddling before a championship with a cheer squad. Tyndall, she notices, hangs back. She has this way of looking down at what seems like nothing, but you can tell how she hovers at the edge of a circle and craves to be let in.

The lesson is from Job, and Casey follows for a bit, but then this teacher seems put out with Job for the way he "Negatively Confesses," whatever that means. The pedal steel and twelve-string in Casey's head blessedly drown all this out. She adores Tyndall studying, how she hunches over the Bible as if she were a drummer, counting and pounding and kind of rocking as she reads. The pedal steel changes rhythm to match her gorgeous friend, who has no idea how lovely she is, and wouldn't know what to do if she realized it. Her flesh is as perfect and tight as a new skin on a drum never touched.

All of a sudden Tyndall insists it is God that says He repents in dust and ashes because, well there it is, and the very next words in the Book of Job are "And it was so, that after the Lord had spoken." So it does read like the Lord said that last part, and He sure enough has put Job through a shitstorm. Why not repent? It's terrible what God lets Satan do. But, whoa. All hell breaks loose right here in Sunday school. Casey watches her pal take on the whole class and the teacher. Tyndall's having none of it. She knows what she sees. She reads what she reads. They're getting wilder and angrier as Tyndall gets calmer and more still but louder and more firm. They have no idea, then, of the fits Tyndall can throw. Drill that volcano! Soon some of these girls are hissing about Demons and the need to purge and vomit out spirits, and a few of them are making these crazy chants like Sufis on TikTok and rolling their eyes back in their heads and gawking up at the ceiling. WTF! It's incredible. At last the teacher is threatening that Tyndall cannot return to Bible study until her Demon is purged. Tyndall declares she's delighted to be excused from lunacy and lies. Just before it all blows up, a tone sounds, and a green light shaped like a cross flashes. Time for worship, the teacher shouts, and claps until everyone but Casey and Tyndall shut up and move.

The girls and teacher stride down the crowded hallways, clearly wanting to leave Tyndall far behind. Tyndall's in no hurry and doesn't seem on the outside to be upset. Anyone else would be a wreck. But when Casey brushes her arm, Tyndall grips her hand fiercely. They enter the worship hall that way to a ton of stares. The worship hall is enormous, white and cream and gold everywhere. Casey wishes she had sunglasses on. Marion and Nora are frowning and huddled with the Olympian teacher and some other heavyset man in a dark suit. Nora's face is bright red explaining something until Marion grabs her wrists and stops her. Finally they all sit down. Casey can see from Marion and Nora's uptight postures that this is a crisis. Lunch may be in jeopardy. A statue in a thunderstorm, Tyndall sits oblivious.

So Casey sings all out about Jesus to save lunch. This gets Tyndall's goat, so many faces turning to see where the amazing voice is coming from. It transports Marion and Nora. Marion has to wipe his eyes when Casey sings "Wonderworking Power of Riches like the Rain" with the congregation. What a lovely melody, this song! But the lyrics treat God like a loose slot machine. So weird. This is way not Oak Creek Church. When the call to rise and accept Jesus Christ as your personal Lord and Savior comes, Marion and Nora shiver in hope, and worshippers around them glance at Casey. But she waits in her pew with her hymnal on her lap. Tyndall pinches Casey's thigh, and it's impressive the pain she can inflict even through a tweed skirt and tights.

In the Lincoln, Tyndall asks plainly, as if nothing has happened, for the credit card and the use of the car to take her friend to lunch. There's a long quiet. Nora goes red again.

"Casey, you sang so beautifully," Nora says, but she's watching Marion like she wants to rip his nose off with her teeth.

"I love being with you all. Marion, it means so much to me to have this time in worship with you and Nora and my friend Tyndall after all that's happened." And she means this, even though saying it feels like an exercise in theatre class.

After a long spell with the car humming and the two parents glaring at one another, Marion at last turns to Tyndall and hands her the credit card. "Can you promise me, Casey, that you'll keep our girl from disrupting Sunday lunch in public?"

Casey nods.

"Unfortunately," Nora says, still giving Marion a murderous bitch face, "Father and I must endure Tyndall's Demon monger of a Bible Study teacher and that fatso Youth Minister. And I have no friend to keep me from disrupting lunch in public."

Tyndall says grace, then drops the napkin onto her lap. "If you don't start talking, I will describe all the effluvia I have lately met." She's fresh off fighting a whole classroom of chanting fanatics who demanded she barf up a Demon, and yet she says nothing about what just happened? Wow, she envies Tyndall this peace, if that is what it is.

They are seated in the atrium restaurant of the John Q. Hammons Hotel and Tower. Hammons, now bankrupt and dead, was the guy who created Southern Hollow Subdivision. Devon and his obsessive dad taught the girls all this history. Like pipes to an organ, tubes of elevators shuttle cleaning staff and the few guests up and down in brass and glass cages.

"I can't see what's right." Casey rumples her linty black napkin. "I need you."

Tyndall's first plate is heaped with waffles and whipped cream, syrup and chocolate chips. It's obnoxious how much she can eat lately. She has a loaded salad plate at the ready, too, but she waits, her chapped lips pursed.

"So Patrick Turin was there Thursday," Casey starts.

Tyndall wolfs down three colors of beets, but watches Casey's chest with eyes gray as lead. One time, Casey went with Tyndall to get her a new security badge at the hospital. The elevator stopped, and orderlies dressed in scrubs just like Tyndall's wheeled in a gurney carrying a corpse covered by a thin, white blanket, head like a dark blue globe rounding the fabric. Tyndall and the orderlies nodded to each other. Then

Tyndall pressed the basement button for them. Otherwise no one said a word. It was like it was no big deal being trapped riding an elevator with a brand new dead person.

"He says he has songs written. And he wants my voice on them. He says I'll never make it out of Springfield with Dwayne and Mitch and Charlie."

Tyndall pushes her empty salad plate away. "Well, do you want to make it out of Springfield? What do you really want? Dwayne, Mitch, and Charlie are good, right? What does 'Making it' in music mean to you?"

"Main stage at festivals is making it. A vinyl you can hand to people and say, 'This is me.' That's making it." Casey is glad Tyndall rarely if ever looks you in the eye. Her eyes are always on your neck, or your hands, or on your chin if the talk gets real important.

"So why can't that be done with New Wave Vultures? In Springfield?"

The scrambled eggs on Casey's plate leak as if they've been submerged in the brine under the buffet's steam trays. "None of us write. We don't have one original song."

Tyndall shrugs. "But you all draw the biggest crowds of anyone." She can now eat really fast and talk, and this is shocking. Where did she learn this? "Who wants to pay money to hear songs they don't know by nobodies from Springfield, right?"

"Tyndall! That's what evil bar managers say."

Tyndall touches her bottom lip. "So, you would just leave them? Why can't you play music with Turin and them both?" Her gray eyes survey everything left on her plate. It's as if there is something more she wishes she had. "If that's what you want, Casey, say it. I have told you so many times how prayer works. Marion's new church even claims you can not only Ask the Lord, but Task the Lord."

Casey sits up straight. Tyndall drags the Lord into almost everything, and a lot of people find this annoying or worse infuriating and alienating. But Casey knows Tyndall walks the talk. After all, here she is listening to Casey. Here she is being a friend.

Tyndall puckers her lips hard to the left—she's really worrying this. "I think you need Time Alone With God. In prayer, lay these burdens and possibilities out for Him."

"If He's almighty, doesn't He already know all this?"

Tyndall's shoulders droop. "It's not for Him, silly. It's for you before your Lord. Prayer may force you to be honest about what you need. And the Lord can make what seems a mess into a pathway. He has a true and beautiful purpose for you. That's not just something we say to justify what feels good."

How is it that Tyndall Hastings, on the autism spectrum, makes more sense and speaks more clearly of Jesus Christ to Casey than Joel Osteen or Paula White, or anybody she just witnessed at Victory Faith Triumphant? A normal high school girl might encourage Casey to leave Springfield. Tyndall's easily that ate up with Devon. And Casey is sitting here giving her the chance. Instead, Tyndall says it's time to stop, be alone, and pray. By the rules of this world, Tyndall Hastings is batshit crazy. "I feel like I need you to say 'No' for me."

Tyndall frowns and rolls the donuts of her sweater sleeves higher. "Casey. God never works that way."

6

In the Hastings home on a Sunday afternoon, if things have gone smoothly at church service, Mother and Father expect the children to nap or remain for at least two hours in their bedrooms taking Time Alone With God, doors shut. In the last month that Ben lived, this practice changed. Doctors and counselors from rehab demanded his door remain open at all times, even if Father felt that denied Faith and constituted a Negative Confession according to the elders of Victory Faith Triumphant. Tyndall learned from eavesdropping that Mother wished the door removed and donated to Habitat for Humanity. A month after Ben's overdose, Father insisted Tyndall renew this Sunday sequester. She hasn't adhered to the rule, not since her thirteenth year when Eve's change made her prowl. She just waits for her parents to shut their door; then she's loose.

One wall to the master bedroom abuts a formal dining room. There a massive antique cabinet dominates the far corner. Sitting cross-legged on the hardwood floor hidden by this hulking cabinet and with her back and head pressed against a wall, Tyndall has listened to 202 Sunday sessions. Before Ben's overdose her parents sometimes negotiated what Tyndall pieced together to be intercourse, or at least pleasure for Father. Now that has stopped and instead, they discuss life in tones and terms that make it clear her parents have long performed like stage actors for Ben while he was alive and for Tyndall still.

Today, very full after lunch with Casey, she hesitates at the dining room entryway. The darkened hallway means the master bedroom door is shut already. Down the hallway, where Ben's old room once was, his doorway sucks all the comfort from the house. At last but too late Mother has her wish—no door on the hinges at the entry to his death room. From the oaks outside, from the curtains, from the chair he died in, a sickly green, light flickers. In movies and television shows she is forbidden to watch, people talk with ghosts, first emissaries to a cavalcade of Demons. What she wouldn't give to speak with Ben! But there... isn't that how Satan enters? Any longing, even a wholesome desire, and suddenly you feel him tightening around your hips like the Serpent around the tree.

She pops the top button of her jeans and eases the zipper down. Touching the antique cabinet, she leans forward to the wall. Voices. So, no sex. Intense. An argument?

Putting her back to the wall and pressing herself into the corner hurts her shoulders as she lowers herself to sit. She can no longer hide her legs, so they jut right out into the dining room. Once seated, she considers standing again. Her stomach bulges and hurts, and yet she can't see it. Her chest is in the way—when did this happen? Every day this flesh confounds her. Rage like a green flame fills her vision. She rests the back of her head against the wall to hear better and get her mind on something besides her body.

Father's voice. Loud.

"But if she's healed, and we believe it, there's Right Confession and Thanksgiving."

"Marion, Tyndall isn't ill. You can't heal what's not sick. She perceives differently and so she relates differently."

"Nothing is beyond the name of Jesus. Is there a Demon in you?"

"You know there is not. In the name of Jesus, there is not."

Silence.

"We must seriously consider the Spiritual Mapping Pastor Micah and the Deliverance Ministry want to do. They wonder if there is some Generational Curse."

"Do they know how Ben died?" Mother asks. Long pause. "You haven't told them."

They holler right over each other.

"Generational Curse? That's ridiculous, Marion Hastings. We know plenty about the generations of our people. Glops of oats all the way back to mud in Saxony."

"I hereby take the Apostolic Authority that I have been granted by God as Steward of this household for the Kingdom of God…"

"First it was my family's genetics. Then it was the vaccines. Then it was testosterone in my womb. And all of it *my* fault. Now more of the same? She is who she is! We don't need this mapping. We need a future, Marion! And she has earned one. We're her parents. We need to keep her out of lion's dens like this Victory madness."

"As the nations which the Lord destroyeth before your face, so shall ye perish: because ye would not be obedient unto the voice of the Lord your God."

Deuteronomy 8:20. It's all downhill from there.

"My roarings are poured out like the waters, Marion Hastings. Tyndall is wired strangely and wonderfully by her Creator. She sees differently…"

"And Demons howl from her mouth and compel her limbs to violence, and now she is expelled from Bible Study, and Pastor Micah fears her Negative Confession in Congregation!"

Silence.

"Marion, God made the morning stars and the hoary frost, and He made the unicorn, which will not harrow your valleys."

"I forbid you to blaspheme in this household! Who is it that darkeneth counsel by words without knowledge?"

So much Job! Tyndall can hardly breathe, she's so full. What a rotten Sunday!

"I'll tell you who this is. It's your long suffering wife, mother to your children, who was not ashamed or afraid and wanted to stay at Oak Creek. But you couldn't take the brethren learning that Ben was addicted, could you? No. And now

I find my family surrounded by health-mongering, Demon-obsessed charlatans who believe Jesus is merely a word to vacuum money..."

"From the wicked!"

"From you and me, Marion! If their Jesus cannot abide and love your daughter as the Lord made her, then I call that Satan."

At the smack of skin and Nora's outcry, Tyndall surges up and buttons her jeans. She rips open the bedroom door. Marion holds a shred of Nora's blouse in his fist. And he cocks his other fist, closed and ready.

Tyndall charges, plants a shoulder in his chest, and smashes him against their dresser. Before he can get a hand to her shoulders, she has him by the throat.

His eyes bulge. He gargles and squirms. Her heart is as firm as a stone.

When Nora caresses her back, sheets of fire slice into Tyndall's flesh. Nora caresses her again. "Tyndall. Let him go."

Tyndall cracks the back of his head against the dresser. Marion's eyes roll. Nora cries out. Slowly Tyndall rises, watching her father, who is now drooling. As her mother retreats, Tyndall stretches her arms out, palms up to both her parents. Marion's eyes whirl and snap back into place, then focus on his daughter, his assailant.

"What is this? What do you make of Jesus that you two would treat each other this way and not listen and love instead?" Her voice is the thunder. "What am I to believe? Nothing from you! Nothing from you anymore if this is how your beliefs tell you to live!"

A long quiet.

"Tyndall. Sweetheart. I think it's time for you to go to your room," Nora says.

"With my door open? Like Ben?"

Her Mother makes the face of enforced stillness when all must be surrendered to God in order to deliver any of His Mercy. Oh, how many times has Tyndall witnessed this expression?

"Yes. All of us. With our doors wide open. Like Dear Ben."

7

Patrick Turin lives in a building that confuses Casey. Four stories tall and across from St. Agnes, the Catholic church downtown, it's called The Wiltmore. All brick, and tucked in across Jefferson Street. How could there be apartments here for anybody but priests or nuns? She pauses and watches the sidewalk and buildings. Behind her, the small Cathedral glows like a box cake. Is this what she should do? She prayed about this, but whenever she prays, she feels fake. Tyndall is so sure about the Lord, Jesus may as well be an app on her phone. Tonight is just jamming with someone to see what she can learn. It doesn't mean anything.

A blind floats up in a third story window. There's a shadow. That's him. Casey lifts her guitar case, heavier with the Glock 43 in it. She's a fallen policeman's daughter, LODD, and at Midwest Tactical or Meemaw's Gun Jamboree, they never charge her for range time.

At The Wiltmore, in its arched entryway, there's a brass panel with black buttons, white numbers, and an intercom's speaker, as if this were an apartment building in some giant city. She pushes the button for 4D, and there's a hiss from the intercom, but no answer or greeting. Should she have announced herself? There's a thump and buzz at the door latch. When she pulls, the door opens. An anesthetizing, natural C echoes inside the building.

A recorder song from childhood toots in her head. C, ¾ time.
Go to sleep before you see monsters.
Go to sleep before monsters see you.

Those lyrics terrified her, such an awful confirmation for a nine-year-old whose father fought real monsters. "Broke fingering!" Just a glimpse of Dad's teasing face flashes in her memory. He refused to say Baroque properly, but he would skip any program on television, even a Blues hockey game, to hear her play or sing. If she ever loses the ability to recall his face—the thought takes her breath away. My father is dead.

She tops the third flight of stairs, and the door to 4D opens with no light inside.

"Close it behind you." Turin's voice.

"Lights on, creep."

Eventually a light flicks on. Patrick Turin sits in an antique chair that has an ornate wooden hood sheltering him, a chair like something from a Bollywood movie.

She shuts the door. The apartment seems larger than the family room and kitchen at home combined, and all the furniture looks really old.

"Ever listen to Joni Mitchell?"

She shakes her head.

With a remote he raises the lighting above a hulking dining room table. On it a laptop glows, and the gold, green, and red-topped bars of SoundBlitz dance like flames in a familiar fireplace on the computer screen. At least she already knows his recording software. Headphones, mics, and cables coil at the ready.

He rises and begins connecting patch cords and headphones. He's wearing a teal coat with tails, a bright yellow peasant shirt, tight black denim jeans and a pair of calf-length gray boots bound by fluorescent laces and collared by fur at their tops.

"Who in the hell are you trying to be?" she asks.

"We are all trying to be. And yet we never become." Even though he's an eye roll every minute, his voice has this texture like sharkskin that makes you want its touch again. He extends a mirror to her with lines of chunky, blue-white powder. "Adderall?"

29

She shakes her head and tries not to make a face.

He leans over the mirror and plants a straw on one of the lines and vacuums it up his nose in one sharp snort. Wincing, he pushes the mirror away with great care. Then he places headphones on his ears and holds a pair out to her. They hang there rocking on his fingertips and make her think of handcuffs.

She lowers the guitar case to the floor then rubs the sweat off her palms onto her jeans. She approaches and tilts her head to him and lets him place the headphones over her ears. She's relieved how careful he is not to touch any part of her, and how his eyes stay on the headset and do not wander down her shirt.

He clicks the laptop and spins a finger over the mousepad then taps it. He watches her with his fingertips at his lips as if he's about to pray.

She rolls her eyes but stops. The woman on the headset sings about a child and a carousel, and she lifts round notes with an open clarity Casey has only heard in her dreams.

When the song finishes, they both remove their headsets. He shakes his head to get his hair from behind his ears. "At the Cedar Shake, I heard a vision. Your voice, like Joni's, but on my songs."

8

—Ride?

Devon cradles the smartphone, scooping the light to him as if Casey's text repairs the smudged, cracked glass. The Otterbox smells of sulfur, and its plexi screen is mired in islands of purple, yellow, and green.

Dad snoozes, head back, mouth open, while a PBS special about toxic algae along the Gulf Coast boils on the big screen in their basement. His stepmom glances up from her Note10, and on her face the candy-colored light of her game clashes with the blue-green flicker of the documentary broadcast. She raises her eyebrows at Devon. Upstairs children's feet thunder across the floors. Sunday night in the Ozarks.

—Got2B early, he types. Soil test.

—After?

—School. Remember?

Casey texts a GIF: a bull's butt blasting poo.

—Wear those rainbow boots!

He waits. On the TV a tiny Asian-looking woman from some place called Pascagoula speaks furiously. Her Southern accent is so wild there are subtitles provided. Shrimp boats bob behind her and glow like the candy blobs in his stepmom's game. America has whole foreign countries in it, and he'll never see them because of Merritt Organics, the business that fails forever. *You don't have to kill the planet to green your lawn!* But do you have to kill your family to run a company?

—How early?

His chest quivers. Anything with Casey is like that awful ache when a fresh can of Copenhagen opens and fills the cab in the ProMaster with nicotine, tobacco, molasses, and raw want.

—5:30.

—Bring earbuds.

Always an agenda with her. Never the agenda he wants.

Stepmom juts her bottom lip at him. She's been watching him. Dad and Devon were alone a long time after his real mom died of cancer. Then at Missouri State, Dad got busted in an affair with his graduate assistant, Sherry Jean Plumly, and now here she sits, stepmom. Baby Sister, now three, doesn't look a bit like Dad, and yet where's the paternity test? Baby Sister is upstairs with two neighbor kids. They're running and making siren noises while Sherry Jean stays downstairs with "her boys" but plays Candy Balls on her giant phone. Devon has seen her driver's license. She's 24 but tells people she's 29. And Sherry Jean will say this right in front of Dad. She lies as naturally and as often as the President.

"That Strong girl, Devon." Sherry Jean has a pug nose and merry, curly hair that she highlights red and yellow. Carrying and nursing Baby Sister left her with a distractingly big chest. Devon jokes with Tyndall to teach him to pray about all this. Sherry Jean grew up in Blue Eye. Once the Tristate Kneeboarding Champion, she still rocks a core like a gymnast. Sherry Jean shakes her head, but her eyes follow the tumbling candies. "She's a user, Devon."

Human biology sucks. How can you suffer a boner and at the same time be filled with loathing for someone? Who really doesn't deserve loathing—Devon knows this. Sherry Jean can't help being from Blue Eye and moving on up any more than Devon can help being a griping white kid from Southern Hollow and feeling stuck. He should be grateful really. Some of his classmates sleep in tents and on friends' couches, never the same place in a week. What does he have to whine about?

"Sherry Jean," he says, "you are a true detective."

Dad jerks awake and blinks at dead dolphins floating on the screen. Upstairs the sirens reach an apocalyptic crescendo. "Nap one minute and the world goes to hell."

When Dad is back to sleep, Sherry Jean sticks her tongue out at Devon, then rises and sprints up the stairs to pound bottoms and stifle the fun.

The Strong house on Lamonta Drive hasn't been jazzed up and made nouveau retro yet like so many around it and up on Meadowview and Cedarbrook. Fading blue paint on furry, patched wooden siding, it looks like the kind of house that would hold a treasure of old vinyl—Black Oak Arkansas and Head East—and kids in bell-bottoms will any second now come grooving down the steps to a waiting Ranchero. It's a split level. The hill on Lamonta is so steep in the Strongs' lot that the garage leads into a lower recreation room like a basement dug into the hillside, and then it's topped with a ranch-style house that creates a floor of bedrooms above the garage and rec. No sneaking in and out of the windows to Casey's high bedroom. The concrete driveway would break your legs.

He texted Casey's mom last night to alert her. She still suffers cop-wife anxieties. She meets him at the front door with a quick hug. In the kitchen, which always feels like a saloon with its dark wood and barstools, she has extra crisp hash browns, a mug of redeye gravy, glistening ham, steaming black coffee, and two sunny-side-up eggs waiting. While Devon eats, she smokes. Her name is Cassie, short for Cassandra, but the Cassie and Casey thing is just too confusing. Tyndall and Devon have called her Mrs. Strong or Casey's mom all their lives. When she turns to extinguish the cigarette in the sink, the ghost of a big elephant tattoo stretches on her calf, the ink faded to a smoky color.

The countertop creases her stomach. She even arches her back and smiles at him. She enjoys him eating the breakfast, and it bothers him how much he wants Casey to look at him this same way, and how much her mom is a projection of Casey, like an older sister.

"What's she forcing you to do today?"

"Not forcing."

She curls her upper lip.

"No, really. Glad to help. And I need her help."

She tops his coffee. Her voice falls to a whisper. "Devon, she doesn't…"

He raises his palm. "Don't. Really. I'm super over it."

She shakes her head. "Devon Merritt, you're a beautiful boy." She's wearing a Missouri State Hockey T-shirt she really shouldn't wear. Then he realizes it's Casey's shirt, and Mrs. Strong probably pulled it from the laundry in a hurry to make him breakfast. "I don't understand what she wants, Devon."

She gazes at him so closely that he has to look away. A mug drips with reddish brown gravy. The ceramic bears a blue circle and a triangle with the letters COPS beneath it. Up on the wall is a framed photograph of the late Officer Strong, his arm over the shoulder of Bret Hull from the St. Louis Blues hockey team. Officer Strong never got to celebrate the Stanley Cup win. Devon cannot look at Casey's mom. When she does this sympathy thing for his broken heart, it's way too confusing. Pornography of the mind, Tyndall calls it.

"This gravy," he says, his voice rough.

She lights a new cigarette. Seeing it pucker her face is a welcome turnoff.

Casey comes down the hall, sandy orange hair in a pony tucked through a ballcap with the blue COPS triangle on it. She's wearing rainbow-sparkled Doc Martens and tattered jeans. Everything in the room stops, and there's a long silence as if Devon and Casey's mom have been caught flirting. "Weirdoes," she says.

9

The jobsite is the rambling stone, bridge timber and barn wood mansion on Third Lake that John Q. Hammons abandoned and left to the weeds after his bankruptcy and then his death. Devon overruled his father, who wanted to run the bid sky high. Devon normalized it. The people who bought the place aren't Hammons, and they're asking for a proposal from Merritt Organics, so they have a chance to treat the lawn without damaging Third Lake, the one lake in Southern Hollow that is almost clean.

The yard juts a peninsula into the lake and shows multiple bare spots mixed with crab, orchard, and dallisgrass. Squeezing on his galoshes and spraying them with raging hot water from the Dodge ProMaster, he wishes he had just let his Dad stay mean. He flicks out two plastic boot coverlets with drawstrings and then kneels. Casey grips the open side cabinet door of the ProMaster and sticks her left boot forward, then the other. He wraps them quickly and touches nothing but her heels.

"Where's your earbuds?" Casey's eyes look sleepy. Drowsiness pinches them so they seem mischievous like her mother's. She holds up a white Blastik, and then, on tiptoes, she pulls open the pocket of his denim shirt and finds the earbuds. Her familiarity with his body and where he stows his gear and the pressure of her fingertips on his chest send a wave like grief down his neck and arms. The COPS and triangle on her cap soften in the peach light of dawn. She has the earbuds Bluetoothed to the Blastik. When she looks up, holding the buds out for his ears, she pauses.

"Stop that," she says. She waits. "Clear your head. Clean up your heart. I want you to hear and feel this. It's new, all new."

He closes his eyes, and she burrows the buds in his ears and drops the Blastik in his shirt pocket with as little touching as possible. For a long time, he can feel the warmth and moisture of her palms on his cheeks and chin.

From the side bay cabinet of the ProMaster, he pulls out the sample box. He hands her the magic marker and sealed bag of lids. Knowing the drill, she kneads surgical gloves loose from a box and pulls on a pair. A sharp latex smell rises.

Casey opens up the magic marker. "Ever seen Tyndall wear gloves like these? Here we got them on, and we're just diggin' in the dirt."

"Tyndall isn't a surgeon."

"Not yet." She numbers the lids and replaces them in the bag. "It was really great to see you two slow dancing. I felt like crying, but I had to keep singing." When he doesn't react, she frowns. "Come on, Grumpy Gus! You have to press the button." She nods at his shirt pocket where the Blastik waits. "How's Tyndall ever gonna deal with you if you're bitchy at night *and* first thing in the morning?"

"You know Tyndall and I aren't a thing, right? We just hang out. It's not dating" He takes the trowels from the back bay of the ProMaster and checks his pants pockets for the flags, extra gloves, and his company cell. Then with a big fake smile at her, he plucks the Blastik from his shirt pocket, holds it up to the sunrise, and presses the button. She has the sample box strapped to her neck and shoulders. She looks like a tiny beer vendor with her box empty at the Cardinals game. They trundle toward the mansion.

In the earbuds, music starts, eerie, old-timey. It's all acoustic. There's a jangling piano, and a snare drum. Then Casey's voice swoops in, but not in any way he has ever heard her sing. He glances at her walking behind him. She's blushing. He stops and tries to focus, points his toe at the first bare patch. He feels dizzy bending to stab the numbered flag in the ground, lost as he pulls out his cell phone and frames and snaps the sample photograph. Another voice joins her, and he feels a chill ripple down his back to his tailbone. He's heard this voice before, singing about vampire dolls and Sofia Castle. It's Patrick Turin.

He looks up at her. He wants to scold her about Turin, what a scum he is, how dangerous, how reckless. But the music stops him. It's as if he hears her for the first time singing, not trying to be Belinda Carlisle or Phoebe Bridgers, but Casey Strong, singing like no one else he has ever heard. She has the sample jar open and held out, but her gaze is gone over the lake. Her eyes are filled with metallic waves and the red sear of first light. She's mouthing the words to the strange new song playing in his ear. This is her ticket out of here.

10

Tyndall rests the earbuds on the cafeteria table. She thumbs the Blastik off and her eyes lock on Casey's shoulders. Devon feels the racket of third period lunch fall away. The huddles of hombres and chicas, the pod of big-shirt-Birkenstock girls contemplating themselves on their phones and clutching Hydro Flasks with ringing metal straws, the brawl of cheer-leaders and football players in Falcon red and aqua—yet here in this triangle is peace, love, and power maybe almost like the three-person God Tyndall talks so much about. Casey waits at the edge of her seat. These two girls have been the steadying forces in his life, all through childhood, through deaths even. His mother, Casey's dad, Tyndall's brother. This new music could end all that right now.

"You sing like that in church," Tyndall says. "When you give yourself up to the Lord and let the Holy Spirit sing through you, it sounds like that. That's really you."

Casey is frowning and making a fist.

"Like worship." Tyndall, the emotional blank wall, goes wet around her gray eyes.

Casey smacks the tabletop. "Does everything have to be Jesus?"

Devon catches her hand. "Hey, it's a compliment. Remember who we're talking to."

Tyndall blinks at him. "That made everything much better." She waits as Casey rages for a bit. Then she places her hand over Devon's and gathers Casey's hand and clasps them all three together. "When you sing in church, Casey, maybe you can't hear this. But when you sing for the joy of it, all out, that's what's here," she nods at the Blastik and earbuds. "That voice makes everyone stop and wonder. You finally got it recorded."

"So... you like it?" Casey asks.

"Of course," Tyndall says. She looks at Devon. "You knew what I was saying?"

He wants to tease her, but he stops himself. "I did. I knew. Casey, Tyndall loves it."

Dwayne and Charlie loom over them. Tyndall releases Devon and Casey's hands and eases back. Dwayne and Charlie both have cell phones out and earbuds dangling.

"What the hell is this on Bandcamp?" Charlie asks.

"Bandcamp?" Casey asks, snatching Charlie's cell and squinting at its screen.

"You and Vampire Cowboy Asshat!" Dwayne adds. There are three pierced and bobbing e-dopes with him, and they each have Blastiks in hand.

Tyndall stares toward Devon, her eyes wide, her expression flat. She's like a machine that has abruptly powered down. Maybe it's the strangers crowding in and the spike in tension. He never knows what sets this off. But her habit of unplugging and disappearing inside herself always scares him.

He reaches across the table to her and snaps his fingers. "Walk with me."

She shivers, and then blushes, even gives a kind of grin—will she ever comprehend what's really happening?

When she stands, though, she's not gawky Tyndall in the funny sweaters anymore. She's suddenly like a full-grown woman. Even furious Dwayne Erb pauses and his eyes widen and drink in Tyndall Hastings moving around the table to join Devon.

Once they're outside the cafeteria in the hallway Devon can't get his hand free of hers, she's so intense. She leads them to the edge of the classroom wing and into a corridor by a gym, which is darkened during the three lunch periods. The Oxy, acid, and edibles dealer, a long, thin kid named Draper, pushes his sagging druggy client awake. They scuttle off in their trenchcoats. As soon as Devon and Tyndall pass a stack of wrestling mats, she hurls him against the wall and wraps her arms around his waist.

He pushes her shoulders back, and she relents, but her mouth drops open. "What more sign do you need, Devon Merritt?" The mats smell like dust and feet.

"What do you mean? I just wanted us out of there. Away from the band fight. Hey!"

She pushes against him so violently his shoulder blades and elbows bonk the wall. Tyndall is taller than he is, and lifting, pushing, stacking, cleaning at the hospital have given her muscles new force. She grabs his shirt at his shoulders and pins him. Her face is not playful or lusty but focused and almost as expressionless as it was when she was listening to Casey's new song. Devon's heart pounds and his hands ache pushing against her ribs. This day is the worst—it's like he's devoured a whole Colorado chocolate bar and is stuck in some kind of terrifying apotcalypse.

"Come on!" She grunts. To his shock she moves her face very close to his, almost nose-to-nose, something she never does. "You heard that with her and Patrick Turin? Devon, she's going to be famous in ten downloads. She's out of here."

"We don't know that." But he can hear in his own voice how little he believes it.

She plants her hands on his hips, bumps him against the wall again when he squirms.

"Tyndall, really. Stop it. Now."

She's so relentless, her hair falls in front of her face. When she sweeps it back with her hand, she is again pretty yet frightening with her blank, gray eyes. There's no laughter, no tenderness, just force. "God made me to love you," she says. Nose-to-nose, her body mashed against him. Her lips rake his forehead. "And that music was Him telling me."

This is his forever friend, his confidante, the strange, brilliant kid he's hung with for so long. "Tyndall, what the hell?"

"Shut up for once. Shut up! And just let me." Her teeth are clenched, and he recalls with heartbreak a medicine her parents put her on that left her teeth clamped and mouth leering for a whole month, she was so miserable and wound so tight. When she was a girl. When her parents were scrambling for answers. This feels like one of her fits of rage.

Now she has them both stuck against the prickly Velcro of the mats. Suddenly as if it were no big deal, she pops his jeans buttons open.

He's shaking his head, still pushing her away, but the more he applies force, the more she presses in. She yanks his boxers out and down, and she has his cock in her fist. He's trapped. Instantly he's swollen fat in her right hand. She grips him firmly. He freezes. Why can't he power down and disappear? "No. Tyndall," he whispers. Unbelievable how strong she is. He can't make himself hit her to get her stopped. And in the past twelve hours, he's been aroused by all the wrong people. He's primed. Pressure rushes, and so does nausea.

"God will make you love me. Let me!" Her voice booms down the hallway. "Casey's gone, Devon. It's time for us to happen."

11

New Wave Vultures practice at Mitch's parents' house on Locust and Commercial Street near Lindbergh's. The Cataldos have a basement with browning sound foam caked on the walls. Mitch's dad played in every kind of band imaginable—doo wop to punk from D.C. to L.A.

Charlie didn't text to offer her a ride, and after the scene at lunch, she didn't ask. No one meets Casey when the Uber lets her out. In the basement, Mitch, Dwayne, and Charlie stand in front of the drums with their arms crossed.

She sets her two guitar cases down, the Martin acoustic and the Fender bass. "Let's get some things straight," she starts. "I wouldn't stop any one of you from recording with anyone else or playing out with anyone else. Don't let me down. Don't let us down. Those were our only rules, right?"

"It's who you're doing it with," Dwayne says.

Mitch counts off on his fingers. "Scary. Violent. Pillhead. Three strikes!"

She waits a moment. "Charlie?"

Charlie's a big kid who used to play football till he got a monster concussion. He has a round, frightening face and spiky, almost white hair. Sometimes he looks like a jack 'o' lantern behind the KORG keyboards, especially when he smiles. "I thought we were a band."

"We are," she says. "But it's not like a contract with a hockey team or something." She kneels and flips open the latches on her Martin. "I'm not canceling anything. We have gigs. We have the Cedar Shake thing till after New Year's."

The three of them pout and glance at each other. Finally Mitch weaves behind his drum set and takes his stool. He points a stick at her. "First time we have to say no because of something you're doing without us, that's the definition of letting us down."

They rehearse like angry robots, and Casey's heart sinks—even when the music's pitch perfect, right in time, it's not solving this hollow feeling. She's to blame.

Patrick Turin meets her outside The Wiltmore and lugs both her guitars up the stairs. Everything was so upsetting, she didn't even ask to use the bathroom at Mitch's. In Turin's bathroom, clean as a sailor's bunk and reeking of Patchouli, there's a poster tacked up above the commode, card stock with a big red fist. The poster reads "Resist Alternative Facts. Stand Way Closer." Boy humor.

On the dining room table his laptop is open, and his Bandcamp dashboard is up. There's the song they just recorded, "Burn Out the Rain," ticking away. She touches the edge of the screen, and in the dark apartment, the glowing square of his face and the gnarl of brush and sky behind him in the photograph turns her fingers an alien gray. So here's this song they recorded together, and its image to the world is just Patrick Turin.

"We need a photograph of us together. I know a guy who'll do a shoot," he says.

She tries to make sense of the numbers and the graph—a blue mountain range under the words PLAYS ~ BUZZ ~ SALES/DOWNLOADS. Beneath the picture of his face is the title "Burn Out the Rain" by Patrick Turin with Casey Strong.

"What's with mean?"

"Means I wrote the song. You sang it with me."

"There're sales and downloads. With means what percent? That's my voice, my interpretation, my guitar, and you're selling it."

43

"There's a party I want us to go to. This isn't worth our time right now."

He's taller than she is. His reach is longer. His biceps and forearms are wiry, and his chest appears lean but powerful in his tight T-shirt. She longs for Tyndall and Devon, or Dwayne and Mitch, always ready to scrap. She wishes she had not let him carry her guitars up here and put them... she doesn't know where. A panic shoots up her arms to her pits.

"Lot of headaches this caused me, Buster. I really would've liked to talk about all this before it went up. Especially before you sold downloads."

He twirls his car keys then catches them in his palm. "Likembé bands from Kinshasa get more downloads in a night than we just did."

"Nope," she says. "Right now. Lay out all the figures, and then we don't have to wrestle again. I sang. I played guitar."

"Sometime Google mechanical royalties. Not now," he says too firmly when she pulls out her phone. "I want you to see this party. We need to boogie."

"Out of Adderall?"

"It's about the music."

"Percentages. Now."

His shoulders slump. "I wrote all the words, played all the instruments except your Martin. And that part I taught you. 75/25."

"Up yours, Buddy. You told me key and chords. The interpretation's mine. 70/30."

He's quiet a while. In the blue light of the laptop, with his big nose and thin face, he looks like a mean hawk thinking on a wire. At last he shrugs. "Makes the math easier."

She squeezes her phone back into her jeans pocket. "Okay, then. Do I get to login for this or are you gonna send me screenshots? And how and when do you pay out?" Before he opens his mouth, she holds up a finger. "On paper. All of it."

"Jesus. We'll never get out of here."

"You're the one threw it up on Bandcamp and made money off it without asking!"

With a snort, he gets paper and pen, and they work it out. He's cold, quick, and rational. She guesses it's because she's already agreed to 70/30. Suddenly she feels like a chump, like he has all the know-how wearing his T-shirt from Jackson Ampworks and his cherry-red Kiton jeans. In her fingers, the pen looks like a needle and the handwritten contract like tattooed flesh. She wants to write that down, to start her a song, but he's standing up now and showing her his cell phone and the time slipping away.

12

He drives a strange old sedan with a lion on the front and lots of leather inside. He calls the car "le Grande Routière." He has to fold the back seat forward—her bass and its case won't fit in the trunk. So now thieves can look in the windows and see choice musical gear.

"We're in Southern Hollow," he says. "Nothing ever happens here."

She checks the locks, which have to be pushed down by hand. "If these get stolen out of your Great Router, I can have cops up in your business till Christmas."

He slings a backpack over his shoulder. "Whenever you think you need to be tough, you drag that casket out."

She closes her fist and swings as hard as she can at his stomach. But he sees it coming. He bends before she strikes, and his abdomen gives no more than hardened wax. Instantly he's got her wrist, but he's grinning.

She struggles.

"If you're gonna hit me, Tink, get something in your hands to hit me with."

She lets out a frustrated grunt. It's a lot to keep herself contained. This has been one rollercoaster of a day. "Does everything got to be a lesson with you?" She jerks free.

"Let's go in here and have some fun and learn some shit. Cool?"

The party is at one of the biggest houses on Second Lake, dark, hulking in front with an aurora of orange light in the back. Casey recalls this is Andy Stone's house. Andy—several years ahead of her—took so many mushrooms and so much acid he suffered an aneurysm or seizure or something (Tyndall would know). Now he lives permanently upstairs, unable to work and with a water bubble on his brain that could kill him any minute. Mindy Stone is a junior. This must be Mindy's party. So Casey's walking into Andy Stone's house with Patrick Turin, the bridge troll of Southern Hollow. Maybe this isn't her ideal trajectory?

Turin leads them through the front door, straight through the house buzzing with Glendale kids and some she doesn't recognize—maybe from Parkview or Kickapoo. Out the back door, a patio glows from tiki torches and a flickering gas fire-pit with freaky blue crystals and dancing orange flames. All around the pit hoodied kids lounge in Adirondack chairs, each kid with a cell phone resting on one arm of the chair. One of the cell phones is playing a song so tinny she can't recognize it. Then just as that song quits, there are guesses shouted, two kids leave their chairs. Another kid joins the circle, holds a cell up, and a new song starts. The sound is abysmal, like listening to a cricket trapped in a coffee can.

"There are speakers out here," Casey whispers to Patrick. She has to stand on tiptoe, until he bends to her. A few of the kids around the firepit give the two of them looks with raised eyebrows, a few wide eyes. She sticks her chin at one of the mounted outdoor speakers above them. "Those could rock the whole neighborhood."

Turin nods slowly. He's not watching the circle. He's watching her.

Someone in the circle blurts out a song title and the name of a band.

"Nope," says the kid whose cell phone creaks out the noise. The one who guessed wrong rises and pulls the hood to his sweatshirt tight. He stalks off. A chick, also in a hoodie, takes his place.

Mindy Stone slinks up to Patrick Turin. In her black dress, she's like a python. She's adopted—mostly the Stones are

pale, white people—but "Mindy" is short for some unpro-
nounceable Hindi name. Her flawless skin is a dark shade
like walnut heartwood, and in the orange gaslight, her flesh
seems dusty and shale gray. She removes a dab pen from her
lips and places it on Patrick's. Then she coils more securely
around him, her jet-black hair flashing with orange highlights
from the torches. Someone in the circle guesses a song correctly—there's applause, and the kid whose cell is squeaking
silences it and leaves.

Mindy's lips part. Patrick exhales and she inhales, his
smoke rolling up into her nostrils. In the firelight, they're like
two dragons in a mating ritual. With Mindy wound around
him and their exchange seeming so practiced, so natural,
Casey finds herself turned on and at the same time disturbed
and, to her surprise, jealous, possessively, even protectively
jealous. Where's this coming from? She's finished just one
song with him and was mad as hell at him minutes ago.

Mindy's voice is tight—she's holding the pot smoke down
in her lungs. "The object is to remain in the circle. Continually
introduce songs so new, they thrill and mystify." She pulls at
the dab pen now. Curling her bottom lip, deep brown which
abruptly changes to a glistening pink, she pours out smoke,
and Patrick vacuums it up his big nose.

"But the sound quality," Casey says. "So rotten."

Mindy uncoils herself from Patrick, then strokes Casey's
left ear lobe. Mindy smiles. She has lovely but tiny teeth, and
it's like she's inhaling Casey now. "Your talent. It can exile you
from simple joys." Her Ls and Ts are delicious. Casey would
love to hear Mindy pronounce a long sentence of nothing but
L and T words. Since her eyes are so black, it's hard to tell how
high Mindy really is. A girl Casey recognizes from gym class
darts up and whispers in Mindy's ear. Mindy excuses herself,
and they hurry off.

He leans down to whisper. "Have some fun. I wanted you
to see this game more than anything." He sticks his chin at the
circle, where applause rises again. "That's your market. The

newest sensation is all that matters. And no one cares where the sound comes from."

Later she's desperately sleepy in the front seat of his car. Patrick puts the keys in the ignition. A football player, a bruiser named Ralph Samford, raps a knuckle on the window. He and Patrick step well away from the Peugeot. Soon they're arguing. She can't see them through the cedar shrubs. But they're getting pretty heated.

Behind her, his backpack rests on top of the case to her Martin. She struggles, shoving the backpack aside, and manages to unsnap and part the guitar case and fetch the cloth sack. She pulls it open and draws out the Glock and its magazine. Glancing over her shoulder, she can still hear Ralph and Patrick fussing. Ralph thinks Turin has ecstasy, but Ralph doesn't have money. She loads the clip into the Glock, and it responds with that reassuring Austrian click. She rests the pistol on the leather console. She turns to settle his pack and the Martin case, but there's the zipper on his backpack flashing in the streetlight. No lock. She glances over her shoulder—the argument is still going on behind the cedars. She tugs the zipper.

In the salmon stripe of the streetlight, she sees rubber banded rolls of twenties, tens, and fives, and a whole pharmacy of pill bottles and a box of snack-sized Ziploc baggies.

The argument skews all Ralph now, and it's getting closer. Casey just gets the zipper shut and whirls around in the passenger seat. The dome light flashes, Patrick jumps in, but Ralph snags the top of the driver's side door. His big yelling face swells into the cab. He shuts his yap when he spots Casey running a fingernail along the muzzle of the Glock.

"Ralphy, I'm so tired. I really want to go home and sleep, okay?"

"Sure," Ralph says. His beery breath floods the car. He raises his meaty hand from the doorframe. "Sure," he repeats, and backs away.

Patrick closes the door. He glances at the Glock, at her, and then grins as he starts the car. They roll away and head toward Third Lake and Lone Pine Road.

She lifts the pistol, points it at the floorboard, and pushes the safety back on.

"That was great," Patrick says.

"So why does Ralph Samford think you have molly?"

Turin stays quiet for a minute. They turn on Southern Hollow Boulevard and cruise toward the big hill after the pool. Casey used to urge any parent driving her to rush down this hill and race up the rise to the railroad tracks. The train tracks could launch even big Chevy Suburbans, all four wheels airborne, and as kids they all screamed with delight. Patrick takes the tracks at a crawl, as if he's driving a fiberglass Corvette.

"Music never pays."

At least he isn't a liar. "So this party wasn't at all about 'the music' or that game? This was a stinking sales call."

"Everything is more than one thing. See. You've learned a lot tonight."

He passes his parents' house at the corner of Southern Hollow Boulevard and Meadowview without even a glance.

"You know how my Dad died."

"I don't sell meth. That's dollar store trash. I don't carry molly, or acid. I don't vend anything whipped up in a bathtub or pill pressed. I only deal excess pharma, what our great American and European drug makers manufacture. Consistent. Reliable. Doctor prescribed."

They turn onto Lamonta, and he stops in her driveway. Mom flicks on the outside lights to the stairs, and then to Casey's bedroom—her sign that she knows how late Casey is.

"There's no 70/30 to this life," he says. "Apartments, guitars, studio time, what do you think is paying for all of this? I don't have some cop trust fund."

"Asshole! Open the trunk."

"Gonna search it?"

50

"My guitars are in it, dipshit."

He pops the trunk, opens the back door and shoulders his backpack. At the back of the car she lifts her cases, quietly, one by one. She's not going to be the emotional girl who slams stuff around and cries. He's beside her, and reaches to take the bass from her. She pulls it away. "What studio time?"

"We'll be in one in the next two weeks or the week after." He reaches for her bass again, and this time she lets him carry it up the steps to the front door.

She's never been in a studio with any of her bands— just home studio stuff on random RAW software, Audacity, Garageband, SoundBlitz, and the arcane but wondrous reel-to-reel in the Cataldos' basement.

He sets her bass down on the stoop. "What we're doing, how we can sound, how different we can be from anything happening now . . . it's all worth it to me." He crams his hands down in the pockets of his Kiton jeans. You'd have to push a lot of pills to afford a pair like that. "What's it worth to you?"

She can embellish a chord, change her picking, her fingering, and she has her voice. But he does have something that's never been there for her—the knack to write the whole song: melody, lyrics, chorus, bridge, build, and end. He's ahead of her, and she's learning from him as fast as she can. But he's ferrying a backpack filled with drugs and funding his music with crime, the kind that killed her father. Figures. *Everything is gray,* Dad used to say, *and nothing comes easy.* "I have a rule. No big decisions after midnight."

The look in his eyes is sad, but for the first time, she could convince herself that he cares. "Casey, all the big decisions in the music grind are made by warlocks after midnight."

"Oh, fuck off with your vampire wisdom shit. Know it all."

"Is this music worth it to you?"

"You'll know if you hear me at your door." She gets her phone out only when he shuts his car door, and she doesn't disarm the security system until she sees the Peugeot's taillights trickle away then vanish on Eureka.

13

Why does this psychologist wear a lab coat? Tyndall has seen neurologists wear slacks and sport shirts like golfers. But Dr. Halston, her new psych, wears a lab coat, and today it's streaked with two black marks along the waist. The incident with Father sent him to the emergency room with a concussion. It marked a last straw for both parents, who felt her previous psych was an ungodly spigot of West Coast liberal elite lunacy. Her preceptor in Saint Martin's Individualized Learning Experience/Shadow program, Dr. Vera Correy, intervened and gained her parents the psych of their choosing rather than one rationed by luck of the draw. Enter Dr. Shanna Halston.

"Does your tummy bother you, Tyndall?"

Shanna has Tyndall's digitized casefile glowing on a laptop which docks into the counter in the examining room. Even with Dr. Correy's intervention, Mother and Father waited weeks for her to see Dr. Halston. Shanna graduated from Evangel and then Northwest University in Kirkland, Washington. She is a Positive Confessor and Confirmed Believer. The laptop's silver light seethes against Shanna's pale skin. Even her eyebrows are yellow.

"We are not changing any medications," Tyndall says.

Shanna looks at the laptop and not at her. That's something to use when she becomes a great doctor, a laptop to focus on. "Quietarol? That's for gastric troubles."

"I spend half my time fighting with doctors to avoid medications that I know are wrong for me. And I spend the other half of my time fighting to get and keep medications I know I need to succeed at the things God created me to do."

"'Half of my time'? Tyndall. You sound like an old country lawyer."

"Read the side effects," Tyndall continues. "Not what's on your laptop, unless you are on the NCBI/NIH PubMed.gov site."

Shanna turns away from the laptop. "What side effects of Quietarol am I unaware of?"

"Ben was prescribed Quietarol because he kept complaining about his stomach to get OxyContin. I know everything about every drug every doctor ever put inside Ben Hastings."

Shanna raises her yellow eyebrows. "So did you take Ben's Quietarol?"

"No. The tablets had expired. I talked with Dr. Lacey about what I learned Quietarol might do for me. He prescribed it."

Shanna makes a face. "What might it do for you, Tyndall?"

"Does. What it *does* for me. In some patients, of which I am one, Quietarol is found to induce an irrational and intense sense of well-being. This is why Clidinium and other anticholinergic agents are preferred for cramps, stomach pains, and/or diarrhea-predominant irritable bowel syndrome. It would be a shame for people to feel intensely well when they are not. I don't have either kind of IBS. In this subject, Quietarol has the unexpected benefit of eliminating anxiety and muting sensory overloads of sound and motion."

Though Shanna smiles, she cannot hide her examining. While she listens, all her bones, neck and chin especially, crane forward and her eyes scour Tyndall. Cascades of question marks flow from her and probe Tyndall's chest, legs, and arms. Finally Shanna says, "I've been warned about you, Dr. Tyndall."

"Quietarol allows me to function without sensory overload in a room filled with blinking lights, shouting and/or crowds in motion. I can attend a basketball game in person. The whole game. I can dance while my friends perform fast and loud music. I can look a boy in the eye when I have to. We are not changing any medications."

Shanna pauses, then types a note. "So... your father had to come to the emergency room. What were your mother and father doing when you entered their bedroom?"

Where the tan linoleum meets the cream wall, an icy, gray snake made of filthy snow forms and begins to creep. Threats bulge along its crystalline spine.

"Father's verbal abuse of Mother escalated to physical abuse. Before he could strike her again, I intervened."

Shanna scans text on the laptop, brushing her fingertip up its display. "That's not precisely what your parents reported."

"It is hard to imagine Mother and Father telling anyone 'precisely' the truth about what I have witnessed."

That got her to leave the laptop alone. She positions a clipboard on her bony knee. "You know, Tyndall, there is a camp school near Rolla for neurocomplex children who have expressed violence at home. Everything is conducted there with calm and personalized, regimented care. But should a child become overwhelmed and express violence, a team of clinicians—padded, face-shielded, and gloved—rises up through the floor like a St. Louis SWAT team to suppress and then comfort the child and pacify the environment back to safety." She says all of this with the cold intensity of the snake advancing.

"Mother and Father sent Ben away to Camp St. Bartholomew, which is in the Ouachita Mountains in Arkansas. When he came back, he slurred his words and he still had smoky voice, but Father said Ben was clean and sober and reconciled to God. Ben would whisper my name in smoky voice when we watched horror movies."

Shanna pauses, then jots a note. "Please. Let's talk more about Ben."

"Dogs in familiar settings can be exposed to double the lethal amount of heroin and still survive," Tyndall says. She stays extra still. All over her and inside her she makes things still, and in the room is just the air vent which ticks and the clock which does not and these poofy chairs that look like frozen custard and on the walls the inexplicable paintings Shanna's son makes. The snake circles. In 38 minutes this will be over for the week. She did not take any Quietarol before this appointment because the stuff dries out her mouth, and it can make her slur her words. It's only for bustling social situations, such as lunch period. If Shanna moves to take it away, Tyndall will turn this room upside down. At last she has everything calmed enough that the snake sighs and waits. "Yet if the dog is taken to surroundings unfamiliar to the animal, half the lethal dose of heroin often easily kills it."

Shanna falls quiet, which is what Tyndall wanted. Tick tock goes the time. Shanna pushes her glasses up on her face. "When you say things like you just did, and there's no change in your facial expression or your body language, do people find that disturbing? Do they know how to understand your intent and your meaning?"

The bulky white lab coat makes Shanna appear anorexic, and the stiff tubes of its sleeves make her fingers seem thin, like red thorns. There's a wedding band flashing. With such frightening, spiked fingers, does she hurt her husband? Does he dread her and refuse her touch?

"I don't know how to understand the intent and meaning that somewhere in the world someone in a lab coat is injecting heroin into a dog until the dog dies." Tyndall says this, then swallows because Shanna makes a hash mark on her clipboard whenever she swallows. It's comforting to control Shanna, even if just a little.

"Let's see if we can concentrate on something a little more positive, then? You believe that your brother, Ben, loved you, right, Tyndall?"

"Not enough to stay."

"Addiction is a disease not a choice. He had a compulsion, a sickness."

"Yes, he did. He wanted heroin more than he wanted God

and Mother and Father and me. More than he wanted to live. That's for sure a disease."

Shanna waits. "What happened the day Ben died?"

Tyndall places her hands on her knees. She wears her old candy striper uniform to every therapy session, even though as an ILE shadow/ER volunteer she's much more powerful than a candy striper now. Her first therapy session happened two weeks after they buried Ben. She wore her candy striper's uniform then and so that is what you wear any time you have to go through this. At night she threw fits, and there wasn't a stick of furniture left in her bedroom but the mattress and the metal bed frame screwed to the floor. In one of her fits, she broke her wrist again. They visited the ER almost as often as she attended school. She can wear whatever she wants, Mother says, as long as she is getting help. When she wears the old uniform now, men stiffen and suck in breath as she passes.

"Ben was not allowed to be alone in his bedroom with the door closed. I came home. Devon Merritt brought me home." She must not tell Shanna anything more about Devon— Shanna might tell her parents all kinds of things. Breaking confidentiality might be a-okay by Shanna. She is a Believer. Tyndall is not yet eighteen. "I discovered I was the only one home, and his bedroom door was shut and locked. I pounded on the door until my wrist and shoulder hurt. I smashed the vacuum cleaner to pieces on the door. It was a Shark. From the porch, I took the metal chair but without the cushions. That broke the door. Swinging the metal chair against the door and ramming it against the door. The door split in a crescent near the doorknob, and there was yellow foam from inside the door everywhere. Inside the room Ben slumped in his armchair. He had the tourniquet band strapped to his arm and the syringe there hanging. His fingernails were blue. His lips were purple. Ben's eyes were brown like Father's are, and so you couldn't see any pupil at all. You had to look so deep in them. Even then you weren't seeing pupils. You were imagining you saw pupils. Diagnostic bias. Because you so very much wanted him to be alive."

Shanna makes what must be her listening-worrying face then writes a long note. Shanna allows herself a lot more faces than Dr. Durian. "The EMTs said you had broken your right wrist, and your right arm into a compound fracture, and you had broken your clavicle. Ben moved a dresser to block the door. A dresser. Full of clothes. Did anyone help you, Tyndall? No one understands how you got to him."

"I just told you I smashed the door with a metal chair from the porch. And the dresser was not full. There were two baskets of folded laundry on his bed."

"This Devon who dropped you off, did he help you?"

She watches Shanna very closely. "I was the only one alive in the house."

"The EMTs thought you were amazing, you know?"

"No, they did not. They called the cops because I wasn't crying."

"Tyndall. The police had to come because Ben had heroin in his room. And because he was dead. The EMTs didn't know you. And your mother and father were not there to help them meet you. It was quite a situation. Once they understood you were neurocomplex, they all thought you were amazing and brave."

Shanna sure has read her file and listened to everybody.

"Why would I be any more brave if I were neurotypical or neurocomplex?" Shanna is about to answer, but Tyndall heads her off. "Ben was dead before I touched that door. Narcan wasn't allowed in the house. Father said keeping Narcan would've been a Negative Confession and would've broken Faith. As a prayer family, we'd already bound the Lord against the Demon of Ben's addiction. According to Father. And his new church."

Shanna's face buckles. That's one face Tyndall has never seen a therapist make, so many shadows and ripples, like a pale, rotting vegetable that shocks you at the bottom of the bin. Eventually Shanna says, "What you do at the hospital now, that's a very positive outcome. Your preceptor adores you. You've taken your grief and given it purpose."

"You mean the Lord has given me purpose." Who *is* this Shanna? What does Northwest University teach? And how much has Shanna spoken with Tyndall's preceptor? How did that conversation go? "Mother should be in here. Not me."

"Do you understand why you are here, Tyndall?"

"Because I destroyed material possessions and interfered in Father's emotional and physical abuse of Mother."

Occasionally Shanna manages flat therapy face pretty well, and for just the right amount of time. "Tyndall, you are nothing if not precise."

This one may be smarter than Tyndall first thought. And she listens. That's dangerous. Dr. Durian never listened to anyone but himself. "Mother's the one who won't forgive herself."

"Do you forgive her?" Shanna asks while making a note. Clipboards could be good, too. You don't have to look at eyes or a face if you are obligated to take extensive notes.

"Of course, I forgive. God commands it. After St. Bartholomew, Ben was very happy for three weeks with us. Everything seemed normal. It was normal to go to the store when you have to run a household and you're out of something. ALDI is right there."

"Does your mother say that? Or is that something your father says?"

"He says that often. Sometimes all to himself. Father can say anything he needs to when it's just me around. Father tells me he's alone even when I'm with him, because most of the time there's no one actually living inside my heart."

Shanna removes her glasses and puts the clipboard and pen aside. She bows her head and strokes her eyebrows with her thumbs, four times. When she looks up, the skin around her eyes is pink. "Have you ever cried about any of this, sweetheart?"

The furnace crackles, and a blower hisses. Hot, dry air creeps from the vent. Exclamation points and minus signs tumble. Tyndall stares a long time at Shanna's lab coat until she can make everything still again. "I am going to be a really great doctor. The greatest. And soon, I will never have to talk with you ever again. Which is great. That means you can help a lot of other people instead of wasting time on me."

"Well, Dr. Tyndall." Shanna arranges her flat therapy face. "Your Father presented a Grade II concussion in the emergency room."

"His twenty-four hours of confusion and amnesia proved a great mercy to his family."

Shanna straightens her posture and sets the clipboard aside. "For now, Tyndall, I am going to recommend that you remain in your home with your parents. For now. But your fate is in your hands. Any further violence to either of your parents—*any*—and you will be sedated, secured, and transported by ambulance to Rolla. Do you understand me?"

All this time in what quiet she could make, the snake had wound around her calves and was icily parting her thighs. How did she miss its slick advance? "See you next Thursday, Dr. Halston," Tyndall says, rising.

14

The studio is way north on National Avenue past Silver Springs Park. In the streetlights, the building looks like a laundromat—one long rectangle of cinderblocks with a red metal roof and hardly any parking. Inside, a black leather couch, a battered coffee table, and a huge mixing and control board and monitor consume the first room you walk into. A fit, older guy with close-shaved hair rises from a chair and hugs Patrick. His name is Jeff, and he's the owner and sound engineer. He bends down to shake her hand and says he's eager to hear what she can do. It's in a speaking-to-children voice.

The mixing board and monitor almost block a bank of three floor-to-ceiling panes of glass. Behind the glass waits a drum set, a Baldwin upright piano, a KORG synthesizer, music stands and mics on stands and a few mics on adjustable booms suspended from the ceiling, and even some Fender amps, the reissue tube amps with taupe casing and silver lettering. Patch cords coil on a tree of hooks. Casey tries to see this as a musical romper room for gifted students, but her heart pounds. Everything gleams super clean and organized. The glowing monitor is SpaceX high tech, and it all looks like it's going to cost them piles of money. At home with SoundBlitz on her laptop she can goof around and make a whole weekend of mistakes and spend nothing but time. Not here.

Patrick and Jeff geek out about the gold velvet paneling in the adjacent soundproof room to the left of the control board and monitor. The soundproof room is thick carpeted and about as big as a walk-in closet. Walling the room is a sparkling gold acoustic foam with sharp ridges. There's not a speck of dust on any of the neatly packed blocks. On the black foam ceiling glow white starbursts of LED lights in black cans—Jeff pulls one down, bragging about them being his own design. He switches it on and off, then sticks the black can back in the ceiling tiles in a new position.

Casey folds her thumbs against her palms and squeezes with her fingers until her thumbs ache. Is the clock already ticking, is the meter running? When does this start costing money? She can't bring herself to ask because Patrick and Jeff seem like boys with toys. She does not want to show them how new this all is to her.

Dominating the soundproof room is an enormous tube mic and the black circle of its pop filter attached with a curvy stalk. The mic, a big, gold canister, is mounted on a fearsome tripod of shining metal with wheels in its base. The tripod supports and extends the canister of the tube mic on a neck-like derrick that bows and swivels and rocks as Jeff demonstrates in slow, careful motions, one hand cradling and easing the sensitive mic. It's like the skeleton of a small, crouching dragon. With one black eye socket, the mic canister forms its golden skull surrounded by the gilled bones of a silver shock mount.

Patrick is quiet now, watching her, and she feels even more the amateur. He interrupts Jeff. "Hey, Casey, let's get your Martin out and go in by the piano and warm up."

"Great idea!" Jeff says. He smiles a lot, which helps, but he's like someone who has had too much coffee, bouncy and happy this late on a Sunday night. "Boots off, everybody."

They enter the playroom, and when Jeff seals the glass door behind them it makes a kissing sound. The air pressure shifts in her ears. Patrick pulls out the piano bench, and sets down his leather binder of typed up lyrics. He swings one of the ceiling mounted mics in front of Casey, and hands her a headset. "So you can get used to hearing yourself and Jeff and me. He can take your volume up or down. He can do anything we need."

Walls of more sound foam bricks make cozy this part of the studio, and the piano and drum kit and music and mic stands are close, but not cluttered. From this side, those glass panes look out on Jeff's blue-lighted face floating above the mixing board. Beneath the console is a thicket of gray and black wires backlit in blue, red, amber, and green.

"Anything tracking?" Jeff's voice comes over the headset super clarified, but his words feel separate from his floating face, as if they are delayed.

"Track this one," Patrick says, tapping the mic in front of Casey. "Just so you can get an idea of what we're working with."

The blue floating face nods. When Jeff sits down, he's just blue forehead, eyebrows, and eyeballs.

Patrick fetches lyric sheets from his leather binder and dithers till he finds what he wants. "Let's do that 'God, You're So Great' thing you just taught me."

"'How Great Thou Art?'" Wouldn't Tyndall be thrilled? Casey taught this to Tyndall on piano after they heard it in church, and they played and sang it a lot as children. She taught Patrick the song because it stretches your voice out from pianissimo to fortissimo in short order. She watches him steadying the lyric sheets, homemade, with chord changes and tone and timbre notations: RISE—Am7, SOBER—F, JOY—C, BIG—G. He typed up something she taught him, and by choosing it now he's building her a calm space and bringing the familiar into this. A drug dealer, a thug, but his posture at the piano is super and his fingers are beautiful.

They start in softly and thoughtfully, and he's singing a baritone murmur that opens the front and center for her. Just before the chorus, she thinks of Tyndall praying, that golden hair falling forward and that smooth skin tightening along her neck. Casey closes her eyes and lets go, all out, even backing away from the mic a bit. The headset is so crisp and clear, and she feels a fist full of redeeming light rising up from the bottom of her lungs, up through her throat and into the night.

They finish, and Patrick turns to look out at Jeff whose eyes are wide and eyebrows are raised. The instant they ended the song, with her eyes closed, Casey felt great. But now, trembling, she kneels and lowers the Martin into its case, while over the speakers Jeff goes on and on about some British missionary in the Ukraine and a German poem thing sung by repenting Russians. Geez! Decaf, Buddy. Patrick is nodding, though.

Jeff apologizes and explains that just two hours ago he had six rappers in here, literally fighting, and he almost called the cops, and at lunch, the white Gospel group from Koshkonong wept and prayed over him, and here they were working on the Sabbath, and for breakfast there was a death metal band with a singer who bellowed like Cookie Monster.

As he talks he leads Casey into the gold velvet closet. She feels like a child being led to a witch's oven. She's put this much together: that glass door will shut, and she will be trapped in here with just her voice and this crouching metal dragon waiting to burn her alive if she does it wrong. She rubs her palms along the thighs of her jeans and frets over balancing Patrick's lyric sheets on the stand and where her water bottle should sit.

"It's the Ozarks," Jeff says smiling at her as he holds out a new headset. "Everyone forgets us, and yet we are the nexus. All this great music."

Patrick, now in the control room, blurts a raspberry—loud as a grinding gearshift in the headset. "Nexus of no escape! Whoever made it out of here alive and famous? Aside from Porter Waggoner."

"You did," she says, her voice grating and childish over the dragon mic.

Patrick scowls, and says "I've a feeling we're not in Aspen, Toto."

She wrinkles her nose at this. Just then something softens in Jeff's face, and his shoulders slump. He's looking at her like her Dad used to, amazed and goofy. Dad kept his hair buzzed like Jeff's, though Dad's never got the chance to show any gray.

"Hey, this is all going to be okay," Jeff whispers. He's adjusting the dragon's head and its black circle of a pop filter, moving it back from her. "Don't listen to us old guys about anything but the sound."

"Ain't that the fortune in my cookie!" She fights the urge to wince at her voice.

He shows her where he wants her to stand. "I know you may have seen people kissing the mic in movies and videos." He looks at her again with a smile. "But you have a crazy big set of pipes for someone your size. Like spinto soprano with a mezzo squatting in the basement apartment. So…"

"Got it," she says. "Don't smooch the dragon."

Jeff grins and looks over the tube mic and its boom. "It kind of does look like a dragon. He's your friend, though. You're going to love how you sound in him."

She massages her face with her fingertips and then palms. Jeff shuts the door on her and takes his seat at the console. Patrick wheels a chair over next to him. She runs through her tongue twisters but rather than just saying them she sings them in scales—Around the rough and rugged rock the ragged rascal ran. Quid pro quo quoth querulous crow.

"Okay," she says, but she doesn't feel it. "Wait. Can I play guitar while I sing?"

Jeff shakes his head. The mic is there to isolate her vocals. A guitar will clutter the track. He explains that all the instruments she and Patrick recorded at home are going to be in the headphones, and how he can make any instrumental track she needs louder or softer, and how she should just let everything fall away and be in the music. They can make as many takes as she needs.

"Ah, no we can't," Patrick interrupts.

Jeff sits back and is quiet.

The room is freezing and soundless, like she's in an underwater nightmare looking out at them and their faces, blue in the monitor's blast.

Patrick catches her eye. "'Lexus from Texas'," he says over the headset. "A little country, but all you."

She nods. Jeff raises his hand and counts her in. Over the headset her Martin chips and rings. Step into it fun and then a big rise after the line about the Lord.

I clipped a Lexus from Texas
Just past the West Memphis Bridge.
The greyhound track broke right at my back,
And I asked the Good Lord to give

Me some sense of his new direction,
A purpose between wicked lines.
I clipped a Lexus from Texas,
Then sought your shoulder divine.

This song Patrick has written—it's all new. It's funny. It's like an old Janis Joplin thing with Porsches and Mercedes, and God is called in. Patrick says it all came into his writing because of her. She feels that fist of light rising in her throat again and pours it all out, digging her toes into the carpet. At last the song winds down.

She opens her eyes. Jeff isn't looking at the monitor but at her, his eyes blank and his mouth open. He glances at Patrick and sticks out his bare arm.

Patrick brushes the chill bumps, whatever Jeff's deal is. Patrick says, "I know. Right?"

Jeff turns back to her. "Casey, that was… I…" He swivels in his chair and looks again at Patrick. "You hear anything we need to…?"

Patrick shakes his head. "Sing, 'Spokane,' please, Casey."

"Listen. Wait," Jeff says, waving his hands above his head. "If she can deliver like that, you two need to bring all the instruments in here and get the level and the mix the same. None of this homemade muddybuzz. I can only push and blur a rotten input so far, okay. If she can do that? Patrick. Jesus!"

He and Patrick get into such a row that she pulls her headset off. There's no crowd, no dancing, no happy recognition from listeners hearing the first chords of a song they love. The carpet beneath her toes gives like a sponge. Even though she can see Jeff and Patrick through the glass door arguing she feels trapped and sinking. There's a clock somewhere that's costing them money. She is costing them money, and she could and maybe she just did do it all wrong. Where's this dream-come-true thing?

Jeff turns red in the face, and he's pointing to his ears. She puts the headset back on. "I just want to say this to you." He stops for a bit. Patrick hunches, face purple in the blue light out there. "I've had a lot of talent in here. But I've never felt that. Nothing like what you just did. You two don't need to cheap out with half-at-home recording. That's not fair to what you are." He turns to Patrick. "That's not fair to what she can do."

Patrick keeps his arms crossed and his head down.

Her heart is going to jump out of her chest. More frightening than failure is that she cares what Patrick thinks of her now. When did that start? Why can't they record it all here if Jeff says that's better? She glances at the dragon crouching and waiting, and wishes she could throw a fit like Tyndall. "Can I at least hear it back?" she asks. "Just once." She puts her palm to the icy glass door. "I don't even know what I just did."

15

Devon cycles through texts on the Merritt business cell phone and backfills his mind with the sound of the ProMaster's AC, a throbbing hum with a dash-shaking rattle every thirty seconds or so. His denim work shirt hangs behind him on the seat as he waits in the Glendale parking lot for traffic to clear. After a sleeting arctic blast, it's a glaring 80 degrees again. The success of a postcard, which Stepmom designed at home, is as exhausting as it is surprising. *Climate change is real. So are year-round weeds. Fight them without destroying the Planet! Call Merritt Organics!* His cell phone pings with outcries from the converted.

The passenger door opens, and Tyndall climbs in and sits down.

"Hey! You can't just do that. Get out!"

Blank mannequin look, not at him but at two soccer players vaping in a banged up Pontiac. "Lock your doors," she says. "I could be a sex-crazed immigrant." She shuts her door, and then blocks a quaking AC vent with her hand. "Your metabolic rate and muscle mass cause you to feel much hotter than it actually is in this space." Rather than adjust the vent, she'll muffle it with her hand until he relents and turns the air down.

He's tried to dodge her for days, nearly impossible at school. He never calls her. If you think Tyndall is odd and robotic in person, she's a menu of voice-activated prompts on the phone. Call wise, she uses her cell phone like an eighty-year-old: emergencies only.

"I want to understand what we're doing now," she says. Her tongue clicks when she speaks lately, as if her mouth is especially dry.

"You and me both."

She seems to watch the gray and yellow piles of vape smoke coming from the Pontiac. "Did that hand job harm you? Are you injured?"

She isn't dressed differently—same style sweater in one of five colors; dark jeans; red Keds with aqua blue laces, Glendale Falcon colors. But her hair is full and golden and not tied back in a pony. Every day he avoids her, he sees her lingering, waiting, her hair washed and lustrous.

She looks right at him. "There was quite a lot of sperm from you."

He tries to calm himself with counting but can't wait till ten. "I told you no. I told you to stop."

"And I have forgiven you. You don't know what God wants from you. Or from us. You never listen to Him. So you can't be held accountable for all your Negative Confessions. I'll listen to the Lord for both of us."

He checks the engine temperature gauge, anything to look away from her. "How is what you did right by anything you're taught at that church?"

"Come to that church and find out."

"I thought all churches hated masturbation?"

She snorts. "You didn't masturbate."

There's no telling if she's joking. Her lips, chapped and cracked lately, are almost always parted and yet her chin juts forward. She seems quite tense. He guesses one of her medications causes this. The expression only softens when she does that unplugged thing. He does not want to hurt her. What a mess this is now!

"Tyndall..." He starts as slowly and calmly as he can manage. "Look. You obsess over things. You lock on heavy, and then you let go. Remember all the dissecting? Remember underwater? No kid at Southern Hollow Swim Club could hold their breath longer than you. Remember car washes? You would pass up Andy's to go sit in a car wash."

She has the best posture of anyone he knows. With her spine erect and shoulders square, it's even more discouraging when her eyes go trackless and her face slackens. He wants to yell at her, but in the amber haze of late afternoon, he's struck with how very pretty she has become. Tyndall Hastings is no longer a girl at all. "Focus! I'm trying to say something. Don't go unplugged on me."

Her jaw hardens. "But you told me to remember! When I remember in my mind, I live again through that past moment. Only it's pure, more pure than the actual living it was." Her eyes lock with his. "Memory can be very beautiful."

She runs her tongue along her bottom lip, and a pang of worry grips his chest. How is she ever going to navigate her college life and medical school with strangers all around her? She's sexy, wetting her bottom lip with her tongue. Right now, if Devon didn't know her, if he were some random guy in college, and she was sitting here with this body, this hair, that lovely face, the dreamy look she just cast, he might read all her signals wrong. He might read desire, when she means nothing like it.

She still stifles the air vent with her hand, her posture locked and erect. "I want to be the one who gives you all your memories that are more perfect than living."

He mashes the back of his head against the headrest and shuts his eyes tight. "Tyndall, what am I going to do with you?"

"I have eleven suggestions."

What is this that has him trembling? Rage? Frustration? Lust? Anyone else would be a pig and just use her till better comes along. But it's not that simple. This is Tyndall. Here's my girlfriend. She has special abilities. In the afternoon light, she's gorgeous. He pulls his denim shirt off his seat back.

"Look at me," she shouts in the voice that others have used on her for so long. "We could be living in the overflow if you will just wake up. I am your Blessing."

What to say to this? One encouragement and he'll never get her stopped. He puts the ProMaster in reverse, and its alarm hoots. When she puts a hand on his shoulder, he flinches.

She watches his shoulders and chest very closely. But she does not remove her hand. He can feel how cold her palm is all the way through his shirt. The AC rattles.

"Devon, what keeps you from me? Please?"

He's shaking, trapped. He doesn't know what to say. "I have to go to work now."

"Yes, I know. Take me home. Give me one of those denim Merritt shirts that I can wear for the rest of my life. Give me that one you have on."

16

Casey's eyes burn with exhaustion. Her ears ring. Kids in the buzzing lunchroom blur like they're all painted by the old French guys in blobs of bright dots. They speak loudly, gesture dramatically, and no one is listening to a word anyone else says. Some hold up cells and film or photograph themselves, hair tossing, muscles flexing, grimacing, grooving to music privately blared through Bluetooth buds sprouting from their ears. "So... yeah-no. Perfect!" Are all of them live streaming, YouTube sensations? Wait. Nope. A few kids exist without smartphones, excommunicated nonbelievers lost in this cathedral of wireless. They blink at their lunch trays and once in a while look up in search of someone. Casey relishes her almost empty table way to the side, a cinderblock wall painted robin's egg blue at her back. At her table a girl films herself in a TikTok for her followers. Next table over, misfits huddle and grouse. Probably would rather be vaping than eating.

A tall girl with bouncing blonde hair crosses the lunchroom and heads directly toward her. The Amazon wears a denim shirt unbuttoned over a tee. It takes Casey several seconds to realize this is Tyndall wearing one of Devon's work shirts with the Merritt Organics badge above the pocket. Casey sits up and tries to focus.

"You sure look happy," she says. "And your hair. Tyndall! Looks great."

Tyndall sets her tray down. There are two lunches piled on her one tray. Under the denim button down, she wears a retro tee with a navy collar. The tee is way too tight, and the upper cup of her bra squeezes her and makes her boobs mound up. PUSH stretches across her chest. Did she mean to do this? Wait, this is Tyndall. She means everything she does. The letters warp and tug. This was a church camp shirt from two or three summers ago. PUSH stands for Pray Until Something Happens. Something sure has happened. Where's the cable knit sweater? Where's the scrunchy?

"I have questions for you about how to keep men happy," Tyndall says.

The girl busy filming herself scowls at Casey and Tyndall. This girl has purple hair and wears a shawl that features a desert planet scape and a golden robot from the movies. She sucks on a metal straw clanging in her hydro flask (which is painted to look like another famous robot). She resumes filming, one profile then the other, rotating back and forth, mechanically. Pink hearts and rosy hugs sparkle all around her shimmering image.

"Keep yourself happy," Casey says. "Look! You're Super-girl. Only with huge boobs."

"Yes. But I want my superpower to be expert hand jobs."

Purple hair robot girl nearly chokes. When she recovers, she holds her phone out at Tyndall like a warning card in a soccer game. "That's on my Story forever now, thank you, slut mouth. Do you just say whatever you want always?"

Tyndall takes her seat then squares her amazing posture to the purple-haired girl. "Yes. Thank you for asking. Now I want you to film somewhere away from us so you don't lose any more followers, please. I am going to talk at length with my loose friend about the care and operation of penises."

Go, Tyndall. If you didn't know her, you would believe Tyndall has never walked into a room and felt like a fraud or cared what others thought. Yet Casey knows Tyndall studies other girls and what they do and how they act and answer. She can have meltdowns of frustration and panic when she gets something wrong or when she doesn't get the reaction she calculated. Anxiety rules her. This makes her all the more fierce when she plows ahead like this. And she's able to do this a lot more lately.

Purple-hair robot girl points her phone at herself, protests galactic injustice to her followers, and then storms off.

"I am trying to change my relationship with Devon," Tyndall begins. Wow, she eats fast. If she doesn't watch it, it'll be a lot more than her chest getting big.

"'Loose friend'?"

"You have had more premarital sex than anyone I know. And you star now and have starred in rock bands, plural, with young men, plural, from other schools, plural, and have traveled with them unchaperoned to faraway places, plural, even across state lines."

Casey snorts. "Have you seen Arkansas? Nothing down there to make a girl drop her skirt. Least not till Bentonville."

Tyndall sits motionless and expressionless for a long, awkward while. Is she angry? Stunned? Hurt? Is she changing her mind? There's never a way to know. She just stops.

"I fully understand the anatomy of the male orgasm."

"Is this really okay for the lunchroom?" Casey waits a beat. Telling Tyndall how you feel about which topics are appropriate doesn't always get the subject changed.

"I am certain from my reading and from what I have viewed online that the way to a man's heart is not through his stomach. That's the wrong organ."

Casey nods.

"Devon has an excellent penis that responds quickly and emits generously without much effort on my part. You have seen it function."

"Jesus, Tyndall."

"Yes, Praise Him. Beyond this emission, Devon did not seem to appreciate my actions. He fought me and told me to stop. He has not requested another hand job, so I must be performing the procedure incorrectly. Instruct me."

"He fought you and told you to stop? What do you mean?"

"That's what he did. He fought me and told me 'stop'. But I am stronger than he is."

Suddenly there is something intimidating about her bestie, Tyndall. Her height, her big shoulders and powerful, long arms. Like unearthed scary Viking warrior queen come to life. Casey recalls a screaming, red-faced fit of Tyndall's that stopped everyone in Sequiota Park, and it took Nora, Devon's mom, and Casey's mom to get Tyndall under control. Devon was there, fishing in the creepy pools of the polluted hatchery, witnessing Tyndall's fit, slack-jawed, a conical party hat on his head. Was it his eighth birthday? Blood and spit and torn clothes—the Hastings' sedan rushed away in a shower of gravel. Now what has Tyndall gone and done?

"His penis presented as extremely engorged and promptly emitted significant amounts of spermatozoa. All positive outcomes."

Some of the cell phone zombies have quieted and stilled at the next table. One greasy-haired kid in a black trench has his tablet raised and its camera turned on Tyndall.

"Hey!" Casey says, rising up. "I'll smash that and spin your butt on the shards!"

"Fuck off, Tiny Rock Star," he says. "This is a public lunchroom."

A hubbub breaks out around him. Even girls who hate Casey and think Tyndall is a weirdo pounce on the kid.

Casey comes around the table and puts her back between the porn collector and Tyndall. She grabs Tyndall's arm below the armpit, and it's almost like a guy's arm, tight with muscle. "Need to whisper. Stay cool?"

Tyndall nods.

"My house. This afternoon," she whispers, lips right against Tyndall's ear. "This is way too much for the lunchroom. You've said way too much."

Tyndall shivers but doesn't jerk away. She nods. "I don't want him to be able to survive without my touch." Their faces are very close, cheeks warm, nearly blushing. "I have never wanted anything like this. It's terrible."

Devon drops Tyndall off in the big Merritt Organics van. Casey watches the feeds from the doorbell and driveway security cams on the screens in Dad's study. Devon wears a ball cap pulled too low for her to read his face. Tyndall's still getting a ride from him? But she's done something to him? He has the van hooting in reverse before Tyndall even starts up the walkway stairs. He doesn't return her goodbye wave. Whoa. That's not like him. Casey goes to the door and hurries Tyndall into the living room. Mom will be home soon, and this is already complicated.

Tyndall sits on the edge of the couch, spine erect, hands in her lap, palms up.

"Mom won't switch the AC back on. You want to take that denim shirt off?"

Tyndall shakes her head.

She sits beside Tyndall, slouches into the cushions. She's looking at Tyndall's back and hair, which glows like honey in the afternoon sunlight. She longs to stroke Tyndall's back and comfort her like she did her mom when Dad died, stroking with just her fingernails until they both went hypnotized and numb. But Tyndall can't stand a caress. A punch, a slap, a push, no problem. But a caress, she claims, burns like fire under her skin.

"Can I run my hands through your hair?"

"No." Tyndall doesn't move for a long while. "I am trying so hard, Casey. Nothing's happening. He hardly talks." She bounces her knuckles against the insides of her knees in something like 5/4 time. "I don't want to be Tyndall, the neighbor girl he has to be nice to because she has 'special abilities.' I want to be the only sun in his galaxy."

What's love going to look like for Tyndall? Autism plus all the Jesus? "What do you mean by he said no and asked you to stop?"

She stills. "I opened his jeans. They were the buttons-only kind. He said stop. He fought me, but he was not able to stop me."

"Did you imagine there might be a reason he asked you to stop?"

"Reasoning is not in Devon Merritt."

"So you just went right ahead and grabbed his dick?"

"After I pulled his underwear down and freed it, yes."

"And then he stopped fighting?"

"I did not say he stopped."

"Was he still saying no?"

Tyndall raps against her knees again. "I believe he said no three more times."

"Oh, Tyndall."

"He must not understand himself. He must be confused. Immediately at my touch his penis became grossly distended. I caused him to orgasm in just four strokes. Copiously. More than I have ever seen on any video. Which means I performed extremely well, right?" She turns to Casey. "Yet then he was red in the neck and face, and short of breath. He stayed a long time in the men's bathroom by the wrestling gym. He would not speak to me after he returned to the hallway. He has avoided me for days. Now he asks to know what he is supposed to do with me."

"Imagine that."

Tyndall twists to the side to face Casey. "What? I don't understand what you mean." She has not moved her legs, so with one hand behind her on the sofa, she looks like a bimbo on a bad heavy metal album cover especially with the denim shirt falling open to reveal the tee she has way outgrown. "Should I suggest he allow me to bring him to orgasm again, but with less fighting so that I don't hurt him? I must have hurt him. I must have done it wrong. Teach me how to execute a hand job correctly."

"This is way not about technique."

Tyndall sits back against the cushions. She plops her hands in her lap again. Then she examines Casey, especially how she sits, slouching, feet up on the coffee table. Her examining you—it's like having a space alien study your body. Her eyes get wide and rove. If Tyndall were a boy staring at her body like this right now, Casey would wring his neck. "When you played that song you recorded, God told me you were going to be famous. You'll be out of Springfield in no time."

"Why is any of this at all about me?"

"If you're gone, that's why God is saying, 'Now it's time for Devon to belong to you alone.' God tells me that. I have prayed for this blessing. I have faith. I have obligated the Lord, and my blessing has already happened. I have claimed Devon." Tyndall slides down and tries to slouch, but rather than relaxing, she's as tense as a bow, as if slobbing on a couch is a new yoga pose. "Devon doesn't listen to God. A walking Negative Confession." She's watching Casey's lap. "If it is not technique, then what do you think I did wrong?"

Casey shows Tyndall her palms and waits until Tyndall nods permission to touch her. She swats Tyndall's knee. "Get your legs up here." Kneeling on the sofa, she guides Tyndall's legs along either side of her. She straddles Tyndall's left leg. Then she juts her thumbs into the belt loops along Tyndall's hips and forces the arch of Tyndall's back flat to the cushions.

Tyndall's eyes, wild like a pinned animal's, rove Casey's wrists and shoulders.

"Feel where you are right now?" Casey asks. "You gave me permission because you know I'm your forever friend." She moves her hands up and digs her thumbnails into the sides of Tyndall's stomach. "You think I wouldn't hurt you. But you don't know. I've never done this." She waits a few beats and then slips her hands under Tyndall's tight shirt, grabs her ribs, and digs in again. "Feel where you are right now?"

Tyndall's eyes narrow and focus right on Casey's neck. Casey's heart beats faster. There are moments Casey forgets how small she is, but here she's hit with one of those times when she feels tiny. Her childhood pal has grown into an

Amazon. If Tyndall flips out, she could crush Casey. And Casey can't stop her.

She moves her thigh deeper into Tyndall's groin, but waits to make sure Tyndall doesn't lose her cool. Then she grabs her breasts, sinking her fingers in. A caress might actually hurt Tyndall. In a flash Tyndall snags Casey's arms at the elbows and bares her teeth.

Casey has trouble catching her breath. "Feel where you are right now? You want me to stop. You don't know what I'll do. You don't know what I'm doing."

Tyndall growls and her eyes lock on the lumps of Casey's hands beneath her shirt.

Casey's voice rises. She's shouting the way that Tyndall's mother did when they were kids and Nora needed Tyndall to focus. "How did Devon feel when you had him by his dick?" Beneath the silky, taut cup of Tyndall's bra, plump flesh strains. She tenses up, knee hard against Tyndall's crotch. This is it. Tyndall is going to snap and whale on her.

Instead the growl ceases. Tyndall's gray eyes grow steady and focus on Casey's eyes. Casey pushes her knee in more deeply and keeps the pressure on her breasts. She can feel Tyndall's heart as well, pumping against her right palm. The tips of her teeth and her jawbone smart. She braces.

"I get it," Tyndall finally says. "He felt trapped. Like this."

Tyndall eases her grip on Casey's arms, but Casey doesn't let up. Tyndall's face relaxes, and in her eyes Casey can see a question forming. Slowly, Tyndall arches her back. Then she rolls her crotch against Casey's knee. She places both of her hands on top of Casey's hands hugging them tighter to her breasts. Tyndall closes her eyes, pauses, then grinds whole-heartedly three times against Casey's knee. Casey can't believe this is happening—this is not where she intended this to go.

But it's thrilling. Her heart starts slamming. Tyndall's breasts feel so full and yet they're the softest things Casey has ever touched. Tyndall starts a fourth grind, then stops, eyes wide almost as if she's nearing a peak.

At last Tyndall exhales. "Like take off in an airplane. But in a circle." She grips Casey's forearms and extracts her hands from her chest. "No more. This feels extremely good, but it is not how I want it. Not with you. You're my friend, and you're a girl. So, no."

There's a purple mark on the side of Tyndall's belly where Casey's fingers bit. "And Devon..." Casey begins, but she's nearly panting. "You may have made him feel that way. Flying. Excited. But trapped and wrong. Not what he wanted with a forever friend."

Tyndall's mouth drops open.

"And then he came a lot, because... Tyndall, that's just animal stuff. He couldn't help it. And you should know that. What do all those medical books say?"

"They are frustratingly silent on the liquid volume of the male orgasm. By no measure an impractical consideration. Why are we women always stuck dealing with bodily fluids that no one honestly warns about ahead of time?"

Nodding, Casey releases her slowly and then moves back. Now it is Tyndall slouching and Casey is the one sitting erect and trembling at the edge of the sofa.

With great care, as if her body is a strange new possession, Tyndall adjusts her bra, then pulls the tee down to protect her flesh. She looks up at Casey. "How can I make him want my touch?"

"How can I make you want my touch?" It's out of her mouth that fast, no taking it back. And she didn't even know this was in her.

Tyndall's forehead bunches. Slowly she sits up. "So do you mean I can't make him want my touch anymore than you could make me want more from you right now?"

Casey nods. Her heart feels like she has plunged off a mountainside after running all the way to the summit.

"He's not gay, is he?"

Casey shakes her head. "It's the friend part. And the who you both are part. And the how long you've known each other part."

"That's too hard. That might never happen. I might never get him to want more from me, then." Tyndall leans forward and adjusts her breasts in her bra again.

Bolts of unexpected desire ache down Casey's arms.

"You must be wrong," Tyndall goes on. "Neurotypicals are so screwed up about all this. People should want what feels good and do what God created us to do."

"Yeah, what about that? I can't see Victory Faith Triumphant encouraging you to become a hand job guru."

Tyndall renders one facial expression she has down—eyeroll followed by the "how can you not know this" jaw drop. She pulls out her cell and swipes around. "Founder, shepherd, and pastor Jack Sprague of Victory Faith Triumphant." She hands Casey the phone.

A tan, fit guy with an Australian accent wears a headset mic and stands before a massive crowd. He holds an honest-to-God arrow at his crotch, pointy side out, and he's preaching about the blessing of his smoking hot wife and how she keeps his shaft polished. All the while he sickeningly strokes the phallic arrow.

"Holy shit," Casey says. She rewinds a portion. It is just too much to believe that Sprague really says this beneath a cross on the wall.

"Exactly," says Tyndall. "If the Lord grants a smoking hot wife the purpose of keeping our Reverend Jack Sprague's shaft polished, then Devon Merritt's arrow needs to glow since he is my man. God already said he is."

"I kind of think you're skipping the part about married."

"I have already obligated the Lord. Devon Merritt will marry me and anything different is a Negative Confession. So I need to learn how to shine his shaft and make him happier than Jack Sprague right now. You show me! I have so much to pray about."

"Oh," Casey says. Her eyes travel her friend's new body. "Me, too."

Tyndall grabs her hands, and this is a great relief. "Pray together?"

"Why not do that thing where you pray over me?"

Tyndall closes her eyes and stretches her hand out to touch Casey's forehead with just her fingertips. "Father God, Lord Jesus, Holy Spirit, I command you…"

17

Dr. Vera Correy calls Tyndall into her alcove where she has three computer monitors glowing. One offers a nine-panel display of camera feeds from all over Dr. Correy's ER. The middle monitor bears the green and gray of a costing spreadsheet Tyndall just finished. And the third shows what Tyndall mistakes at a distance for a colorized sweet gumball. But then, no, the spikes end not in points but in burls, like the clubs on a playing card.

Dr. Correy has straight black hair and a long, white face. Her eyes are the soft brown of a minister's shoe leather. She clicks her mouse, and the monitor shows a whole cluster of these clubbed balls. And then another where they are all red.

"No chain," Tyndall says. "Not streptococcus. What is it?"

"What may be a new virus in China. An ophthalmologist has shared it. Chinese authorities have detained him." Dr. Correy takes her hand and squeezes it. They both share the occasional need for this contact gesture.

Tyndall has learned from Dr. Correy of jealousies among hospital staff, envies Tyndall often fails to perceive. This gesture is one source. Mother calls Tyndall's lack of perception one of the Lord's greatest blessings. Nora believes this lack frees Tyndall from the world's sinful noise and vanity. Some illusions are worthy of our cultivation and may even yield positive medical outcomes. They operate like the soothing falsehood that Quietarol deploys on her heart, mind, and nervous system. The mayhem, the disorder buzzes and strives, but the chemistry lulls her neurons with hope. Nora sometimes steeps herself in Hope, the right-minded Hope of Jesus Christ, Our Lord and Savior, but also irrational hopes. Tyndall has witnessed illogic sustain Nora through the worst from Marion, and from Ben.

After Ben's overdose, Dr. Vera Correy attended when Tyndall came to the emergency room. Dr. Correy displaced the lead physician, as she tends to for any neurocomplex child presenting on her watch. To the family's surprise, after closely following Tyndall's counseling and even observing a session of her physical therapy, she showed up at the Hastings' house, unannounced one evening. In a low monotone, she recommended to Tyndall and her parents that Tyndall enroll in an Individual Learning Experience/Shadow program. It was to be of indeterminate length, and Dr. Correy would be her "preceptor."

Southern Hollow neighbors, the Correys live beside First Lake. The family goes back in Springfield even before the Civil War—miners and blacksmiths, and one was a nurse. Dr. Frank Correy is Saint Martin's Chief of Surgery. Vera, his spouse, runs the ER.

On the back porch that evening, Dr. Vera Correy stood rather than taking the offered chair, one of the metal ones like Tyndall used to smash Ben's door. Vera held quite still, making her recommendations and answering Marion and Nora's questions. Despite her monotone, she offered a great blessing from the Almighty, nothing short of it. Marion trembled as he witnessed, at length, the awesomeness of the God they all served. Like Dr. Correy, Tyndall stood, motionless and unplugged, as Devon calls it, her heart in turmoil that this woman doctor, who had followed every step of her injury and recovery in such a scientific manner, now visited the Hastings' back porch and endured Marion Hastings.

Nora, though, had long been observing Dr. Correy.

"You don't have to answer this, Dr. Correy." She popped a hand firmly over Marion's fist to shut him up and freeze him to his chair. "You know, as Tyndall's mother, I mean you no offense. We're so grateful. All you've done. Where are you on the autism spectrum?"

Dr. Vera Correy's eyes rested on Tyndall's shoulders, and she was silent long enough that all but Tyndall grew nervous. In that time, Tyndall watched a white lab coat of authority burn away to reveal a blood sister standing there with long black hair and brown eyes behind which tumblers were rolling as if a locking mechanism were striving to sync open. *Another like me. Struggling to quell the roiling world and answer. Like I do.* How did Nora perceive this first?

"My mother noted deficits in developmental milestones," Dr. Correy began carefully, returning Tyndall's stare, "signals that medical science would not recognize and codify for a decade. Mother intervened when recognition and vocalization did not manifest. Much like you intervened, Nora, didn't you? Early. Very early. And she fought for my life when no one understood her. No one believed her." Nora glowed as if the Holy Spirit had lit her like a candle. "Please allow me to return some of the bounty of the Lord's great Mercy and Love."

Even this nod to the Almighty did not revive Marion. He wrestled with the contradiction that the Angel of God's Glory might also bear a lifelong affliction such as Tyndall's. How could this be? God is perfect. And He redeemed us for our own perfection of health, mind, and great wealth. "You're not Catholic, are you?" he asked.

With effort, Tyndall swallowed the thought that her father would not be any better of a man even if she cracked his noggin against a dresser every afternoon. Nora smoldered, her cheeks red, her eyes narrowed on Marion.

Dr. Correy erected a smile—a practiced and fashioned expression, just as Tyndall had developed and rehearsed a warm smile she could present to hopeless classmates. "Frank is Presbyterian, Judge Hastings. You don't have to be Catholic to be employed by the Sisters of Mercy. Your daughter has so much to offer. Please say yes."

In her alcove now Dr. Correy clicks her mouse, and on the screen the spiked balls shift and pulse.

"An ophthalmologist?" Tyndall asks. "It invades through the eyes? Why detained?"

"Detained for sharing. And for calling this virus new." Dr. Correy lets loose of Tyndall's hand. She draws three squares on the screen, fences around each spiked ball. "When doctors are detained for speaking the truth, then the truth… may prove terrible." She grips Tyndall's shoulder. Any witness would think Tyndall is being reprimanded. "I need to talk with the staff. Go to Supply. Get a clipboard, a notebook. I need a physical count. Face shields, head caps, gowns, masks, and gloves."

18

Jogging down Utica, Casey spots Devon sitting on Red Rocks, the four huge boulders in the Correys' yard bordering the Wainwrights', two families that sided with and still get along with Devon's dad. Devon can stroll their waterfronts like a paladin. She has her hair in a pony and a ball cap, and she's wearing tight leggings and a St. Louis Blues pullover hoodie. The leggings worry her—it's not easy being around Devon anymore.

Behind her as the sun rises, those huge picture windows on the Merritt house glimmer with a brassy frosting, one more eco-technology the Merritts obsess about. Inside the house, you can stand at those windows at night, and no one outside can see you, like you're at a big casino hotel. The light that comes through them at night—the moon, the houses off the western shore of the lake, and the lighted tennis court that no one uses—turns so golden that her skin and the white Oxford shirt of Devon's, the whole scene all looked fashioned in ancient parchment. His parents were away second honeymooning. Devon slept after him and Casey had sex. Past midnight, and Casey knew she needed to dress, slip her shoes on, gather her stuff, and leave. She didn't love him. They just fit. She trusted and knew him. Experimenting, they found they had a natural symmetry where she could climb on top of him and slide herself right over his thing and just ride it without it entering her. Built for each other. They both got crashing peaks from this. It was pretty safe, and for her there was no pain, and that matters when you're built really small.

But soon it was no longer just thrills for him. He grew tender before and after, wanted to know where she had been and who all she had been with. That night, with his parents gone, he started talking about a future. She didn't love him like that. What he wanted she couldn't make real. In that golden light, a sad music rushed over her—C, G7, A-minor, F. A leaving song. Her body wanted to stay, but her heart and mind knew she had to go.

What if he had awakened and found her in the Merritt family room wearing his white Oxford and nothing else, body swaying with music only she could hear? What would've happened? Would he have wrapped his arms around her and convinced her to settle for a forever in Southern Hollow? To settle for safe. To settle for steady nothing in the heart. To settle for a great house and nice stuff. She had never wanted more to hold a guitar and write a song than in that parchment light. The music transfixed her for what seemed like a drugged hour. But no words came, only the feeling and the chords.

He woke up to her handwritten note: "I don't love you enough. We gotta stop."

So what's he thinking now, with Tyndall?

He looks up from the water and sees her. So much for her chance to jog on by. She balances along the top of the stone border to the Correys' driveway, hops down in the grass and walks to him. The stink of the lake hits her. Like rotting broccoli. Out on the water float globs of goo that glisten in brown, gray, and an oily blue-green. Some of them are as big as a corpse. This used to happen only in summer, but with these hot and cold swings in the weather, this goop and stink may last all year. One of the lake's vicious swans paddles by, neck swaying, grace gliding through filth.

"You didn't fix it?" She motions at the water.

He flips her the bird. He's not smiling.

"Want to be alone, Lake Prince?"

"Can't live without you."

When she stands on tiptoe at the top of Red Rocks, she can just see the roof of Tyndall's house. She can feel Devon's eyes roving her bottom and legs.

"So... it's none of my business." She turns and sits near him, pulling the Blues hoodie down her thighs. "But Tyndall's made it my business."

"She'll do that."

Casey nods. "Okay, not trying to be funny. Not trying to be nosey."

Devon waits and keeps his eyes on the lake. "Tyndall has always been kind of our project together, hasn't she?"

"Or we're her project."

His jaw buckles. Dad used to say this rippling along the jawline was your warning that a suspect had reached the end of his rope and was ready to fight. But watching Devon, she's not so sure. Some people can keep a fight inside them all their lives.

"You know how she gets stuck," he says. "Car washes. Periodic tables."

"Cutting stuff up."

"Yeah, that. So, I'm hoping I'm a thing she's stuck on and this will go away."

Casey stares him down.

"Oh, shit."

"Yep. So you told her no? And tried to stop her?" When he lets out a long breath through pursed lips, she touches his hand. Her calluses make her fingertips numb. She can sense the warmth of his body, but nothing about the texture of his skin comes through her fingertips. It's as if her fingers end in ovals of hardened wax. "Sorry. Tyndall can't help herself. She says everything. No filter."

He nods. "She was violent. It was violent, the whole thing. But not like one of her fits. She was in control. She wanted... It was almost like she..." He rolls his shoulders. "I thought about hitting her, but, I mean, we really could've hurt each other if we went at it." His face is pale, and his eyes are dazed and wide like someone after a car crash.

"You said no. Why?"

His mouth drops open.

"Come on. That's not exactly a guy thing to do."

"This is Tyndall, Casey."

Casey shrugs. "She knows what she wants. Better than most of us. She has it way more together than most of us. Life plan, I mean."

"Tyndall is not like anybody else. And she doesn't have it together like anybody else. When she has it together, it's because she forces it." He slides off the rock. Just when she thinks he's going to stalk away like a big baby, he leans back to rest below her. It's an odd pleasure, the perspective of looking down on someone. She risks pushing her heels against his shoulders. She's ridden those shoulders at rallies and football games and concerts.

"Are you ashamed of her? Would you be ashamed of her?"

His neck reddens. "Not so much ashamed. I mean from the outside, when you first see Tyndall, you got no idea anything is different. I just can't believe... Does she have, you know, the ability in her mind? Is she old enough in her heart to make... I mean, don't you look at her sometimes like a little sister?"

"Devon, everyone is bigger than I am."

"Not size. I just don't feel equal." He turns toward her. "I don't feel I can make a decision like what she wants when she's... I mean, can she think like an adult about sex?"

"Can anyone our age? Can you?"

"Hey now! I've dealt with your cold shit. In a pretty adult way." He swallows. "I told her no. I told her stop."

The urge to hurt him and mock him is almost too much, but she edits herself.

He goes on, "So if she can't think about that, about sex or love and what we're doing, in a grown up way, in the same way, equal, well... then this could all be very wrong."

"Who thinks the same way as anybody else? About anything? Ever?"

He mopes like she just threw yucky lake water over his head. Tough shit. Grow up.

"Devon, Jesus! Soulmates? That's fairy tale noise. Does your Dad honor and cherish as an equal the mind of Sherry Jean Kneeboard Goddess?"

"Hey."

"No, really. It's just good sex. She's got abs and thighs like a UFC fighter. And I'm pretty sure Sherry Jean has a real different picture of what matters." In bars of sunlight, the water smokes, gnats whirl, and the swans arch in two dal segno marks. Easy to imagine that what you're seeing is beautiful and clean yet beneath the surface bubbles a polluted horror.

"You're not really appealing to my better angels here."

"Is all your better making you worse?" She watches him. "Wait... you are ashamed of Tyndall. You think she's too retarded to make a choice."

"No one says retarded. They taught us not to from when we were little. I haven't said that word in years. Since Pershing."

"Which is too bad, because now you're living that word, and you don't know your nasty self because you can't name the way you're living."

He backs away from her.

Casey presses him. "If you don't let her choose how to express what she desires, you're saying she's not equal to you. She's behind you and beneath you. She's retarded."

He drops his head, crosses his arms over his chest. This isn't easy stuff. She's pretty amazed that the two of them can tackle it. And there's a pang inside her, like she's losing something convincing him. For a second, it chokes her.

"Now we understand why you said no. Do you still need to say no?"

"But if I don't love her?"

"Don't kid yourself. We both love her. Learn something. Make each other feel good. Even if it's only for a little bit. We're in high school, Devon. Does every kiss have to end with a wedding ring and a mortgage?"

19

Thick house carpet on its floorboards, and Mitch's car always smells of gasoline inside the cab. It's an ancient black Porsche with so many Bondo spots the band calls it the Dalmatian. Inside it's freezing, except for a square of heat along the side of Casey's right foot. In the cold, the seats are stiff, and you have no trouble divining the springs beneath the upholstery. Her bass in its case juts between them from the joke of a back seat, and her Martin mashes her knees. Mitch rebuilt the car with his dad after they found its shell in a slough.

New Wave Vultures have only one Cedar Shake show left. Tonight, the cash in her pocket bulges like a wallet all by itself. Something blew up on social media, and all these geezers showed. Mitch brought in fedoras, one for each Vulture. After wearing them for a whole set of Simple Minds and Jesus Jones, Mitch gave the corniest speech in the world about America and this being their senior year and second-to-last show, and then the Vultures passed the fedoras out in the crowd. The hats came back overflowing with cash. The Cedar Shake manager raged, and Mitch's face and neck still blaze from that argument.

"I almost don't care if he never has us back!" Mitch hunches when he drives, too, and if he's pissed and at the wheel in his battered black trenchcoat, he looks like an eighty-year-old. He's holding a can of deicer in his left hand as Casey hovers near the wheel. When the cobwebs of ice close the only hole Mitch can see through, he lets loose of the wheel, and starts cranking down his window. She grabs the wheel and steers for him. It's very late—they've been through the whole after-show chore of unloading Dwayne's van at Mitch's house. It's a Thursday, a school night with freezing fog, so Sunshine Street is thankfully clear. The Porsche is so old there's no power steering, so guiding it from the passenger's seat while squirming between two guitar cases is a core-bashing workout all to itself.

"So," she grunts, overadjusts. They rock and weave. "Something I want to ask."

He sprays the window. An ozone stink like dish soap mixed with apple juice momentarily overpowers the gasoline smell. It's a wonder they're not high or dead.

"Casey Strong!" Mitch stabs the scraper on the deicer can against the windshield. Blue sparks of ice fly out into the night. "Did ever a woman since the creation of the Ozarks interrupt a man during such an operation?"

"I can't make this any crazier!" She's laughing, and, to her relief, he is, too.

Once they've recovered, she asks it. "So what would you think about Patrick and me playing a set before the last Cedar Shake show?"

He bows up and starts snorting. "I cannot believe." It's best to let him go on awhile. "Not on brand. Nothing New Wave about this Oregon Trail folkmuck you're playing. I mean, what are those songs? That piano! They all sound like smash hits from the Mexican War or something! And he's a thug. Oh, My God, Casey Strong, the choices you make!"

"But think of the people in the door, Mitch. Come on. Sixteen million humans all over the globe have watched "Sofia Castle" on YouTube. Sixteen million."

"There are over six hundred thousand abortions a year in the US, but that doesn't mean I want to be part of one."

She catches her guitar case before it cracks him. "Mitch, you love money."

"I ought to stop this car right now and pitch you out of it, but I don't think I can get the damn thing started again. No!

And do not take this terrible idea to the band. Dwayne will clock you with his Tele. No."

The engine rings along. He's downshifted. "When we're done with the Cedar Shake," he says, "I think the Vultures need to take a break. And you either get Turin out of your system, or, I don't know, get famous, or get addicted." He sprays and scrapes again.

The steering wheel seems even heavier as she hauls it to keep them off the median. "Mitch, what are we doing here? Really?"

"I'm trying to get your tiny butt home without killing us both." He has to wait on the wipers to move aside before he scrapes. It's a bobbing and weaving dance. She thinks of the months she has watched him hunched at the drums, the myriad beats he has down pat, the falsetto he can sing. He's amazing.

"In bands, I mean. What are we doing? And I mean the whole of Springfield musicians. All of us." She watches him dodge the blades. "You're so talented. We both have something. Why the hell are we not super famous, Mitch?"

"There is a lot of talent here. Dwayne, even Punkinhead Charlie, they're quality. But we're stuck in the flyover. Where's our coastal elite, right? Branson?!" He turns the wiper blades off, but they stick at wild angles. It's now snowing in the car, a blue glitter hanging. "Look at Billie Eilish. Her and her brother, right? Los Angeles. Famous family of actors already! Mom and dad both. Dad was in that movie where the sharks fall from the sky."

"Oh, now that *is* famous."

"Well, it's sure more of a network they got than your cop widow mom... or my dad!" He glances at her and dares third gear. "You got to grab whatever joy and coin you can out of what the Lord gives you. How many kids can't do what we do, but think they can? Or, hell, maybe they can, but they're sitting out in that audience and staring at you and wishing it was them? They're not even listening, they're so desperate for their chance. We're lucky." He sprays, but the deicer piddles across the starscape of the windshield. "We're the ones playing music, on a stage, and people are putting cash in our hats."

"But I feel like there is something more for me, Mitch. Like more people than just 150 above a law firm next to a brewpub in Springburg should know my music."

He twists in his seat and drops the deicer can behind him where it gongs on other spent cans. They turn into Southern Hollow Subdivision on Ventura Boulevard. "We all feel that sometimes. If the Lord says you're ready, He'll move it all for you. Until then, just sing."

"So I want to ask the Lord, what are we doing wrong here in the Ozarks, then? We're in church all the time! Even you with your weirdo Catholic stuff. But Porter Waggoner? I mean, the Ozark Mountain Daredevils? That's just one or two hits. Poof. Gone like frost."

"Fool's Face," Mitch offers. "The Morells. Big Smith. My Aunt Rosie dated that poor guy from Jordan Border who killed himself. They were fantastic. Or so I heard."

"Find me any records of theirs, will you?"

"Big Smith has all kind of stuff you can download." He eases into her driveway. His teeth chatter in the cold, and his lips are a light blue. "Casey. You're threatening to live out the oldest music story in America. Drag guitar to crossroads, make deal with Satan, die drinking poison, gain fame decades later after some Jew steals all your music rights."

"Fascist Trumper!" She whacks his shoulder. "I wish we were in the Mississippi Delta. At least we'd stand a chance. What New Yorker ever poked around here with a recorder and an invite to Carnegie Hall?"

He throws his hands up. "Here's a conspiracy theory: No one ever listens to my conspiracy theories. So they must all be true!" His face softens. "Look. A dream can be a fine thing, but if it's so big and burns you like a fire, with no real outlet… That's not a dream. That's a nightmare."

"So wait. Can a dream be like a car heater that actually works?"

He crams his fists down in the pockets of his trench coat. "Every bullshit Hollywood movie peddles dreams come true. Every stinking karaoke-contest TV show teaches that discovery equals instant forever success. No one sells patience. No one pushes craft. And no one ever shows you the joy of just making great music without mass, screaming fandom."

"Come on, Mitch. Is that just what you tell yourself?"

"It's also what I'm telling you. You're from Springfield, Missouri, but you get to play music on a stage, for people, for money. You decide: Gift or Curse." He bows his head. She's never seen Mitch look this worn down. She's wrecking his good thing. "Look. Don't worry about me. Every high school drummer with a basement and a chill family is guaranteed a band. I hate Patrick Turin. And I think you're really wonderful. Just, please. Don't fool yourself into getting hurt."

20

Tyndall demands that he take her to Barnes & Noble. Casey's birthday is coming up. Tyndall is terrible at gifts, and they can both go in together on a present.

Black and gray slush slops at every intersection, and mounds of sooty snow lurk at the corners of each parking lot. No need to wash the outside of Dad's Dodge Charger. He clears the inside of all the sucker sticks and spent juice packets, blue cleaning gloves on his hands and carpet stain remover at the ready. Something about the roar of the shop vacuum puts sound to the empty feeling in his heart. Is he going through the motions of something ceremonial but meaningless? Is this a date, but with no goals to it? He doesn't need to get to know Tyndall any better. And it's no natural part of her pathways to know more about him, or anyone else. He's avoided her for much of December and the holiday break.

On the front steps, Sherry Jean bounces Sister on her hip. The child is so chubby, she looks like a grumpy version of the Michelin Man, rolls on rolls, skin tight as can be. Sherry Jean smiles at him and grabs Sister's wrist to make her wave. Devon lets the shop vac hose howl against a floor mat. The carnage around the space that normally holds Sister's car seat overwhelms him. Why does the family that fought to clean up the Lakes now own a carbon-barfing Dodge Charger? Why does fitness queen Sherry Jean cram a toddler with mounds of refined sugar? Listening to candy-covered chocolates and jellybeans rattle up the shop vac's tube, he feels like the world has lost its axis. It's the suburban Ozarks. Don't like your convictions? Wait five minutes—they'll all change.

Nora invites him into the Hastings' living room. No television. Only a sofa, chairs, and a coffee table carrying stacks of books by evangelists. Above the sofa is a new piece of art, a luminous painting of Jesus Christ pointing toward his heart, which is exploded and projected forward, almost like a diagram in a biology text. It's a painting Devon has seen elsewhere, though much smaller, and on the backpacks and in the lockers of Latinas.

Marion stands from his upholstered chair. He had been reading the Bible under a lamp. Marion shakes Devon's hand with showy firmness, and motions to a wooden chair across from him. "Mother, I believe you have some organic green tea we bought just for Devon." Marion smiles at him, a warm, round face crested by thick, shining white hair.

Devon presses his palms to his knees and wants to ask the painting why Marion insists on this. But you cannot take Tyndall out of the house unless you spend time with Father.

"That painting trouble you, Son?"

He starts to answer, but pauses. Marion's smile and the silver wetness quavering at the rims of his eyes give him that look of an elderly man desperate for you to stay and talk.

"I wish it were more... all together," he says. "The heart, those rays around it, seem... like a medallion. When everything else is so soft. The light is soft."

"Yes. Soft. I would say almost like our lightbulbs used to be before Obama-DiCaprio told us we were too dumb to buy them."

Nora arrives with two green teas. He and Marion thank her, and she departs. Sherry Jean would tell you to get your own damn leaf water.

"Forgive me," Marion says. He looks up at the painting. "I do see what you mean."

Forgive me? When has he ever heard that out of Marion's mouth? Maybe Tyndall really did break his skull? They both sip tea, and he thanks Marion and the now absent Nora for being so thoughtful to have it, and organic, on hand. "I know it's not your stuff."

"Hard to imagine why it's not." Marion makes an exaggerated face. "Hey, so with tea, how does it get to be certified as organic? I mean tea's a bush right, on a hill in China? It's a leaf that's fermented and dried. And those Chinamen, they'll dry out a food product under the exhaust of a dump truck, right? Run it over and over. So do the Chinamen get to say 'organic'? Or do we gather a bunch of Harvard-educated bureaucrats who are the only ones who can say if a thing is 'organic' or not?"

There's the old Marion. Usually conversations with Marion feel like contests. He was a lawyer, and then a high up judge, who resigned after exposing tons of corruption. Retired, he always seems much older than Nora, and he's heavier now that Ben is dead. He's leaning toward Devon, smiling, eager. Like Tyndall, he has these learned and practiced ways of relating with people, if arguing and fussing can be called relating. Yet, like Tyndall, Marion can't pivot, even though his pathways don't always lead to any real conversation.

Devon finds a coaster on the coffee table and sets the cup aside. "Mr. Hastings, do you ever worry… does it ever hit you that we've lost… there used to be a reality we all believed in, a starting point. Before Mom died, she was our starting point, a center. She kept my dad grounded in a reality that wasn't way over here." He stretches his left arm way out. "Or like you, sort of way over here." Right arm and hand way out as far to the right as it can go.

Marion holds the tea closer to him and sits back. "Your mother was a really good neighbor, Devon." He straightens his shoulders with a wince. "Grounded, steady." Marion frowns and looks intently at him. "Son, I find myself sometimes at a loss when I want to talk with someone—and pardon me, please—who's not a believer in Jesus Christ. There's a great poet, from St. Louis I understand, who said that Christ is the still point. While I think that's mostly right, there's far more to Our Savior than that. Christ is as well a starting point. A rebirth from folly and death. Jesus can ground and steady a man. I worry how a young man navigates without comprehending that love. So you see, because there is the commandment that we must spread the Gospel, the Good News, well, I have trouble not starting there."

Marion's gaze wanders down the hallway, toward the bedrooms of the house. For once he feels Marion is not fretting at how late his daughter can be, but worrying at something else. "Let's try not starting there." Marion waits a bit. "Devon, are you all right?"

Whoa. "I think so. Thanks for asking." The instant he says it, he hears his mother's voice. "You know… it's like there are people I counted on that are all out of whack now."

Marion sits forward, nodding. "Devon, that's a thing that most men feel, for sure, but usually not until they're much older." He sets his tea aside and rubs his forehead with his palm. On the backs of his hands, his pale skin has age spots now, like algal blooms. He looks down the hallway once more. No Tyndall. Marion is about to say something, but then Devon can see the wheels stop and reverse.

"While I have this chance, Devon, I want to thank you for treating my daughter so well." The Hastings' house falls so quiet, it's like a funeral home after everyone but the dead have left. "The Lord made the unicorn that will not harrow the valleys after you, will not abide thy crib." Marion sighs. "But you treat Tyndall with kindness and respect. For me, she is a starting point, a home base. Son, I worry all the time. When Nora and I are gone, where will she be?" His voice bucks with emotion. "No one to take care of her. No one for her to take care of." Marion stops. His cheeks and neck redden. It's the most genuine conversation they've ever had, and Devon's heart is drowning.

At last Marion reaches out and thumps his knee. "I can't help myself, Devon. God placed Good in you. Timbers of cedar. You have that in you, like your mother did."

Tyndall arrives in Glendale colors—a light blue and white-striped short-sleeved tee, and tight, cardinal red jeans. It's sweater weather, even inside. Who's dressing her? Her face darkens. Marion is not done talking. She stares at her father as if she might lower her head and gore him. Marion pays her no mind.

"Innate good, from God," Marion goes on. "I'm afraid the world is always going to seem a whirl and a mess to you, Devon. But you will know what to do. I'm sure of it."

Tyndall snorts. "You listen to him about God, but for years ignore what I tell you!"

"Bracingly forward," Marion says. "A surprise every minute of the living day." He gallantly rolls his hand as if formally presenting someone. "I give you Ms. Tyndall Hastings."

"Stop!" Tyndall says. "No one else gives me. I give me." She looks down at Devon. "Get up. Barnes & Noble could go out of business at any minute."

21

He opens the passenger door for her, and she settles in the Charger. She drapes her long puffer coat over her legs and rolls the collar and sleeves in a bundle like a muff. Her face, which seems rounder and softer, glows rosy in the cold. Her hair flows down golden onto the shoulders of the tee. The sleeves squeeze her upper arms. Her chest could sway any man. Maybe Casey's right? Maybe he's being an idiot? But then he remembers.

Pressing the ignition, he warns her he will need to run the defroster. She unbuckles and sets and resets the temperature and fan level until it's precisely to her tolerance while he idles in the driveway. The car cannot move until she completes this. He can't take Eureka to Eastmoor then Cedarbrook. Instead he must wind all around the easternmost streets of Southern Hollow, past Glendale High onto Ingram Mill, then west up Battlefield to Barnes & Noble, otherwise she won't even get out of the car. There's no smile, no nod, no thank you as he accommodates her quirks. She sits imperiously, her chapped lips pursed as if she's chewed something sour. Once in a while her gaze fixates above the houses and apartments, and then she chants a clot of words, nothing he can catch. If he asks her what she is saying or seeing, she'll go blank as an iced over pond. They might even have to head straight home.

At Barnes & Noble, the parking lot is wild with cars cramped by charcoal piles of ice and snow. Add to that it's the January Saturday before school starts back. Not used to the Charger and its long snout, he bumps a concrete parking block hard. Her body trembles, and this takes his breath away. Tyndall stares down at her chest.

"I carry fat now." She unbuckles and guides the belt across her so that no metal touches her. It's a slow, practiced ritual he's sat through many times, her holding the belt out far as it can stretch, the belt hooked only by her thumb. So formal. But today, set against the tight, striped shirt, her quirk emphasizes her outsize bust. "Nora had to special order bras for me. Over the internet. Nothing in all of Springfield would fit these."

Compliments can backfire. Agreement could crater her. Sympathy she'll call out as dishonesty. Trapped, he stares at her fabulous chest and waits to see if this is going to be a theme all afternoon or just a blip. Her body has changed in three weeks.

"I've never cared one way or the other about food. As long as it was ready." She rolls the puffer coat tighter. "But right now, I could walk into that bakery and wipe it out."

He decides to risk it—he knows not to caress her arm. Grip it and squeeze it and keep hold of it until she tells you to let go. Her upper arm is softer than he remembers, but he feels that firm core beneath. She whirls to look at his hand gripping her arm, then briefly at his face. Her expression is flat, but her reactions are quick. It's like being around a hawk. Is she alarmed? Offended? Relieved? Aroused? Is he about to get a talon in the face? No telling. At last she places her hand over his and presses it tighter to her. Her gaze travels to a blackened pile of snow.

"Do you think it's any of your pills doing this? Making you hungry?"

A long pause. If someone were to look in the window, and see him gripping her upper arm this tightly, the stranger might think this was a fight, that he was about to open the passenger door, and push her out into the parking lot. But this is how we settle down.

She swallows, and her mouth seems dry from the sound of it, like a seal cracking when her lips part.

"Why don't we stow your coat in the back since we're not going to wear it?"

She hands it to him. That's progress. Okay, so we might make it into the store.

"I want you to hold my hand really tight and walk into Barnes & Noble with me," he says. "Then after we pass the registers, you do whatever you want to."

She looks directly at him, "So many quirks you have," she says. No smile, no change in expression. "Do this, this, and then this."

He smiles. "Yep. Loads of quirks." He's about to extend her joke and say that she is his most pronounced quirk, but he stops himself. He recalls Marion's face, about to say something, but then halting. The skin of her neck and face is so white and flawless, it's like snow. Snow and ice suit her. There's a gray crescent shadow and a rounding beneath her jaw; her chin has doubled. Somehow this soft change warms his heart.

"Let go!" she blurts. "Starving." She's out of the car before he can get the ignition off.

Inside the store, Tyndall turns heads, partly because of her striped, short-sleeved tee with no coat, but mostly because she's an extremely busty, tall and attractive blonde with a strange expression, almost as if she's horrified to have been dragged into a bookstore. Past the registers she still grips Devon's hand. There are not many tall, beautiful people such as Tyndall in a Barnes & Noble in Springfield, Missouri. Any that are will be in the café speaking loudly on a cell phone or flipping through a free magazine while waiting on some nerdy stepkid in sci-fi or avoiding the disillusioned third wife whose only romance comes from paperbacks in which virile dukes shapeshift into forest creatures. Casey's mom once shared one of these fictions with Devon. Tyndall pulls him around a corner and down a row of manga. Three middle school boys in red puffer coats look up. Their eyes bloom. Devon imagines a giant cartoon thought balloon inflating above all their greasy heads: "Boobies!"

She stops at the music book section, and Devon begins the hunt. Every hardback book Devon shows her contains slick photographs of one band and costs too much, or it's a biography or memoir of one band or singer, but printed on paper that feels cheap, almost like newspaper, and it also costs too much. They are high school kids on a budget, if you can even call it that. He, Tyndall, and Casey, they're from that set of Glendale kids whose parents can't buy them cars or won't, whose parents don't chunk them allowances, and don't fly them to Snow Mass or Padre for spring break. Tyndall has work, sure, but it's all volunteer. Devon works, and his father pays him whenever the freelance accountant and the bank says he can.

A clerk in khakis and a green polo drifts over. She's wired up like a fast food worker at a drive-through with a headset and mic. "I'm sorry," she says into the mic, "No, we don't sell Kindles." When she has finished what must have been a phone call, she pulls the headset down so it collars her neck. Tyndall grabs Devon's hand again and squeezes it. As the clerk approaches, Tyndall drives his knuckles into the side of her breast and ribs as if his hand were a purse she means to protect. In spite of this, he readies to do the talking.

"Maybe I can help. What kind of music do you listen to?" the clerk asks Tyndall. She has a buzzed haircut except for a purple curl at the top of her forehead.

Tyndall looks away and drives Devon's knuckles so deeply into her breast that the clerk stares at Tyndall's smooshed chest.

"New Wave," Devon says. "Gift for a friend." His hand and wrist smart, but his knuckles float in a padded heaven.

The clerk, still locked on Tyndall's chest, manages to ask: "Like... 1980s bands?" Her voice roughens.

Devon nods. The frozen clerk doesn't see him. "Yes," he emphasizes.

Tyndall is still looking away with an urgency, as if some psycho killer is about to leap over the shelf of Mystery & Crime and attack her.

"Okay." The clerk rolls her shoulders. "Sorry. Great big day. Don't mean to downgrade you, but check this out." She leads them to a bargain bin in the middle aisle.

The clerk holds up a large white book, bound like a Bible. Tyndall has his hand still crammed into her. Her other arm she now has across her stomach, so that both hands grip him. She jerks her head at the book. With his free hand Devon takes it from the clerk and holds it up for her. It's titled *HOW MUSIC WORKS*, and below that is the computer speaker symbol and some guy's name.

Strawberry flecks break out on the clerk's cheeks. Her eyes have yet to reach Tyndall's face. "So, yeah, no, perfect. This was that guy with the giant suits. Looked kind of like Dr. McCoy. Burning Up Your House. Way New Wave. Big..." She blushes.

Tyndall will not let him go, so he has to flick his left wrist to open the book. Cool type and pictures. Stays open like a hymnal. Tilting the book, he can float the pages forward and backward in clumps. He would say to Tyndall, This is crazy. Let Go! But, nope. This is being with Tyndall. His hand is deep in her flesh. Her heart thumps against his knuckles with such force, there's a recoil down in his wrist. He's turned on and at the same time concerned and confused, worried she will embarrass herself, and, yes, embarrass him. The clerk's bottom lip quivers.

"Hey. This might be the guy whose band wrote that song 'Heaven' that Casey sings."

Tyndall nods. "Oh, yes. That blasphemy."

He manages to get the book closed and flips it over to show her the price on back.

Tyndall nudges him hard with her hip.

The poor clerk, she's a dumbstruck Q-tip by now, arms at her sides, hands flexing and closing. In a trance, she pulls the headset back on and fumbles at its wire and controls. "You've been a great help," Devon says, and he means it. Without her this could have taken forever and might not have happened at all.

The book costs so little at the register, Devon forgets himself, and comments how this feels like cheating, it's so inexpensive.

"We need more? This is not enough for a gift?" Tyndall's voice is super urgent.

Customers stand back from her and look warily at the two of them.

He gets the book paid for and leads her away from the register. "We can go to the bakery or to the car," he says. He catches himself using the loud, firm voice that Nora and Casey turn on Tyndall. "Bakery or Car."

Her expression flattens, her posture straightens. She's unplugging. "Bakery," she whispers. Some in the line of people at the register are still staring. You would think they have enough neurodivergence around them to roll with her outburst, but no. They still gawk.

At the café, she's stopped pulling Devon around. He stands her in front of the pastries. His heart is still thumping with worry, and with lust, which makes things worse. Who knows what set her off back there? He watches her gray eyes coursing over the pastry display. All at once, she's at peace and taking in something pleasant, bent forward, brushing her hair back— and she's a knockout. In the space of three minutes with her he has experienced his topmost anxiety, surges of lust, peaks of frustration and hollows of self-loathing, waves of adrenaline to defend her, and now a gush of awe. This is his childhood pal grown up into this lovely form. She's exhausting.

"What would you like?"

"The bottom shelf."

"Okay, but which one?"

She glances at him. Her lips form an O, like she's about to tell him how dumb he is. "The bottom one. The shelf on the bottom."

There are five cheesecakes across the bottom shelf. "That's $200."

"I'm worth every penny."

He gets them two slices and bottled water, but she demands a Java Chip Frappuccino. She finishes her cheesecake at a rush. Astonished, he pushes his, untouched, to her. She doesn't hesitate. Finished with that she attacks the pile of whipped cream and chocolate sauce on the Frappe with her spoon. Only when the topping is gone does she lift the Frappe and drink. She sets it down, and her eyes travel back to the bakery case.

"Get me a slice of lemon, and then another strawberry, and then a dark chocolate."

What the hell is this? Sure he remembers some cafeteria lunches before holiday break when she seemed to have two servings on one tray. But he's never seen her obsess like this about food. Car washes, dissection, crystals, sure, but none of those fixations were harmful to her. He weighs the options— if he says no, she might fly into a fury. Sometimes her meltdowns seem timed and convenient, even weaponized. But that's not fair. He's watched Nora negotiate this tension, too. Just the threat of a fit seemed to get Tyndall anything she wanted, and whole days were arranged and rearranged around her demands. Yet she never seemed grateful about these adjustments. She didn't even seem any happier.

"$9.24. That's cheaper than a movie. I can't sit through a movie. You buy the slices and bring them, one by one, to me. And a Java Chip Frappuccino with each one. Lemon. Strawberry. Then dark chocolate."

He shakes his head. "That's a ton of sugar and caffeine. You'll be up till three a.m."

To his relief, she takes this without upset. "Are you and Nora consulting?" She sits back and stirs the Frappe. "Do you call each other at night and talk about how fat I'm getting and how much I've been overeating? She calls someone about that. They talk about my whole body. Every part. Then she weeps into the cell phone. Is it you she calls?"

"Maybe she's worried about you? I mean, this is new. You said yourself you never cared that much about food. Is there a pill that's new, that's making you do this?"

Her neck and cheeks glow red. "When I am a great doctor, I will stride into Barnes & Noble, and they will have five cheesecakes waiting for me. Waiting in beautiful boxes you can see down into. And Gina will help me out with all five so I don't have to carry anything, and I can protect my hands. My precious, my precise great-doctor hands."

"Gina?"

"She found us Casey's gift. Her name was engraved in white on her hunter green tag. When I am a great doctor, I will do anything I want to, whenever I want to."

When she talks, she can leap from pits of despair and confusion to summits of confidence. He no longer talks her down from these heights. Maybe she can be a great doctor? She's working in situations at the hospital beyond anything he imagined she could handle. But there it is again, rearranging reality to avoid her meltdowns. That's not actually living in a real world together. How is someone ever going to love her if they always have to dodge what's real?

He reaches across the table and opens his hand. She downs the Frappe and pops the empty cup in his palm. She's grinning. A joke. She says she doesn't kid, but she can. He sets the cup aside then holds his hand out again. Her expression fades to blank, but the new roundness to her cheeks makes her seem full and satisfied rather than hollow. She takes a deep breath, then rests her hand in his, and he grips her fingers tight.

"Tell me about the new pill. What is it? How much are you taking? What's it do?"

"I really must have the lemon," she whispers. "And the dark chocolate. On one plate but not touching. And another Java Chip Frappuccino."

It will go on and on, this bargaining. Unless they leave, and then there might be rage, a fit, and then home. Or even after departure, more bargaining, as if it were perfectly rational to drive away from but then return to Barnes & Noble, stride right back in, and then resume eating an entire shelf of pastries.

"You have shown me the cheesecake," she says, as if it's all his fault.

He watches her from the counter after he places the order. Without a phone, without a book or magazine, she sits erect as a royal in a portrait and stares over the periodicals section into the weak January twilight. Is she at peace? He hopes so. He yearns for her to be peaceful, inside and out. Her posture is magnificently straight. Beneath the tee, her bra seems to bite into her back and carve out a parabola. Men in the café steal glances at her. A middle school boy with his mother gawks. They have no idea the trouble their appetites could get them into. Even grown women take her in and glance with raised eyebrows at their tablemates. He sets the plate down, and the Frappe. Scooting the plate out from her, she turns it and checks to see that no food is touching. No thank you, no sign of gratitude. She makes him go get her two new forks and a new spoon.

These she doesn't eat with gusto, only precision. It's so much rich food, his stomach hurts watching her. Four slices now, devoured. She then dissects and consumes the whipped cream and chocolate sauce and begins to drink her second Frappuccino.

When she finishes, he asks, "The new pill?"

Her gaze follows a barista. "I should have eaten the lemon after the dark chocolate. Get me another lemon."

He shakes his head. "No, Tyndall. The new pill. Tell me about it."

She pushes back from the table and rubs the top of her stomach where the table's edge must have been creasing her.

"What's the name of this new pill?"

"Quietarol. Why ruin everything? I'm having a great time. This is a great time we're having together. You should get me a slice of the lemon. Or the blueberry! I didn't try the blueberry. That's the only one I haven't tried. It's the right time for the blueberry."

"We've had a lot of sugar and caffeine." He swallows. It

feels like he's the one on edge. "Tell me about Quietarol. Did you take it before you came here?"

"I took three."

"Three? Are you supposed to take that many?"

"Mine is a non-intended use and self-directed, though doctor prescribed."

"You took three pills at once? I've never had a bottle of medicine that told me to take three pills at once."

Her gaze lapses down the aisle of tables, a desert of Formica and linoleum. He feels like he's battering her. But taking this much medicine alarms him.

"Have you never been prescribed Prednisone or another steroid after exposure to poison ivy or a lingering congestion or a sprain?" she asks.

If he suffered inflammation, his mother gave him turmeric. All these pharmaceuticals! "What does Quietarol do besides make you hungry?"

"I took three Quietarol so that everything could be still and nothing would overwhelm me, so that I could be a perfect girlfriend for you."

"It makes things still? It calms you?"

"Yes, a lot. Like nothing else I've ever found."

"Well, you weren't very calm around that clerk, Gina."

Tyndall snarls something to the side. Then, as if she has finished off a Devil on her shoulder, she turns back to him. "Think of this: You took me to Casey's concert downtown. You took me to two basketball games. Think of the places I have been with you lately and everything has been perfect. I have been perfect. Think of lunch period. I have presented so few problems. These are outcomes we should celebrate. With blueberry cheesecake."

"So you took Quietarol before lunch periods, too, then?" She nods.

"You've been eating a lot more at lunch."

"I would eat the whole world if it meant I could be normal for you."

This stops him. She frequently says things in extremes.

STEVE YATES

When she talks about the future, she always predicts spectacular achievements. She can't just become a doctor; she will
become a great doctor. Sometimes you can ignore these excla-
mations as just Tyndall being Tyndall. But, like everything
she says, she means it, to her core. And like a lot of what she
says, it's bananas. There are obstacles, consequences, dues to
be paid, but she doesn't seem to acknowledge any challenge
between her and the ideal she proclaims. In middle school,
for a whole semester, she talked relentlessly about becoming a
tiger trainer. But this one gets him. She wants to love so much,
any price is worth it. And it's him she wants to love.

In the car, she asks if he can disable the seat belt alarm. He
gets out in the cold. With the heavy passenger door propped
against his backside, he adjusts the belt so there's a giant loop
of extra slack. She holds this away from her, as if the belt were
a boa constrictor.

"Does your stomach hurt?"

"It is distended."

Crouching there next to her, he offers to lean the seat back.
Her eyes widen and her face creases, but then, as he reclines
the seat, she clutches her side and looks around. "Oh, that is
better."

He doesn't wait for the thank you. No thank you is coming. He closes the Charger door carefully. The motor chugs.
Tyndall now reclines herself as far back as the seat will allow.
With both hands she's holding the belt downward in a broad
loop of slack. This causes her arms to mound her breasts up,
and they were already plenty present. The stripes and tight
shirt only emphasize this. He's going to go stark raving mad.

His breath shudders. "Tyndall. You have shown me the
cheesecake."

She glances over at him, and, to his dismay, she smiles.
"Did you know that the Dodge Motor Car Company removed
most of the firewall shielding between the cabin and the
engine of these vehicles to enhance that terrible noise we're
hearing? Engine rumble makes male buyers feel more virile,

111

and they would thus buy more cars from Dodge. And in a bonus to the company, the cars could be made more cheaply because there is less heat shielding between the driver and the engine. In case of an engine fire, the driver, feeling so power-fully viriley male, will be consumed by flames more rapidly than in almost any motor car on the American roadways. The Dodge Charger!" She speaks more rapidly than she normally does. All that caffeine and sugar must be bashing through her. Her smile, though, is lovely, and it's so big, it now pinches the corners of her eyes.

"Are you happy? You seem very happy."

"Yes, thank you, I'm extremely happy."

"How come?"

She looks out toward the crawl of traffic on Battlefield. The sky is navy blue, darkest at its crest, and there's a hon-eyed glow to Springfield in its twilight. With all the cars and concrete and searing streetlights, and tar-drenched shopping center roofs, this is to Devon a dismal nightmare, devoid of nature. But maybe Tyndall sees a whole different vista?

"I feel we have experienced a very successful time together. We accomplished the gift buying. We worked through and overcame your neurotypical obstinacies and your left-wing, granola-nutball resistance to pharmaceutical medicine. All boxes checked. Well... so far."

He tenses, ready for a demand that they now go back inside for the blueberry.

"I want you to drive behind the Venture building," she says.

Mystified, he drives down the parking lot, which steadily becomes emptier at its southern end. Then he turns behind the derelict Venture building, a big box like a K-Mart but long ago closed. Around the back, an alley opens made by overgrown cedar hedges and the crusty sheet metal of the abandoned store. He creeps—this is the kind of cranny where you'll find tweakers in a battered hatchback with a mobile meth lab ready to blow.

"Tyndall, this... What do you want back here?"

"We treated a couple in the emergency room Thursday night, who got stabbed and robbed while they were making out back here. It's time to make out. All the other boxes have been checked. This is where to make out. I have to find these places for us. You don't know a thing about the world. Only grass and phosphate and compost that smells awful."

He slams the brakes, and she clutches her stomach. "A couple got stabbed back here?"

"Yes, but that was well after nine p.m. It's not even six o'clock." When the car doesn't move, she looks over at him. "Do you want to start right here? Is it time to start?"

Backing out of the alley looks iffy. He pulls forward—she's still chattering, now listing all the stores that have failed in the Battlefield Mall and this adjacent strip mall. They reach a concrete gulch beneath what looks like an abandoned loading dock. He's relieved to find it empty, no tweakers, no junkies. He can turn the car around here.

She grabs his arm. "Perfect! Look! It's like a canyon."

Rather than argue he cuts the car off. She unbuckles the seat belt and guides it away from her with care.

She glances over at him, smiling. He leans back against the driver's side door and crosses his arms. What to do here? His mind, heart, and body wage war. He does not want to hurt or belittle her, but at the same time, he's exhausted and fed up, and he's aroused. He would love to have his hands on her chest again. But couldn't she become overwhelmed in the midst of kissing or touching her? Couldn't she throw a howling fit?

"Okay," he says. "So boxes have been ticked, and you're happy."

She nods.

"All right." This is hard—he's speaking to her like he might talk with a child, but he doesn't want it to sound that way. Or does he? God, what a mess! He wants but doesn't cherish, and that seems gross. "What box is next? What would you like me to do, Tyndall?"

"I want you to do something Casey did for me and to me."

113

A sinkhole capsizes in his mind and swallows his understanding. "Casey did something to you? For you?"

"Yes." She still doesn't move from the reclined seat. "She pressed her knee into my privates. Then she grabbed my chest and squeezed really hard. Pushing in circles around here with her knee while she did this was violently exciting. I want that again. But I want you to do it. Not her. You."

Her breath seems short. She places her hands on her stomach, gingerly, like Sherry Jean did when she was big and pregnant with Sister. It hits him that Tyndall might get sick in this car that he spent the whole morning cleaning. That realization plus this Casey news proves useful—karate chop to the boner.

"Casey did this when?"

"Before Christmas. When you were being so difficult. After I gave you a highly effective hand job. I asked her what was wrong with you. And I wanted to make sure my technique had not been at fault. She assured me it was not." She strokes her stomach, and her cheeks redden.

"Are you going to be sick?" He asks. "Please don't throw up in the car."

She punches his shoulder. But then rests her hand again on her stomach. "It's just that when I breathe in, I feel like I'm going to split wide open."

"You ate way too much, Tyndall."

"Thank you, Nora," Tyndall sneers. Her breathing is shallow and sharp. "You know… I eat sometimes just to make her mad. I eat seconds and thirds of pie and ice cream in front of her to see how long it takes for her to weep into her cell phone." Her eyes narrow at him. "She doesn't call you?"

"No, Nora doesn't call me. Do you want to lie down flat in the back?"

She strains to turn her head and look at the back seat. "Is that how you make out? I wondered with all this console and gear shift and steering wheel, how to manage it."

He checks the loading dock and alley to make sure no one is about to ambush them. When he opens her door and helps her out, it reminds him of grudgingly helping Sherry Jean, who claimed to be miserable all the time when pregnant. He restores the reclined passenger seat to upright, slides it all the way forward, then opens the back door, sits her down holding her arm firmly. "Lie back now, okay? Roll your coat up for a pillow."

She complies, watching him closely. Once she's fully stretched out in the back with the puffer coat rolled behind her head, her feet wiggle, like an excited little girl's. For a moment holding the back door open, he does want to "make out." He pops the trunk. Back there, Sherry Jean keeps a blanket and pillow in a giant Ziploc storage bag. Sherry Jean claims to get car sick at any speed above 45 and forces him or Dad to drive all their interstate trips while she curls up asleep in the back. He opens and spreads the blanket out and is about to drape it over her.

"We don't need a blanket. I don't need a blanket. Do you need a blanket? Is that to hide us? Do we hide under that? Just get in here with me."

He rests the blanket on her legs. Then he grips her calf. "Tyndall. Stop for a minute. Think. If I mash a knee into your privates right now, what will happen to your stomach?"

She holds her stomach protectively but starts to argue. "They're different. They're not connected. Not that much." She frowns. When she reaches for the blanket, maybe to cast it away, she cringes. Then her gray eyes cloud. She's beginning to get the picture, but he can tell she doesn't like it.

He leans in and flips the blanket's hem to cover her chest. "Okay. We're going to drive real slow around the lakes, nice and easy, and you're going to be still and tell me all about what Casey did to you and for you, and all about Quietarol. Everything. That will tick all the boxes for a wonderful date."

She pulls the blanket up but looks at him. "How? No, it won't." He closes the back door, sits in the driver's seat. "For one thing," she begins the instant he's seated, "I did not have the blueberry cheesecake. Gina will be glad to bring it out to us. It was clear to me how much she wanted to touch my breasts. You should want to touch them as well. There may be something wrong with you, Devon. We will have to work on this. I am going to be a great doctor, and I foresee a very positive outcome for you if only you will listen to me."

He starts the Charger and looks at her a long while in the rearview. Here he has a buxom blonde stretched out in the backseat, a babe who wants him to "make out" with her. And instead, he's going to drive her around the Lakes of Southern Hollow and let her talk until her stomach settles, and then he'll drop her at her parents with a handshake.

She's gone quiet and watches him in the silver rectangle of the rearview. The appalled expression she wore in the bookstore returns, but he knows it doesn't mean anything he might think it means. The sun is down, so the light is a sputtering tan from a security lamp above the abandoned loading dock.

"What's wrong with me, Tyndall?" he asks. "I shouldn't care if your stomach hurts. I'm a boy. I'm supposed to just take things I want, but… You look gorgeous tonight."

She folds the blanket down to her waist, makes two fists, and pounds the back seat four times. Her head tilts to stare out the back passenger window. "I would give anything for God to change me and wake me up instantly normal," she whispers. She crams her fists against her closed eyes. "Because then you could be normal, too."

He shifts the rumbling Charger into gear.

22

The bell above the door to Hoover Music is the old-fashioned real deal, and its jingle should be merry, but today it's not. The fourth or fifth Hoover to run the store has announced on Facebook its closure January 20.

When she and Patrick enter, the owner strides over. Brian Hoover is tall with pale skin, chocolate brown eyes, and an Afro-poof of kinky, brown hair. Casey took lessons here as a child from a guitarist who now tours with the Ozark Mountain Daredevils, Dave Painter. She was Dave's only student who could read music. One time she brought in a Yardbirds song to learn, and Dave fell to his knees and wept a thank you. Brian Hoover was the first person to suggest she sing in public with a talent show band his daughter put together at that dinky private school, Greenwood, where the rich oddballs go.

Brian Hoover is so soft-spoken she has to stand on tiptoe to catch his greeting. She hugs his waist, though she knows this may send him away in a seizure of embarrassment.

"Patrick," Brian says, nodding to Turin. "I heard you two were collaborating. That's wonderful. I'm eager to hear the music you make."

Even in the gloom of a business closing this darling man encourages another musician and projects a positive vibe. Casey grabs Brian's hand and buries her cheek in his shirtsleeve. The twelve-string, six-string, and bass guitars hanging and gleaming; the stacks of amplifiers longing to shout; the chrome-trimmed, glass cases loaded with pedals and picks and rosins and strings sparkling like gaudy fireworks; the brass of the saxophones and trumpets blaring orange light; the lemon yellow walls and speckled, tan linoleum floor tiles welcoming her home—in this store, Casey is a child again waiting for the door to Dave Painter's teaching studio to open the music to her. And yet she's a musician now, a young woman maybe even, clinging to Brian Hoover's sleeve. She has cash money in her pocket, all her Cedar Shake savings, a roll of dough she never would've earned but for the musicianship she learned right here. This space changed her life. Now it will go away. It's like another death.

"I want her to see and play that Seagull Echo, the blue one," Patrick says, leading them across the store, all music business tough.

They head over to where three Seagull electrics by Godin hang. Seagull stopped making electrics to focus only on acoustics, touting sustainably made and fair labor practices—Tres Canadien. These three guitars are rare treasures already. For Casey, the sustainable stuff was exciting if you were Devon or that Swedish badass, Greta. But Seagull locally sourced and politely priced its instruments right out of her reach. She bought her Martin acoustic and her Fender Jazz bass from Hoover with a big chunk of her portion from Dad's life insurance money.

"Plug it into that Jackson," Patrick insists.

She elbows him.

But Brian hooks up the patch chord. "A Jackson will sure bring out the best in it." He fits the guitar with a Hoover music strap. Then gingerly he hands the Echo to her.

The neck and body stocks are dense and solid. She tunes quickly by ear. A heavy guitar on the shoulder, weighty as a Gibson she once tried. But it's much more compact than the Gibson, and that's important. A big guitar can make a small player look like a circus act.

Brian kneels at the amplifier. "Where would you like to go?" he asks. There's a light in his eyes, a curiosity.

Why is this place closing? Her eyes sting, and she can feel the tears welling. "Oh... let's go all Will Sergeant. Bassy, clear, bit of reverb."

But she doesn't have to tell Mr. Hoover. He knows Echo and the Bunnymen and all the history of Liverpool sounds. He's already dialed it in, and now stands back.

She plows into the bold, opening hook in B, then adds fills and nicks since there are no drums or keyboards along for the ride.

To her surprise, Patrick knows the chorus, and when she strokes up the big B-7, they both sing out. He can really do Ian McCulloch, and she has sung long enough with him that the harmonies twist in eerie swoops.

There's usually a jaded impatience while someone thrashes in a music store. Shoppers cringe, though they all jones for their own turn to whale away. For her and Patrick, though, the store stops. People round aisles. Clerks come to the counter's edge to witness. Even the death metal kid's eyes bulge, and he drops his hand from a starry Ibanez he wants to steal to watch this tiny girl sing about lips and swans, grace and water, kisses and sugar.

She watches Patrick's Adam's apple when he sings. His pipes rumble, like a big V8 in a Mustang. The new clarity he has encouraged from her locks with his voice and lights up its canyons. Together they sound matched and yet unlike any two voices she's ever heard. Their sound colors this home place. She stops before it becomes a full-on show. Blushing, she squeezes the guitar to her stomach and strokes its neck.

Brian clears his throat. "That is what it sounds like when everyone cares about the music they make instead of how famous they may become."

She's about to go waterworks but Patrick grabs her arm and bends to her ear. "I'll take it from here. 70-30. Matches your eyes. Great optics."

The Seagull Echo Electric by Godin fits like a beautifully made shotgun in her hands, one of those high-end brands that she and Dad practice-fired at Bass Pro Shops, but he never could afford. She wants it, but she doesn't want to turn a thug loose on Brian Hoover to get it. To give the two of them space, Brian kneels and powers down the Jackson amplifier.

Patrick hisses in her ear. "Let me do this for you. This is the only way to survive in music. Vicious and ready to be vicious again."

He unwinds the price tag from the neck and stalks toward the counter.

Brian flashes a smile at her. "It does match your eyes, Casey." He glances at Patrick's wake to make sure he is out of earshot. He bows to her, hand on his chest. "Thank you for making music here." Casey fights her instinct to wrap her arms around his neck.

"Oh. Don't worry about me, Casey Strong." His eyes travel to Patrick waiting to haggle at the register. "I can say no to anyone. You'll need to master that." His face has a quality like porcelain, a white that glows deep inside his skin.

She pops the store's strap off the guitar and hands the strap to Mr. Hoover. Then she follows Patrick up to the register. He glares down his nose at her.

"Price tag," she says, holding out her hand. This will cost her everything she made at the Cedar Shake and then some. "I don't want your money or your vicious shit."

He starts to speak, but she shows him her palm. "Wait in the car or we both leave now. Those are your only options." The clerk stands back from the register.

Stewing in the car, he pops the trunk when she exits the store. He's already collapsed the back seat to help her ease in the new guitar.

She sits down and buckles in. Then he whirls and points at her. "Don't ever fight me in front of other musicians."

She returns his stare. "Hey! There are places in this town that belong to me. You're not going to pollute them. I don't care if Jack White records you. Hoover Music raised me."

She's never seen him this pissed. She wishes she had the

Glock from her Martin case. He boils awhile, and she lets him. Red stains his face like a bad, cheap wine. She pats her hip for her phone, and its bulky, reassuring rectangle in her pocket soothes her.

At last, he twists to see behind him in the parking lot and jams the Peugeot in reverse. "This softhearted crap will keep you right here stuck in this backwater."

"Need me to call an Uber, Mr. Big Shot? I know where I am. I know my way home."

23

Casey always marveled at the old Victorian mansions on Walnut Street. This place where they're supposed to debut, Write On Book Stop, occupies one of her favorites. Cream with a terra cotta color bordering the front door and sills, wrought iron shielding the bottom half of even the upstairs windows, Write On Book Stop looks like an AirBnb in some rich kid's Insta pic from Italy. But then pasture grass and starving shrubs in the rocky clay front lawn bring you right back home to Springfield. Where's Devon when you need him?

At the door, a gallant bald guy with a milky eye and a Payne Stewart cap lifts her Fender Super Champ and her Martin in its case. A smiling man with a lovely black beard takes her Seagull case. Patrick sweats it behind them with his drum kit and accordion. They set up in a living room jammed with motley chairs, loaded bookshelves all around, a giant, screened off fireplace blocked by a killer retro green sofa. The high, recessed ceiling glows—it's made of those tiles of hammered metal and painted eggshell white. On the floors, hardwood shines like in a commercial for wax cleaner.

There's hardly any room up front, and the handsome guy with the lovely beard gets flustered when she wants the store's PA amp, a spiffy Ion Tailgater, up on a table and in front of her mic. She tries to explain—you're singing to people's shins if you don't raise this. She looks to Patrick for some help. He set this gig up. But he's obsessing with where he and the drums should be. Then, when she finally convinces Lovely Beard, he says they'll have to stay for an author to read. They can't tear down right after. And to save hassle the author will want to use Casey's mic. Super. Twelve people mill around, chatting or sulking. All young, pale. No one owns an iron, a comb, or a vent brush. From the look of it, these are all smarty pants college people. The bald guy with the milky eye sits right in front next to a slouchy, round guy draped in a field jacket. They're both staring at her. She's used to stares, but not from such close quarters. In one lunge, Milky Eye could grab her and bounce her on his knee. The author Casey recognizes from the poster—piles of lush, brunette hair, great lips, this kind of 1940s look, sailor tee and a cute navy blazer. She has her book cradled in her left arm, vicious red Xs and the word EXTINCTION on the cover. Oh, Lord.

She turns to Patrick. At least the store has a PA for her, and they don't have to push both vocals through Patrick's JBL. "You hear that? We play, then we're stuck. Hope you like some fancy book readin'."

"Chill, Tink. This is exactly the backdrop. And I'm not who I am. You're not who you are. Incognito. This is guerilla. Big YouTube reveal."

Up on a speaker stand, the JBL PA has a mount for a camera, and Patrick has a GoPro screwed to that and focused down at him. He's got his Busker-Do drum kit, a bass, snare and high hat that can all be foot pumped, front and center. It's very old timey, one-man bandish, his set up. Two girls already recognize him as the Sofia Castle guy—they're huddled up and comparing him on their phones. Casey will end up a side decoration, no more important to his act than the lady hula lamp at a Bel Airs show. "If I'm not who I am, it would've been a great idea to tell me who I'm supposed to be," she snaps.

He grabs her hand and holds it steady. "Settle down. We're going to blow the roof off this place. Okay? Check these two mics." They check and set levels. This feels awkward. Every "test" blurted out stops conversation. People glare. No one came to see music tonight.

A gorgeous woman with dark hair and an almost Mediterranean complexion glides over. Huge brown eyes. The lady leans down to Casey. In her aqua top with flowy flute sleeves, she's like a cascade, and Casey rises into it, deeply turned on. Oh, this is all Tyndall's fault. She wishes her Martin wasn't between them.

"Trigger warning," the woman whispers. She gets even closer to Casey. "Violating so much here, sorry. But you're *tiny*. How old are you, really?"

Patrick drops the hand he was holding out for the lady and goes glum.

Casey looks up into the lady's eager eyes. She can smell cocoa butter on her warm neck. *Why am I not who I'm supposed to be?* "Help," she whispers. She grips the lady's arm. This lady moisturizes and lifts weights; there's a rope of muscle back of her elbow. Her skin feels delish. "Bad man took me. Want Mummy."

The lady recoils then glares at Patrick.

"Kidding," Casey says. "I graduate in May. Everyone thinks I'm eleven."

The lady puts her hand on her chest and breathes deeply several times. She's trying to smile, though. Casey still clings to her arm. "It's okay. If I were literally half an inch shorter, I would qualify as a little person, officially. Then it wouldn't be okay to ask me anything or say I'm tiny. When I am, right? Figure that out. Half an inch." She doesn't want to let go, and her nerves are racing, making her chatter.

Patrick hands the lady a card. "For the introduction," he says.

The lady's face rumples like there's barf stains on the card. "Alberta?"

Patrick gives her a vacant stare. Jesus. What is he trying to pull?

She frowns. "Okay, look," the lady says. "Wherever you're from, whoever kidnapped whom, Janice set this up, and then quit on us. Yesterday! So, you can play two songs. But then it's the author's night. Got it?"

So this is going to be their debut. In a bookstore. Where no one has come to hear them play anything. It's clear from reactions to the author, this is her homecoming.

"Ask him to put this on YouTube or Facebook Live," Patrick whispers. He nods at Milky Eye, who is absorbed in his phone.

"I could've had ten pals up in here and put this on YouTube," Casey says. He banned her from promoting this. He was to handle everything. Guerilla marketing.

"Not authentic," he says.

"We're in Springfield, Missouri," Casey says. Her teeth are clenched. "You said nothing here is ever authentic. Remember?" She's seeing red now. The crowd is larger and louder. People are hugging the author and making a wonderful fuss. This is the author's happy night—what the hell are she and Patrick even doing here?

Patrick jerks his head at Milky Eye.

Casey turns with a smile to the man who helped her already. He lowers his phone and beams. The round guy in the army field jacket leans to her as well. These two are sweet, and she can feel protection flowing from them like warmth from a fireplace. She risks putting a hand on Milky Eye's shoulder. She speaks in her outside voice, "My kidnapper, the guy with the drums, would like to ask you how your eye got that way. That okay?"

To her surprise Milky Eye stands up, and so does Field Jacket. Patrick gets right next to her, and rests an arm across her back, grabbing her shoulder in his claw to rein her in.

"Any way you could film this to YouTube? Insta? TikTok?" he asks. "I caught you looking at Vimeo, and I knew instantly you got taste. You can make it authentic."

Milky Eye and Field Jacket look at each other, wide eyed, then back at Patrick.

"My cousin's kind of out of it," Patrick goes on. Casey can feel him glaring down at the top of her head. "Long road trip," he adds.

"How's it authentic if you ask us to film it?" Field Jacket asks. "I mean, for starters, shouldn't we want to do that?"

The wine color creeps along Patrick's neck. This is already such a mess.

She grabs Milky Eye's hand. "Please. Film us. Pretty please. I have to ride in a car with him all the way back to the cellar in the woods where he keeps me." She sticks her guitar pick out like a key and rolls her wrist back and forth at the mimed lock.

Milky Eye snorts and shakes his head. "Fine. You two are strange."

Patrick hands him a business card—where did he get business cards? "If you'll tag @PatrickwithKC. Like it is on there." He points at the card. "Appreciate it, man."

Patrick takes his stool, scowls at her, points a drumstick at one of the lights in the room, and then at the floor where he must want her to stand.

The lady in aqua glides back over. All these nonconformist college types settle down instantly. There's thirty people in here now. "Our manager, Janice, who can't be here, arranged a treat for us." She raises the card Patrick gave her and bobs her eyebrows.

Casey is relieved to see that Milky Eye has his phone up and is filming. She bows to him and mouths Thank You, blows him and the camera lens a kiss. Field Jacket is watching the phone, but just then his smile grows wide and sinister.

"Patrick with KC, cousins all the way from the sand oil fields of Alberta, Canada, are debuting here at Write On Book Stop. In Springfield. Wow! So, wow, here they are."

Canada? Cousins? Sure, look at their freckles. She bats her eyes at Patrick. WTAF?

Patrick gets the Busker-Do bass drum to thumping and he clicks the sticks on the rim of the snare. No denying how precise in time he is. She pulls the Martin up, and they launch into "Lexus from Texas" just like they've practiced and practiced. The sound deadens in the long rectangle room with all that metal overhead and the crowded upholstery, bookshelves, and people. She notices some of the listeners have leaned toward the phone Milky Eye holds up, but they're grinning too much. He's doing something funny. Milky Eye and Field Jacket, though, are pretty absorbed watching her. She's just figured out how the room vibrates and where to put her voice. Right along that shadow in the raised part of the metal ceiling, that's where she's going to throw this. She heaves it up there, knowing the sound's going to shower down on them like it's raining bells. Patrick's eyes bulge when she hits full tilt. Everybody gets really still. Even the gaggle watching through Milky Eye's phone leans back. The author's mouth drops. At the last, Casey diddles a quip of a country lead, and they close on a big C and a pish of the cymbal.

"Holy. Shit," says Field Jacket.

Oh, thank God, there's applause. Field jacket leans in whispering to Milky Eye, who nods and then adjusts something on his phone. Casey lowers her head, folds her hands on her Martin, and dips a curtsy. She's wearing a yellowy tartan skirt over amber tights, celery pixie boots, and a rust-colored, princess vest with silky panels and just a wife-beater tee under it. Freckles on her arms glow. The volume of applause rises after her bow. So... it's for her. She looks at Patrick, who jerks his head at her Fender Super Champ.

Some guy stands up. "Know any Neko Case? That was great, kid. You could totally sing Neko Case."

"Shut up, Nathan," says a chorus of women.

She closes her Martin away and whisks out the Seagull electric, kneels to the amp to adjust. Meantime Patrick is yapping about "Spokane" and all this deep meaning of being trapped and unnoticed, and how a place can be a shelter and a curse. How one Spokane can connect you to a whole coastal and elite culture and another Spokane can be a nail through your feet. Good God, brighten up the house, why don't you? Like these smarty pants bookworms won't get the song. She dials in clean with high tone and reverb. She rearranged

"Spokane" once she learned the Seagull's strengths, and the song has now got waves and swoops like those old Crowded House songs her mother grieved to over and over. He wanted it to sound like the ocean. She gave it to him, but with white caps of mourning.

When she stands up ready, Patrick and his yap have glazed the whole bunch. Even the lady bookstore owner with the aqua blouse slumps droopy-eyed.

"It's so nice to be let outside to see others," Casey says in her most girly voice. Every woman in the room jolts. "In the darkety cellar where Cousin keeps me, my only play purties are Hellbenders." That's got 'em. Everybody's sitting up straight now, alarmed and confused. "Y'all are so shiny with your metal in your noses and all the paint on your skin."

She looks over at Patrick, red in pinot noir rage. Screw him. You're not who you are. She moves the mic stand. She's going to smash the glass windows and sing wherever she wants. Alberta? He pumps four beats on the cymbal, and she starts the chirping lick, like playing a Keith Richards barre chord that adds a hammer on with your middle and ring fingers, releasing, stroking up then attacking down for the chirp and wave, so it bounds, ocean waves with peaks and hollows. One deep breath, then Write On Book Stop disappears. No one drowsing, no one wanting Neko Case, no author waiting. Just her voice, the guitar, the time signature of the bass drum and cymbal, and now the accordion comes in right where the ocean breaks against the heart. It's not volume you need with this song; it's texture, and everyone is still enough she can make her voice clear and varied in the Ion.

Here I am where all our mountains
Never face your waves of famous fire.
But my Spokane cain't rage by an ocean—
It's scarred by gravel roads sewn in wire.

It's a pretty story-song of a doomed long-distance love between two kids in two Spokanes, one out west and one here. Patrick can write. She envies that. He eases them out of it on the accordion as she quiets the guitar down to just dead strings trickling like drizzle on a back windshield. She's ooo woooing a melody that matches the accordion. It works great mic'd, and the people are so quiet, she can project it right at their scalps. She's getting this spine-chilling crackle from deep in her lungs. She's asking so much of her voice, it's like she can feel her heels levitating. Her lips shape a kiss, her tongue pushes at her bottom teeth. Since she's on note with the accordion, it carries till you don't know which is making the ooo woo ooo. Two three four and done. There's a pause this time, a long, scary one.

At last, Neko Case Nathan jumps up pounding his paws, and suddenly they're all standing and clapping. She curtsies. Milky Eye is still filming, but his eyes shine soppy. She dares to stand aside and swirl an arm to Patrick while bowing so they acknowledge and clap for him. He's going to be sore. He nods at her amp. "Turn that off," he says, loud, in Dad voice. One more curtsy. Then she rests her Seagull in its case and kneels at the amp.

The lady in aqua thanks "Patrick with KC" and after some more clapping, she starts introducing the author. Lovely Beard bends down to her at the Super Champ. "That was amazing, kiddo," Lovely Beard whispers. "Do you all have a CD we can sell?"

She has the Super Champ powered down. She rubs her palms on her skirt and looks into his eyes. They're bright blue, like Devon's. He's darling, a Sensitive. She really shouldn't do any more of this. But whose fault is it that they don't have a CD? And why bother to play here without one? Him and his guerilla backdrop. Cousins from oil sands?

"I'm not allowed to speak with you unless Cousin can hear me," she says loudly.

The pale look on Lovely Beard's face is awful.

The author stands over the two of them now.

"That was *so* good," the author says, bending down to her ear, touching her arm. "Are there really Hellbenders in Canada?" She looks curious and sincere, and probably she does want to know if there are rare Ozark salamanders in the oil sands of Alberta. Behind them the crowd is clapping for the author.

Patrick is sitting on the hardwood floor, his back against the bookshelves. He's fiddling with his phone. "Forgive me. I must return to my Lord and Master," Casey says.

The author looks wide-eyed at Lovely Beard, then at Casey.

She flips her skirt and plunks down next to Patrick. She grabs his hand and clutches it to her lap and smiles up at the author, the woman in aqua, and the bearded guy, who are all blinking and puzzled. Patrick gives her side eye, then jams the cell phone between their two hips, but he doesn't let loose of her hand. "Way to go, Cuz," he says, deadpan.

"Okay" says the author. She says some stuff about Missouri State and thanks a lot of people. Then she starts reading her book about extinction, and Casey is relieved the Ion still sounds fine where it is. She can feel Patrick's phone vibrating against her leg. Something's blowing up. She looks him over, stiff and pissed. But the phone is sure buzzing. Isn't that all he wanted? The author reads about all these islands vanishing in water, and the women in the story get what's happening but the men ram their heads up their butts. Rains a lot here in Springfield, too, now, right? Huge applause. Everybody stands clapping. Casey joins. Wow! Who knew people would sit through stuff like this and give it a standing O?

Back at the Peugeot, he's silent and careful as they load. The lady in aqua and Lovely Beard approach the car holding hands. "Just what is going on?" the lady asks. "Your plates are from Missouri," he says. "We're concerned. About her," they say together.

Patrick holds his door open. She sits buckled in in the passenger seat with her hands folded in her lap, her eyes to the front even though she wants to watch the lady's every move. "It's an act," Patrick says. "We live in Southern Hollow. I take her to her mom's tonight. She's back at Glendale High School tomorrow."

They look at each other. "So that was all..." The lady stops. "That is so disingenuous."

Patrick stares at them. "At its core, can performance really ever be genuine?"

Yeah, go deep. That'll solve everything. He shuts the car door. The phone is still buzzing, buzzing. He glares at the two bookstore owners until they walk slowly back into the house, still holding hands.

She tenses when he reaches for the phone. When his arm moved, she really felt he was going to hit her.

"That kidnapping thing was a lot," he says.

"You told me I wasn't supposed to be myself. Woke 'em right up."

"Why can't you just follow my lead and shut up, then sing when I tell you?"

Before she can tell him off, he flips his phone over. "Look what he did to us on 'Lexus from Texas.'"

On the video, she approaches the camera. Just as she bends to blow Milky Eye a kiss, a filter swims and transforms her head and chest into an orange cartoon kitty-cat. Patrick is a smiling turkey, red neck and wattle behind the drums. But they launch into the song. It sounds as amazing as she felt it to be. It's a funny song anyway. So she's a kitty-cat?

"Hey," she says. "Look at there. Kitty me's got some titties!" She gives her shoulders a shimmy. In real life, Casey has the chest of a Little League shortstop.

He lifts the phone to him and swipes. "And this is what he did on 'Spokane.'"

This video has no filter, and this one Patrick has cast to his hundred thousand followers. She's front and center, and Patrick has the drummer's curse, back and to her left. The Seagull Echo does match her eyes. It pulls some blue out of the tartan, and even radiates metallic tones onto the rust red silk of her vest. The phone buzzes and buzzes.

"1,000 likes, 200 loves, 48 casts, no 52, sorry. Just since we stopped playing and I shared his video. 340 loves now." He lets her take the phone. "Dig the comments."

"Whoa," she says. The buzzing against her calluses feels like a thrumming shock from an outlet. "We're kind of a thing."

"You're kind of a thing, Tink." He starts the car. He's not smiling.

24

You want organic lawn care, but you don't want to sacrifice. With the new LawnGenie System from LawnMagi, you don't have to. Devon's shoulders droop. Ordering spring inventory in the Merritt Organics supply room, he's opened a key supplier's website and discovered LawnMagi has morphed. It's no longer just a provider of fertilizers, grub outs, and soil builders made with no animal byproducts, no manures, no biosolids or other waste material. LawnMagi is suddenly much more. They'll take a satellite image of your yard, send you an easy-to-follow soil test kit with prepaid postage, process your sample's data, and then ship you a constant year-round supply of *Organic Guarantees to Lawn Care Glory. We've worked super hard to make this easy for you.*

He types in Casey's address on Lamonta and quickly builds a profile. The cost estimate that LawnMagi generates staggers him—it's so low. But then, why not? LawnMagi will send Casey's mom a box, like those gourmet-meal-in-a-box people. All she has to do is get a spreader or buy an overpriced, branded LawnMagi Balthasar Blaster. Then she has to trot around the yard and do all the leg and back work that Devon at Merritt Organics would do. LawnMagi just replaced him with DIY lies, cardboard shipping boxes, and an AI chat.

"Hey, what's the hold up?" Dad's voice in the respirator sounds like he's submerged.

Like Devon, Dad's got on safety goggles and a respirator dust mask, gloves, and green Merritt Organics coveralls. Dad loves equipment. Merritt has closets full of branded coveralls, and garden gear. Sherry Jean designed the Merritt Organics logo, and if you have a logo designed by your hot, new wife, well, then you have to buy lots of paraphernalia to stick it on, right? The lease on this supply room is crushing—*but* it has the logo printed gigantically on the roof so private airplanes taking off and landing at the dinky Springfield Downtown Airport can admire it. Merritt could easily build an extension onto the back of the garage at home and fulfill most of their actual volume. So much waste!

Devon backs the website up to the landing url for the LawnGenie Program. Of course, LawnMagi already has a kickass YouTube video for the new service. He clicks play. Bouncy K-Pop music starts. Lithe and wise-looking women slip on garden gloves and open the bright cardboard box from LawnGenie. *So easy. You don't want to sacrifice.* A British voiceover pronounces LawnGenie as if it were a style of French lace panties.

Dad pulls off his safety goggles and watches the whole thing. "Well, that has to cost way more than us, with the shipping and all. And the satellite."

Devon hands him the estimate he generated. "They don't have a satellite. It's just Google Earth and an algorithm."

He squints at the estimate. His lips begin to curl. "Damn. Click around and see if there's an affiliate program like at Amazon. Maybe we can work with these assholes?"

"You mean for not with. Why would we even order from them? They're out to kill us. They will kill us."

"You don't know that. And do you have another weekend for us to scout a new supplier?" Dad puts his goggles back on and gets the seal at his nose down tight. "I tell you, Devon, we're not going to make money at this until I can get you through high school and have you in here kicking butt all the time. Time is everything in business."

Devon lifts his clipboard and inventory tally off the cluttered, soiled desk. "You want me to order all this for Spring from a company that's ready to eat you alive?"

"They're not ready, and yes." The bulk of a respirator mask, goggles, and the billow of coveralls make most men seem menacing, even apocalyptic. But not Dad. He seems thinned, like a filament in a sputtering, green Christmas bulb. "What is it with your generation? I swear to God! It's all your one way or no way. And it's always all end of the world."

Devon shrugs. "Okay, then. Sink the business before I graduate. Then I won't be stuck working here." He doesn't wait for his Dad's angry reply. "I have to get going anyway. Tyndall's making me dinner."

Dad pulls his goggles and respirator off. "Now, you want to talk about waste, Devon. You with that Hastings girl. That's a waste."

Devon builds the LawnMagi order, clicking as if Dad isn't there.

"Son, the Hastings are evangelical zealots and worst of all Trumpers. And I'm sorry to say this, but that girl is going to offer nothing but problems all her life." When Devon keeps working, Dad grips his arm at the elbow. "Look at me. You're around her a lot lately. You're not kids anymore. On the outside, she's one hell of a good looking girl. But on the inside… Devon, autism doesn't go away. With those crazy, evangelical parents, if you screw up… if you even *think* about her sexually, they'll want you two married in a shotgun flash. You don't need anyone right now. But when you do, you need to marry someone who brings something to the table, who adds something to what you can do."

"Don't even," he says.

"Your mother added so much to who I was, to who we are."

"That's not fair. She's gone. And you can't say what you're saying right now and be married to a kneeboard champion from Blue Eye who could be my sister."

Dad's face glows. He picks at the clay-reddened elastic straps to his goggles. "I'm not saying this to you because I did everything right. I'm saying this so you have a chance. Think about who you are. Think about what she is. Think very carefully about the choices you make and their consequences. I didn't. And here we are."

Showered, he's drowsily watching the President and a bunch of suits and a lady in a scarf talk about some virus in China. If it's only as bad as the mildest flu and will go away in summer, why spew this on TV? Boop, a text from Tyndall! The world really is ending.

—don't drive walk neighbors

What? Fine, it's downright cold outside, so the blueberry cheesecake he's picked up at Barnes & Noble won't suffer. Tyndall's house would be a three-hill hike if he took streets and sidewalks. But walking the lakeshore, it's only four houses and then the stream and spring to her cul-de-sac. The gray lake shimmers in wind, forms and reforms like a tray of magnetite in those games he and Tyndall played as children. Tyndall gripped the magnetized iron pen and drew geometric spirals over and over, as hypnotic as Escher puzzles.

Tyndall answers the door and yanks him inside quick. What the hell? Usually it's Nora greeting you, and then you wait listening to Marion for thirty or forty minutes until Tyndall appears. He's barely kept his grip on the cheesecake box.

He hands it to her. "The blueberry you didn't get to try."

Her shoulders slump. Already she appears frustrated. "I took only one Quietarol. Like you insisted."

He breathes. It's been a long Saturday. "Where's Nora? She usually…"

"Marion and Nora have a Couples Weekend with Jesus. C W^2 J. They are trying to save their marriage. At Lake of the Ozarks. They can't come back till Monday night. It's a Victory Faith Triumphant Lockdown."

"Oh."

She's wearing another tight T-shirt with stripes, and a jade skirt, shiny, like something Casey would pick out for her. Tyndall in a skirt!

She leads them to the dining room table where she has arranged two paper plates, a pizza box, and a bottle of sparkling grape juice. She sets the cheesecake box down and stares at it. "So, you want me to take more Quietarol and then eat till I'm ill again?"

"Of course not. I just thought…"

Her eyes are focused on his shoulder. "But you said our last date checked all your boxes for you."

Never tell Tyndall even a tiny lie. "We're having dinner, right? A little dessert after."

She stares at the boxed food. "I want us to do something else first." She's opening and closing her hands. "We discussed this while we drove around last time. What Casey did. I want you to do it to me. My parents are not here. Will not be here. They've Positively Confessed their Faith in Jesus Christ to save their marriage, and so they have to stay in lockdown till Monday at 4 p.m. at Tan-Tar-A. That's 91 minutes driving from here."

He thinks of his dad fiddling with the soiled strap on his goggles. Every credit card maxed, and here they just promised $1,700 to a company that will devour them faster than army worms. Sherry Jean Plumly was Dad's teaching assistant. And Dad got her pregnant, at least that's what Sherry Jean says. Who am I supposed to listen to here?

"Did Casey help you choose that skirt? It's pretty."

"And the shirt," Tyndall says. She points at a silver stripe and then at her gray eyes. She inhales sharply, steps forward. She cups his fingertips and squeezes them. "I'm trying so hard. Don't you dare do anything tonight out of sympathy for the strange girl." She pulls his hands to her chest. "I want you to do exactly what I tell you for forty minutes. Then I will do everything you tell me for at least six minutes. Unless I say no if you have a bad idea." She looks at his neck, and he sees the struggle in her eyes—she strives to read his every signal.

"So you need forty? But I get six."

THE LAKES OF SOUTHERN HOLLOW

A smile. He makes Tyndall Hastings smile. "Oh, you might not take even five." She swallows, and there's that dry paper sound. "I'm going to be amazing. I've read 87 magazine and book pages and watched 16 videos." She's almost skipping as she jerks him by the hand down the hallway to her bedroom.

25

At Patrick's apartment she and Patrick have the mix from the studio downloaded. Four songs—all they could afford for now. That's not even an EP.

"So... what's the goal here for you?" She has her headset off, and she's wishing there were a vocal exercise that would clear the ears and mind. They've listened and re-listened to these four songs, after playing and playing and recording and rerecording. She's worried she has stopped hearing, that the track burned in her head is too loud and its groove too deep for her to catch any flaw in what's playing through the headset.

"It's about emotion, and it can be about narrative."

Oh, God. Deep ways, here we come.

"I want the lyric particular enough to be new but at the same time the song has to belong to the listener way before the chorus starts. That's where the great songs live." He licks his lips. His voice is dry, and she wonders what he's on. "That's the balancing act between 'Never heard it like this before' and 'That's exactly how I feel.'" He flattens his hand and teeters it back and forth. "Nail that, then the world says, This is our song."

"I meant, what is your goal with only four songs to work with?"

"Let's just get these right. It's you who keeps stopping the playback."

She puts her headphones back on, and he presses play again. They both have pencils and pads and watch the counter.

She's over the rush of hearing her voice at this level and clarity. They're seated together, thigh to thigh, at the big, formal dining room table. He's running the mix through SoundBlitz so they can watch the peaks and valleys and log those times where Jeff needs to rework.

She's amazed and energized that they can work like this in close quarters. They've had a lot of physical contact—almost like her and Devon when they were kids playing and fighting; like having a big brother all of a sudden. With New Wave Vultures, whole basements of space, whole stages of distance kept everyone virginal and scratch free. Only in Dwayne's van were they ever pressed together, and the farthest they ever traveled was Fayetteville. She and Patrick have been in close quarters a lot, rehearsing and listening in the studio. She's grateful there are no weird sexual come-ons from him. Nothing really sexy about him. Although his skin, with all its dots, is pretty fascinating. All of his red freckles are nicely round and mostly the same size, like beads of oil on the surface of a homemade soup. He's an actual ginger. And lanky and muscled. He smells like cheap soap and a mouthwash Dad used, Chlora-something. It's getting late and this is a school night, but here they are hammering away.

She stops the play again.

"What? Tink!"

"You can hear that," she says. "Some patch chord Ohming away."

"It's raw, right? It's what we made, ourselves. DIY."

"We didn't make that. That's racket. Muddies the bass. It sucks."

"70-30 says it stays."

She pulls her headset off and tosses it against the tabletop.

He stands. She rises up, and pushes his chest hard.

"Don't throw my gear around. This stuff costs money."

When he moves to shove her back, she lunges. He's got her by the shoulders. She grips his arms at the elbows. She's determined to get him off balance. They're snorting. In a whirl, her foot snags under a leg of the table just when he gets leverage and wrenches her around. There's a crack.

He releases her, showing her his palms. "Oh, shit. Ow. Casey, I'm sorry."

Gray circles swim in her vision. Down she goes.

She's in too much pain to argue when they swing into the parking lot of an urgent care. He keeps saying he knows this Doc. His dad, Mr. Turin, did some lawyer thing for him.

The doctor's hair hangs in greasy strings, and he breathes through his mouth. His breath smells like a sewer grate. Patrick tells the doc everything that happened when her foot tangled and caught. But he leaves out the why. Then he and Patrick whisper for a while standing close together, the doctor with his back to her and hunched. Patrick keeps his hand in the middle of the doc's back, as if he's leading him off somewhere secret.

Finally the doctor straightens up. "Not without an X-ray."

"Sure. Right. Of course," Patrick says.

She has her hi-top unlaced and is sticking it out at both of them. The doctor stands there with his hands jammed down in the pockets of his grimy lab coat.

"Will somebody get my shoe off before it's stuck on me?"

In the X-ray room, the tech yawns a lot. When he stabilizes her foot, she howls. Back in the examination room again, the doctor gets her a plastic boot, a big clunky thing like from a sci-fi movie. Patrick pays cash for everything, and then there's a big hurry to get to the pharmacy before eleven p.m. The late-night pharmacist takes her driver's license and asks when she's going to Europe. Tour starts immediately, Patrick tells him.

"This is a lot," the pharmacist keeps saying. "This is just a whole lot."

He and Patrick get in a row. She slumps in the vinyl waiting seats, sweating. Her foot feels as if lightning bolts are separating it from her ankle. "Jesus!" she yells at both of them. Patrick points at her foot and waves a folder the doctor gave him. They don't even write her driver's license down like they used to for the snot pills that cookers used for meth. They just squint at it.

Finally at Creamy Doodles he gets her an ice cream sandwich and has her take two of the opioid pills. She's never had this medicine, but she's in so much pain, she just does what he says. The diner is scalding white inside, with sparkling jade benches in the booths, and a shining checkerboard tile floor. There are two bottles, a small one, and a huge one.

"I cannot believe you," she says. "First you break my foot, and then you wangle the whole deal into a score. This isn't a pill bottle; it's a pill barrel. I could open a pain clinic!"

"Pipe down, Tink! You're all set," he says, eyeing the empty diner. This is a fun place where your parents take you for a milkshake after soccer. The two of them are skeezing it up. "I'll leave you with thirty. Now shut it."

"I'll shut up for fifty. Wait. So, when are we going on this European tour? You made that up? Patrick!"

Back in the Peugeot, her spine glows warm. Her shoulders, neck, everything relaxes. Her heart rides up on a note, G sharp, and then suddenly a whole chorus showers over her chest and swirls warmly and lovingly deep into her stomach. He's driving her. He took care of her. He bought her crutches. Everything feels different. Everything feels so much better.

"You're gonna have to explain all this to Mom," she says.

"Oh?"

"Yeah. I feel really wack."

Of course, her mom is up. A cop's wife, she has already lost a loved one. All of a sudden Patrick is like an adult and meets all of Mom's confrontation with straightforward answers. They struggle to get her up the stairs, one helping on each arm. She has never used crutches and she's hopeless and feeling pretty elastic. She tells her mom more than once that she started the fight. Inside she slouches on the living room sofa, her crutches on the floor. She hates them already.

"I did what I thought was best, and got her immediate attention," Patrick says. "Ortho specialist tomorrow. Here's her referral. I'll pay for everything." Her mother is furious he didn't call, that he, a stranger to her, made any decision about her daughter, a minor. "Right," Patrick says, "but I had to act. If we waited till tomorrow, we'd be stuck the whole weekend waiting for the specialist. And she'd be in terrible pain."

So adult all of a sudden. Like her new big brother got a law degree and knows medicine almost as much as Tyndall.

Around her head and heart, this electric blanket feeling wraps snugly, and every once in a while sends a loving surge down the insides of her arms, sometimes dizzying like that moment before an orgasm or an upchuck—she can't really tell which, it's that intense. Both. Waves. She sees the lake at night out the windows at Devon's, and the lights across the lake, one big light throbbing. She's in that beautiful family room of Devon's filled with midnight lake light, the whole surface shimmering like brushed steel, and she has her clothes in her arms. Some sound must have escaped her, because Patrick and her mom both stop grousing and look at her. She doesn't much care.

"This is really screwed up, kiddo," her mother growls.

"Me or him?"

"Both!" Mom glares at Patrick. "What did they give her, and what do I do?"

Patrick reminds her that a pill bottle is in her coat. She pulls it out and hands it over. Her Mom spins it. "Whoa! I didn't think they prescribed this shit anymore."

"My foot is way broken," she says, and snatches the bottle back.

"She should be fine to sleep. Sleep with that boot on," he says to her firmly.

Mom pops up from the sofa and grabs his arm and drags him to the foyer. "Listen, Buster," is all Casey hears until Patrick comes back with, "I'll pay for everything, and I'll see you tomorrow morning at seven. Do not let her sleep without that boot on."

26

"These pills are like music. I can hear music."

His Peugeot has warmed, and she's wearing a cashmere wrap that he says is from Tuscany. They're headed west on I-44 to Webb City. If the scenery outside weren't so flat and horrible, she might even feel glamorous. He's bought or rented a cute trailer for all their gear. He said something about a classic Peugeot with a towbar being a metaphor for his life so far. Maybe that's supposed to be funny? He's not good with humor. He's like the Wings kids at Glendale—the ones who memorized *The Little Prince* in French—real interesting for about a minute, but smirk humor, never funny, not even to each other.

Two influencers, both named Jill, broadcast on YouTube from Webb City as The Jillions. She's seen them a lot, followers in the millions, and they know music. Rock stars with new songs or video albums dropping make Skype and Zoom calls from Los Angeles, New York, Portland, from the road, from backstage at Bonnaroo. The Jillions discovered that screaming wolf-child from Wyoming, Sheryl Feral, and they were the first to interview those chicks from Nassau, Crotch Rot, the comedy punks who are dropping their first album video by video and now boast preorders in the stratosphere. How the hell two teenage girls from Webb City became influencers of anything is a YouTube miracle. But then she doesn't remember The Jillions ever telling anybody where they're actually from. She didn't know where they were from till Patrick described this whole scheme to her. She's skipping school to do this.

But what's school when you're hobbled on crutches, right foot jammed in a Darth Vader boot, and you're hammered on Roxicodone?

While he drives, she's watching clips from the Jillions' channel on her phone. The backgrounds behind them change, even during the same episode. Crashing surf, towering sheer mountains, leaning jungle temples, whizzing lights in city nightscapes. They do this thing where they react to new songs sent in. Unlike the two black guys who listen to old white people songs and always jam with joy, these two white girls sneer and gag and eye roll. Sometimes they groove, though. They look so alike. Same dad maybe? She loses her train of thought as a surge of sunshine radiates from inside her. D, G, Bb sustained 4. She doesn't even care about the boot. Or the surgery coming, or the pins. Pins mean more pills, he tells her. Yeah, he let that slip, like she's some dairy cow with bouncy opium udders.

"Could you write the music down?" he asks her.

"What?" He seems pretty far away. The old leather in the car glows like caramel, and the early morning light outside spreads a crystalline smash of blue and white like after an ice storm. Billboards for Advanced Prosthetics LLC and Indian casinos flash by.

"Drink that Gatorade," he says. "You gotta get your head clear. What if this is live?"

"You won't admit it, will you? But you're so Southern Hollow."

"What do you mean?"

"Joyless. All business," she says. He stole these sunglasses she's wearing from Ross, or says he did. Who steals from a Ross? You're already shoplifting just walking in there. It's hard to find sunglasses that look anything but ridiculously big on her. But these are great. They're silver ovals like safety glasses for wicked Asian lab workers in some monster movie. The Gatorade glows blue and its surface trembles. She doesn't want to drink it or do anything that makes this feeling go away. It's like the flu when one of these damn pills wears off. "So who are we supposed to be this time?"

"Tink? You're all over the place. Just let me do the talking."

"No. Who are we?"

The leather on his driving gloves wrinkles up as he tenses. Yeah, driving gloves. And a teal scarf, an olive green car jacket, and a Canali orange knit polo and drawstring linen chinos. Six degrees outside, and he's dressed for some beach in Europe.

"Shouldn't this like already be figured out? I mean we don't have CDs pressed. We don't have labels. We don't have a logo. Do you really think Patrick with KC is a name?" She hears Mitch's voice in her head, and she can see him hunched and shaking a finger.

"CDs? Could you be more 2016?"

"Fine. Bandcamp uber allus. But this name! Patrick with KC? It's so morning show, Kidz Toonz, or something. Trout Fishing in America. Yay!" She raises her fists, fake cheering.

"We're almost to Mt. Vernon, and you want to change our name?"

"Why not Turin & Strong? That's kind of badass. Our last names are way cooler than our first names."

He's quiet a while. "We're in Mt. Vernon, and now you have the best idea you've ever had, ever?"

"Yeah. See? Turin & Strong. So much freaking better than Patrick with KC. So better." Suddenly inside her, everything goes hollow and dull. Can she feel her foot hurting? Or is it the boot, squeezing her, and all this sitting? Stay ahead of the pain, right? No one deserves to be in pain, the stringy-haired urgent care doctor said.

"It doesn't change anything about 70/30. It's still with."

"Whatever. Yes. I signed it." She pulls the pill bottle out of her coat.

Frowning, he glances at her. "Does it actually hurt? Or are you just over a crest?"

"Is there any part of my show that I can just run, please?"

"Hey. I do know a few things about pills, Tink."

"You know one thing I think we should keep, in public?" She uncaps the bottle and knocks one out. They're so cute, grainy blue, like Devon's eyes. Stamped with a bold square around an M. On the back, 30 floats above a tranquil line. Amazing. So little makes so much happen. So just because some corporation produces this pill and stamps it and doctors say, okay, that makes it different from meth cooked in a hick trailer, or molly whipped with fentanyl in a Chinese lab, or bathtub acid tabs from Silver Springs Apartments? She stares at Patrick, lanky, ginger, all dolled up in this Italian designer gear. A tweaker, jacked on meth, shot her dad. How are these pills not just a designer coating for the same Satan?

"Tink?"

"Fighting. I think we're charming when we fight." She puts the Roxie on her tongue and sips the blue Gatorade—blue meet blue! "Like an old black-and-white comedy couple."

He watches the interstate. For a while she's not sure where he is—angry, dismissive, condescending. He's stony. She knows this much about these pills: in a minute, she's not going to care about anything but the music. And it won't matter if that's the music she and Patrick can make together or the music she can now hear unleashed inside her.

They pass giant stone hands praying and billboards for an airport and for The Bitter Sweet Art Gallery.

"Oh, My God," she says. "There's the name for Turin & Strong's first album. The Bitter Sweet Art Gallery."

He grins. "So many ideas today. You're really zooming." He signals then turns the car onto a wooded road. "Focus with me a minute. Time for background." One Jillion's dad owns nine microbreweries between here and Boulder, including The Cellar in Webb City, he tells her. That's how The Jillions got their start—acts coming to the brewpubs would appear on The Jillions' YouTube channel live and later even remote to hype what brewpub Dad had going. It took no time for managers and publicists to find these "authentic influencers." But when DAP debuted their song "Anthony Lamar Smith" on The Jillions, it supernovaed. It was even on that geezer show on Sunday morning television, the one with the happy sun ball face. The other Jillion's dad has still more money. He inherited a bunch of abandoned lead and zinc mines that he flipped into subdivisions. So, fragility alert, it's pedal to the floor white privilege with these two. Patrick turns the Peugeot onto a narrow, winding, but paved drive that carries them deep into the trees. At last they stop at a huge gate, wrought iron suspended between big stone pillars.

He idles just short of a keypad and camera that arches on a steel post from the side of the paved drive. The camera looks fixed, so right now, only the front panel of the sedan should be visible. He thinks like a criminal. "We're talking about a lot of money here," he says to her. "So... no half-baked posturing about Righteous People's Music and rejecting middle class success markers. Don't you dare go all blue collar, dead cop's daughter on me."

The air turns fuzzy and peach colored above the prickly winter forest crowding the Peugeot. She probably shouldn't have taken that Roxie. She's going to have to ask him for more, and soon. But that huge bottle that he kept, they were all pre-scribed for her anyway. Skeletal trees claw the air. Clouds bulge downward, the gray of rotted beef. Inside, she feels a grinding like she's stuck in one of those old angsty Feelies songs.

"Have you even watched The Jillions?" she asks. "They don't talk about money. Ever. Why would that even come up?"

"Because you."

"It's an interview. Right? If they ask us things, we answer them."

He smolders. "Well, they also don't have bands play live with them in this studio anymore now that The Jillions are huge famous." Uge, he says. He drops the H in huge, like some Glendale kids will do. "Everybody Skypes or Zooms. The reason we're here, face-to-face, is because of how great you did at the Book Stop, and that video I shared. Right now, this instant, we are Megamillions jackpot lucky."

She drinks her Gatorade down.

"Good. Now I have some bad news for you. Those Roxies can screw up your voice. They're gonna make it harder to get big air, and if you're not careful, they'll make you fry out, high and low. And not a pretty fry. I want you to drink Gatorade till you're sloshing." He roots around in the back and opens a cooler and brings up another Gatorade. "Drink! There's a bathroom in there. Probably seven or eight of them."

She opens the Gatorade but leaves it in the cup holder and stares at him. "You can really be a buzzkill, Buster."

"We're here to get famous, not high." He unbuckles his seat belt and puts out his hand. "Gimme your pill bottle."

"Nope," she says.

He lunges. His knuckles slam her chest and plunge into her coat pocket so quickly, it's like a dog bite. Sudden, ferocious. He has her pill bottle in his fist. Her ribs and arm burn where his nails raked her. Her breath is gone.

"Drink your Gatorade."

She raises the drink but has to put it back down. She's shaking.

"When we get in there, we have forty minutes before they want us to play. You have to warm up and you have to know where your limits are, high and low. You have to learn what it's going to take to sing with this stuff in your system." He tips the pill bottle at her then tucks it in his coat.

27

All those times she thought, *now he's going to hit me*, none prepared her. Stuck with crutches and boot, she can't move any equipment. He unloads all their gear with his usual put-upon martyrdom and vigor, as if nothing's happened.

The place is an office building in the trees, glass and brick and two, maybe three stories. The interior is a searing white, and even in this winter gray light, it's like you've stepped into Heaven's waiting room. But it's hard to care about all this, hard to be dazzled. A thought is not nearly a fist. If her world were a picture, he just tore it to pieces, then jammed the fractured mess back into the frame.

A security guard meets them, uniform, Beretta, and everything. He leads her to a cushy chair and takes her crutches and sets them where she can get them.

The Jillions come in, and they're both in matching big orange and white blouses with teal yoga pants. They do their hair exactly alike, angled bobs with crazy long bangs and bolts of orange highlights. They're super thin with big brown eyes, like two manga characters.

They make a fuss over her boot and crutches. "How'd you do this? Were you skiing?"

Patrick waits, already starting his sulk.

"Him and I fight like brother and sister," she says. "We just got a little too wild."

"Art and pain, right?" Patrick does his best Heathcliff.

The Jillions grip each other's shoulders and look in each other's eyes. They both talk at once, super excited, like kids on a Ritalin rebound. They do this on their YouTube, a sort of freaky twins' language. She gets the gist—they want her to perform "Spokane" and "Lexus from Texas" and anything else she wants to do, but mostly they are all jacked about what they call "genuiwinnity." Her and Patrick fighting—that's genuine and winning authenticity.

"Huh," Casey says. "Thought it was just a sore foot."

Patrick coughs. "Hey, anything for you two. But we want to change our name. And we want to announce our name change on The Jillions."

The Jillions grip each other at the elbows and spin, screaming with what seems like delight. Tyndall loved spinning when they were little, and now Casey can't get this out of her head. Vertigo and worry, how she would spin frantically, arms locked with Tyndall's, but so purposeful, no one was having any fun. These two spinning Jillions, squealing like kindergartners, hold the fate of Turin & Strong, if that's who she and Patrick are about to be. Worry, too, that so far they haven't given Patrick much respect or recognition for "Sofia Castle." Are songs devoured and forgotten just as soon as the next YouTube blows up?

Chattering, the Jillions and the silent security guard lead them deeper into their compound. Banquet doors open to a studio bigger than Patrick's entire apartment. White walls, less searing because they are sound tiles, white linoleum flooring—the only interruptions of the white are three green screens, the black and silver of cams on tripods, the silver and black of mic stands, and gray extension cords. Even the folding chairs are white. The place smells sharply of lemon verbena cleaning solution. "We haven't had an act in here in how long? How long?" they ask each other. "Plug in, warm up, and all that. Okay, so we're not going to do this live, or anything. Okay? Way better? Way better." The Jillions ask and answer each other. "We'll broadcast it later with a bumper before it. Like, 'Hey we were going to do this, but...'"

The security guard shows her to the bathroom, waits outside the door for her, and then helps her to a folding chair. Patrick's got everything set, his Busker-Do drum kit, accordion, his Pantheon, her Martin on a stand and her Seagull. The Jillions have a white Yamaha upright in here. A gorgeous piano just sits here, lonesome in Webb City. It took Mom and Dad forever to afford the battered upright at home. There are three Gatorades by her chair. The security guard closes the banquet doors, but posts himself inside the studio. Patrick gets her attention and points to the four corners of the room. At the ceiling, tucked into each corner is the blue dome of a security camera.

"Anything you say can and will be used against you," she says.

He nods. "They're watching. They could even record warm up."

"So what's the plan, A-hole?"

He smirks. "Warm up." He hands her the Martin. "'There is a Ship.'"

They launch into it, and she immediately feels what he warned her about. It's as if her lungs don't care anymore. This song doesn't call for force and sustain right away, and it has plenty of lows to feel out that range. Ugh, the betrayal, the water, no wings; she'd like to whack him with an oak. So what part of singing this feels beautiful and right because there's a pill in me, and what part is actually beautiful and right? There's a nauseating whirl for you. She settles down when he plays all the flute parts in a solo on the Pantheon, and she keeps rhythm. He's really a beautiful player, tasteful, not showy. And he maintains a respectful difference between the old-timey raw twang of his own songs, and a cover such as this. Some players "make it their own" and ruin everything. At the last verse, she wrestles it together and, just to spite him, she throws out a sustain and carry that's total showboating. They finish. The security guard wipes his eyes, laughs, and apologizes.

Patrick bobs his eyebrows. "Low sounds good. Gatorade."
He points to it with his pick like she's forgotten where it is.
"It's cool if this isn't live."

"Yeah, but they could throw it all out. Trust me. I can still
screw this up for you."

He ignores her, and watches the cameras. Over at the
Yamaha he plinks high, middle, low. It's a 52" and it sounds
fantastic. "Okay. 'Rainy Night House'."

That'll work it all out. A5. This is one of several covers he's
chosen for them to fill a set. She's not so sure she can carry it
with this stuff in her. But then watching him show off for 22
bars of piano, she gets pissed, and goes for it. His sweetheart,
Joni Mitchell, is breathy up that high, but this morning Casey
Strong is not. When she nails A5 without breaking or whispering, he closes his eyes, and his back shudders. Just one
shot of ecstasy where she has him. If she could only keep him
there. But why does she want to keep him there? Why does
she care to give him any peace or pleasure?

He sits with his eyes closed after the song ends, as if he's
meditating. Thug. "Tink, I kind of hope they recorded that."

She sticks out her tongue.

He snorts. "Your tongue is blue."

"Of course it is, guzzling this antifreeze."

The Jillions return along with a heavyset kid in washed
out black jeans and a faded black button-down shirt. Maybe he
sleeps in his clothes surrounded by cats? It's like Phoebe Bridgers
dresses him. He sets up everything, all the cameras, the mics,
and cords. Chubby bulges of pale skin peek through his buttons.
She's beginning to feel that way inside as the Roxie washes out—
pale and fishy, a stale filet on a plate left out all night.

It's harder to sing sitting down, but she's small, and with a
Martin or a Seagull in her lap, she can't slouch. She tries to sit
Tyndall straight. They play two songs. They have rehearsed
enough that she loses herself, and the music blossoms in the
milky white of the studio. The Jillions ask them to play that
song they practiced earlier with Patrick on piano.

So they were watching warm up. Patrick goes into a long explanation of the song and songwriting. It's not even his song. Is this some coping thing with him, these lectures? She's scared about the high notes. This drug—it's like a belt around the mind and the heart and the lungs. She does some deep breathing, while Patrick glazes the Jillions. What the hell is he talking about, cohesion and tension and water? Jesus. He's worse than Devon lecturing.

"Do you believe that?" the Jillion on the left asks her.

Oh, Lord. "I don't really try to say stuff that's deep. That would come out like lies." Shit. She made it even worse. She swallows heavily. Suddenly her mouth is full of spit when it should be dry. He's red and his jaw is a fist. Rage-face emoji. "But sometimes Patrick writes something that makes sense to a lake full of people. Even if we haven't really thought about it. He just wrote it, and I sang it. And suddenly it's deep, cold, what he's said, how I sang it, deep and cold and everyone connects."

"Oh, My God! Yes!" The Jillions exclaim.

Her nose is about to run and her eyes feel drippy. And here they are filming. Patrick starts into the spiel about Turin & Strong, their new name. She doesn't have a tissue. He doesn't have a tissue. The Jillions don't even have pockets. Here we go with an Ambien on authenticity, thank you, Patrick. A ball of wet pulls at her snoot, about to wobble loose. She snorts it up, a rip-roaring slurp of snot. Patrick's eyes widen at her.

"Hey, deal with it. I'm from the Ozarks."

Both of the Jillions' faces rumple like wet laundry. The Jillion on the right flashes a hand in the air, and Frumpster hovers, about to halt the camera.

"We don't say anything about where we're from," The Jillions say together.

"I didn't say a thing about where *you're* from." She pauses. If she's blown it, well then, hell, rip it all up. Her foot's throbbing and she can feel the shards and the balloon edges of the swelling cramped by the boot. "I grew up in Southern Hollow

Subdivision in Springfield, Missouri, I'm from the Ozarks, and I'll slurp snot and hock a loogie if I don't got a tissue. K? My foot is killing me, and my nose is running 'cause earlier I was wacked on painkillers, but now they've wore off. Let's play Joni Mitchell and then 'Spokane.' Patrick?"

The Jillions look at each other. The Jillion on the left stabs the air above her head twice. Frumpster touches the camera. "Oh, My God. So much genuiwinnity!" the Jillions exclaim. They turn in their chairs and stare at Frumpster. He glares back.

Casey loves him. Dark circles under his eyes. He's so bored with this. "I got it all. I can edit out whatever!" Frumpster says, like he's told them that a thousand times.

Patrick stands. "Let's give Casey a bathroom break. Let's blow our noses and clear our throats. You're going to sound goosey with all that in you." He lifts her crutches with such controlled anger, it's like he's positioning two rifles.

When the security guard steps forward to accompany them, she feels better about it. Patrick gets tissues from inside the bathroom. The security guard stands apart from them but he's watching as if they're going to steal soap or towels.

Patrick hands her a wadded blossom of tissue. "How do you do that?"

She blows hard three times, then hocks a loogy into the wad.

"How do you almost trash the whole thing, and then suddenly it's 'So authentic!'?"

After spitting in the tissue again, she feels blasted and hollow. The crutches make her armpits ache.

He pulls the pill bottle out of his coat. When she lets a crutch fall, he loses his concentration. With a swipe that scrapes his hand, she snags the bottle. The clatter of the crutch on the linoleum fills the studio. The Jillions whirl to peek over their chair backs. Frumpster pulls at his pocket and whips out his cell phone to film. The security guard steps forward. Patrick glows red, but he's trapped. She slips the bottle into her pocket.

"Kneel down there. Pick up my crutch."

Steaming, he complies.

"Now go to the car. I'm freezing. Get that Italian shawl. Then we're gonna play the song they want. We're gonna play our beautiful song, 'Spokane.' And we're going to nail it."

She nods to the security guard, who steps right beside her, his eyes on Patrick. Patrick shakes, he's so enraged. It's going to be a long, terrible ride home. But she has the cure for that, rattling in her pocket.

"We're Turin & Strong now," she says. "They're waiting."

While he loads gear into the trailer, she slips the Glock from her Martin case into the shawl. The security guard monitors Patrick. After they played some more, it came out during the interview that she was a Line Of Duty Death cop's daughter. You could see, the minute the guard heard it, Casey gained a champion. He escorts her to the Peugeot. He's beefy and clearly keen on squat-thrusts—he's got butt cheeks like two motorcycle helmets. Catching his eye, she shows him the pistol then slips it down into the passenger door's grab tray. He nods, waits till Patrick's at the car door.

The security guard holds up his cell. "Don't hesitate." He points the phone at Casey and then to his heart. "I know who you are, tough guy," he says to Patrick.

They idle waiting for the big metal gates to open before he says anything. "What you just sang, what we just did in there, that's going interstellar. Go ahead and take that Roxie you're wanting. In fact, when we get home, remind me to load you up good."

She runs her finger along the safety of the Glock.

"You're a proven asset, Casey. You don't need some beefcake cop fetishist to protect you. Not from me." He turns to her. "Go ahead. Take the pill." Those high cheekbones shadow his face and make him seem lean, fit, and fox-like. Such a handsome monster.

"I'm cool. I'll ride it out." Her legs and arms cramp the instant she says it.

A watchful pause, then he nods. "That's good, Tink. We're gonna make some great music together."

28

At school Tyndall grafts to Devon, a soft, insistent presence. No one notices or cares. For much of Glendale, these two have always been stuck together. The cool kids buzz instead about spring break and who'll be skiing where, who'll be drinking at what beach, who'll go visiting Northwestern with mom. He and Tyndall have grown perennially, like dollar weed evading the cool. Now as seniors, they're ineradicable. Her arm and hips press against him. Why did he ever care what anyone thought? And as for all his sweat about whether she can handle thinking about sex and sexuality, now he's wondering if she understands it all better than he does.

At the cafeteria lunch table, she's hunched over her phone and picking at her lower lip. When he grips her thigh, she straightens up and stiffens as if she's receiving an injection.

"Did you know, Devon, that humans have evolved membranes covering the eyes and brain to separate those organs from recognition by the body's T cells that would otherwise devour the eyes and brain as foreign cancers?" She grips his hand and digs her nails in.

Squeeze harder? Remove your hand? He can't read her. So he's trapped, and at her mercy. It's intense, like that moment before you start swinging in a fight. Then with no explanation, she releases his hand, and goes back to her tablet's screen.

The instant he relaxes his grip, she turns on him. "Harder not softer! Ding Dong."

Sexually Tyndall works like an electrical switch. When on, she's direct and urgent about what she desires. Off, she's icily focused on her latest obsession, this virus in China. Now that he has seen her skin's ripe perfection and had his hands on her body, his id burns with concrete tactile and visual demands. Her nearness drives him wild. They suffer chastely—they own no private space. With Tyndall, though, there's no predicting the switch's position, and there's no sensing what you might get once the current slams on.

He drives them in the ProMaster to the Merritt Organics office off Division Street. It's Sunday evening. Dad's with Sherry Jean hoping the baby will sleep and he might get some.

Tyndall's on a jag about droplets and how long viruses can live on various surfaces. He feels like a sexist pig hardly registering a third of what she says about all this. But if he listens and responds, will there ever be an end to it?

When he turns the van off, she stops. "I'm so glad. I want to check your PPE." She unbuckles. "What is Merritt Organics doing to be ready for the coming pandemic?"

"I thought we could maybe…?"

Mannequin look, and those gray eyes make her stares a powerful defoliant. "Use your words, please, Dum Dum."

"I mean… No one will bother us. Dad's never here on a Sunday." If she's so obsessed with him, why doesn't this click? Here all her pet names for him—Ding Dong, Dum Dum—involve his insensibility. He sighs. "I thought we could be alone."

"Agreed. Without distraction, we should be able to check all your protective gear much more efficiently. You're thinking clearly on this Sabbath!"

"I thought we could pleasure each other. I want your body. I want to be with you."

She sits back in the passenger seat, eyes riveted to his left shoulder, lips pursed as if something gruesome oozes down his windbreaker. After a minute like that, she runs her eyes over the office's entrance. "I don't wish to have my clothes removed in a former aircraft hangar filled with soil amendments." She looks him up and down, and he feels like a crushed insect. "But this is positive. You should desire me at all times and constantly scheme to entrap me alone while I devise ways to satisfy your libido and yet remain unimpregnated." She grabs his arm and shakes him. "Young love!" She opens her door but turns to him when he doesn't move. "What's wrong with you? Come on. I don't have to have my clothes off. And the sooner we finish you, the sooner you can concentrate with me on your PPE inventory. I'm extremely concerned that you and your father are not one bit ready, even though I have explained every pathology and even shown you photographs from Wuhan."

—Dinner? Bambino's?

Hours later with no response to his text, he calls. No answer. Voice mailbox is full.

Almost midnight, he's dozing off and his phone buzzes on its charger.

"What do you need?"

He sighs. "Well, maybe that is the question."

Long silence. "I can't come over there. You can't come over here."

Now that feels like some progress.

"You have no solutions?" She sounds angry. Surely it's just that her voice becomes threatening when she whispers. She grunts. "Here's an idea. Think about me all night long. Then you'll be all plumed up in the morning. You'll be no trouble at all. I'll help you before school. You help me after. Bring towels."

"Tyndall, why's it got to be… it's so like… like a formula with you. I want to take you to dinner."

She hangs up. When she's done talking, that's it.

Driving her to school in the ProMaster, he worries that her eyes seem so sleepless. Her lids and the skin below her eyes puff a pink and brown. She's muttering to herself. They drive into a subdivision where construction has halted. He swings the ProMaster into a wooded cul-de-sac. Down a slope, the framing of a house teeters. There's a yellow sign with a bank logo at its top staked in the red yard. No construction activity.

Tyndall snaps back to reality and looks all around. "You didn't say there was a job you needed to do before school. I didn't bring boots." She's wearing the Merritt denim long-sleeve shirt over a red tee stretching the words TRUMP AMEN tight as can be. On her feet she wears Glendale red Keds tennis shoes with aqua blue laces. "Do I need to wear boots every day? You have a boot fetish, don't you? Casey wore boots all the time." She straightens her arms and clenches her fists, a dangerous precursor to a fit.

He unbuckles, twists, then jerks his backpack from behind his seat. Working fast, he extracts the towel, and extends it to her. She halts.

"But you said we've become formulaic?" She doesn't take the towel.

Holding it out, he feels he's begging, desperate and idiotic.

She growls. "If you were forced to fill in a Daily Operations Report on me..." She pops a fist against her thigh. "The whole spreadsheet would be about nothing but sex, when she wants my sex and why. Your sex is the least interesting thing about you, and your need for it the most annoying. And yet you say I fixate on things! That I have led a life of obsessions. You live a pecker-led life. I could lead you around by your pecker for years. All of you men would be better off gelded!"

She pulls her phone from her backpack, taps around and then sticks it at him. "We need to focus on this."

He lets the towel drop to his lap, and takes the phone. To his surprise, it's Casey, in a very bright, white room playing guitar and singing. She's so pale, and this old lady's shawl is draped over her shoulders. How small she is, like a frozen princess in all this white. He pauses the video and exits full screen to get his bearings. Whoa. This is The Jillions. This is big time. She's performing wonderfully, though she sounds really sad. The words to the song seem sad. She's stuck in that big, black boot. She's missed a lot of school. Tons of shares and likes on this.

"Look at her skin color and her eyes," Tyndall says. "Now watch at the end of this. See how her nose is running?"

Devon laughs when Casey goes off about where she's from. "Go, Southern Hollow!" he says, pumping a fist in the air.

Tyndall snags the phone and stares at him.

"What? Look at her represent."

"Devon, we need to talk with her. She's taking way too much pain medication."

He's about to ask how in the world she can know that, but the realization floods over him like a charley horse. It's not just her hospital work. Ben—that addiction and then death lets her see this.

She unbuckles. Then she scoots across the bench seat and lifts the towel from his lap. "Raise the steering column, please."

"What? Tyndall, wait."

She grits her teeth. "So now we're not doing this? Oh, Mighty Jesus, Holy Spirit, make my man make sense!"

29

Casey doesn't answer Devon's voicemail or his texts, not even DMs. Tyndall shows Devon the comments section on Casey's Insta. Every kind of emoji, crazy GIFs, marriage proposals, pleas from young musicians, whole songs from self-proclaimed songwriter/poets, and so much venom about her making the Ozarks look bad. How dare she say she's from the Ozarks when she's from suburban Springfield? Was she even born here? A DJ that Sherry Jean follows threatens to spit tobacco in Casey's eyes and shoot her with his old .45 because she's a snot-nosed city kid. Hate and rage just makes the hurricane of fame blow even harder.

It takes Devon texting Mrs. Strong to get a bead on Casey and when they can see her.

Saturday morning, they're just up the steps from Casey's driveway when the front door opens. Mrs. Strong comes out on the porch with her finger to her lips. She squeezes their hands in hers, a scaly greeting. She cleans houses, offices, and nursing homes, so her hands are a craggy wreck. She turns and shuts the front door behind her carefully.

"It'll be so good for her, seeing you both. This broken foot. Oh, My God. All she does when she's here is play guitar and take pills. She's on the laptop all the time. She's in the basement being interviewed by some outfit right now, so you can sneak down to the edge of the stairs. But watch it. She will throw stuff at you if you make a sound. Tyndall!" Mrs. Strong raises her own chest with the backs of her knuckles. "The boobs!"

Tyndall glances down at her chest and then back at Mrs. Strong's. Tyndall grips his hand. "How many pills a day and what kind?"

"Oh, some crap that thug Patrick got her. Roxie something. Can you believe, just the two of them on a tour they're planning? And they aren't dating, they aren't a thing, but they fight like they been married a decade. And this surgery they keep putting off because my insurance isn't, and Patrick says he's going to reimburse us when he 'raises the funds.'" She makes air quotes. "I'm like, Let's see your bank balance, Buster."

"Roxicodone?"

"Yeah, that's it. Roxicodone."

"With or without acetaminophen?"

"None of that. There was some big deal made about how this Roxie didn't have that in it. The liver, right?" Mrs. Strong touches her stomach about where the liver might be. "So you're still with Saint Martin's, Tyndall?"

Tyndall leans away, but nods at Mrs. Strong. Tyndall's gripping Devon's hand, and this makes their passage through the entryway and into the living room awkward.

Mrs. Strong watches this clinging, and you can tell from her eyes, she knows something's different between him and Tyndall. She's so much smarter than the jobs she has to do. "Devon, did you ever think Tyndall Hastings would turn out to be such a bombshell?"

But now they are at the basement door, so no one can answer her. He and Tyndall tiptoe down and wait at the bottom of the steps where the carpet ends. Devon helped Officer Strong lay this linoleum. It leads to the garage and connects carpeted stairs to shag carpet in the basement where there's a giant wraparound couch. A laptop glows silver, and they can just see the top of Casey's head over the back of the couch, orange-yellow hair wild.

They can't hear the other end of the conversation. But Casey asks, "Ruthie with a guitar? Who called me that? I'm sorry. Who's Ruthie?" Long pause. "So Ruthie from a crime show.

About the Ozarks? Great." Another pause. "I'm the daughter of a murdered cop. Line Of Duty Death. So, no I think that sucks, even if I've never seen the damn show, which N O P E, I will not be." She's quiet for so long Tyndall starts to count on her fingers the seconds passing. "No, no. Look, I'm not playing 'Spokane' unless Patrick's here. We're Turin & Strong, and you can Zoom back and patch that in later or not. Up to you." A pause. She clears her throat and says, "Sure..." Then after a deep breath, she speaks in a much peppier voice: "Look for 'The Bitter Sweet Art Gallery' on Bandcamp. It's a thing." Pause. She snorts. "Soon as I can get this boot off my foot, I'm there at McSwiggans. I promise. Much love and crazy rhythms, Hoboken!" Her head bobs as she waves goodbye.

The light off the laptop changes colors, and Casey's head wags as she plucks earbuds loose. She has to stretch to look over the back of the couch. "Hey, look at you two!"

Spent tea packets and torn and rumpled Songwriter's Journal pages wreath the laptop. Casey grunts and lifts the Darth Vader boot and plunks it on the glass coffee table. Maybe it's the wash of the laptop, or its light bounced off the open, lined pages of the SWURNL, but her skin looks gray-blue, and her eyes droop. "I'm so tired of playing happy, I could scream, but that would take energy."

"Hoboken?" he asks. "As in New Jersey?"

He waits to see where and how Tyndall wants him to sit. She points right next to her on the couch. Once he sits, she wraps her arm around him and pulls him into her. It's more like a tackle than an embrace. Casey watches this with a smile.

"Oh, My God, you two goobers, so finally it's true!"

He feels himself blushing. Then his stinging cheeks grow warmer when Tyndall shows an appalled expression, one she doesn't mean. Mouth stuck open, eyes wide. "New Jersey?" he asks again.

"What?" Casey blinks but so slowly, he feels like she's dozing off. She swallows.

He looks to see if Tyndall registers how vacant Casey

seems. But Tyndall has her eyes locked on Casey. He can't catch her gaze. "Weren't you just on a Zoom with somebody?" he asks. "You said McSwiggans, and love to Hoboken."

"Ugh, it's all one big mess." She points at the boot. "I can't get this off because Mom and Patrick are all in a fizz. And then there's this virus. Tyndall, what is all this? I mean, Turin & Strong is in the top five all time most watched on The Jillions. Top five! And Patrick says three songs from The Bitter Sweet Art Gallery are smashing it on his YouTube. But it's like the governors of New York and California are going to close the whole world."

Tyndall is quiet for a while watching Casey's every gesture.

He nudges her. Though Tyndall's face still holds the appalled expression, he can see in her gray eyes the rattle of worry he's feeling.

"May I see your bottle of Roxicodone, please?"

Casey closes her fist and pushes it along her thigh. Her yoga pants bunch and ripple. "No. Look. You don't gotta worry about me. This needs pins and is all screwed up and, trust me, it hurts. But... don't come in here and play doctor."

"Tyndall's your friend. She's been worried about you. So am I now."

Casey grins, and it's scary. It's like she's wearing a Casey Strong mask. The rest of her face is so dead, only her lips move. She's even thinner than he remembers, which doesn't make sense. If you can't exercise, and you're trapped in a basement, how do you get thinner?

"Ain't that a plot twist? Here I wanted so bad for you two to enjoy each other and get it together. Now here you are, together, and I don't think I like what's in your heads."

Casey lets that sit for a while, as if what she says is something deeply philosophical. With a grunt she reaches over and lifts up her guitar. She strums a few chords, then she closes her eyes and shimmers into a song by Troubadour Molly, very bubbly and worldbeat. Her playing seems even more accomplished. Witnessing this used to be enough to stop him—the wonder of a kid he's known for so long, a girl he's dated, he's been naked with, picking up an instrument and playing this, trills and rises, notes like coveys of glowing, exotic night birds. But today, her guitar playing is a shield, a way not to face her friends.

"I'm not going to sit respectfully through another performance right now," Tyndall interrupts. "Casey, you show all the signs of someone using too much pain medication. Let me see your eyes."

Casey stops her playing with a discordant bang. "Get the hell out of here."

"Whoa," he says. "Dial it down."

"No. I'm trying to do something. I'm trying to make something happen here. This could be my dream come true at last. I don't need flack. You're not a doctor. You're a gofer in an ER that uses you up. You barf spreadsheets and count sponges. For free!"

Tyndall doesn't move, but she's nowhere near unplugged. He can feel her shoulders and ribs rising and falling.

"Out of any of us, Tyndall has seen herself what this looks like. Ben is dead."

"These are pills, genius. Doctors prescribe them. Scientists make them. Ben was shooting H. You roast that crap in a spoon with a cigarette lighter."

"Ben was abusing heroin because he could no longer obtain the pills that the doctors had prescribed then denied," Tyndall says. "This isn't about what I do at the hospital. Though thanks for the respect on that."

There's so much ice in the room, it's like a horror movie where suddenly you can see your breath. "You know, Tyndall and I didn't have to come over here. But we wanted to because we care, especially Tyndall. You were so bad, she could see it in The Jillions video."

"Oh, no, don't give me that Rain Man insight bullshit."

The basement door to the garage opens, and Patrick Turin strides in. He carries a grocery sack and a pack of energy drinks hooked on his thumb. Used to be no one came in that door but family, and here Patrick Turin dangles a jingling key ring in his right hand.

Devon stands up from the couch. Tyndall gives Casey a look, then stands as well.

"No time for homeroom reunion," Turin says. "Sorry, kiddies."

Tyndall heads toward him. "Do not let her take any more Roxicodone than it says on her prescription." She stamps her feet and blocks his path. "It's for acute pain after injury, not for long-term pain management. You need to get her back to her attending physician and get her something with a longer release."

Turin smirks, glances at Casey, and then fully and openly undresses Tyndall with his eyes. "When we do this video, I want her in a cage dancing." He shimmies and shakes his chest. "Bow-chicka-bow-wow."

Tyndall plants a hand in Devon's chest and stops him.

"Three minutes, and they want us playing." Casey's pointing at the laptop. "Leave, you guys!"

"Okay. We leave," Tyndall says. "But I'm going to be checking on you all the time."

Even though he's seeing red, he takes one last look at Casey. She has Turin clearing her tea packets, tissues, and mess from around the laptop. They're both on task, like Tyndall and Devon were never even there.

At the top of the stairs, Tyndall calls for Mrs. Strong, then hollers louder again when there's no answer.

"She's gone to work!" Casey yells. Tyndall's shoulders slump.

Turin sticks his head out the door to the basement. "Really, beat it, will you? We got a Zoom audition, and you two are just noise. I want to see the front door close and watch your behinds recede. Especially yours, Big Momma."

Tyndall grips Devon's hand and they take the sidewalk through the fog toward Utica and the Merritt house. The sun can't burn off the fog and so the thickened air nearing the lake brightens until it glows. Familiar houses—the Correys', the Jutes', the Carltons', the Hansons'—seem farther away and yet much larger in the clogged atmosphere.

"That was worse than you said."

"I didn't say anything about what we would find, Dip Dip. But yes. That was bad."

She had talked a lot about Ben as they debated this visit. That's what he meant. So literal. You're never having the conversation with her that you think you're having. "Well, now what?"

She picks at her lip. "It's going to take everyone around her. I'm going to have to teach you and Mrs. Strong how to administer Narcan. We'll have to carry it all the time."

Swarming fog makes the air frantic. From the street, a car hisses, but you can't see how large or how dangerous until it's right on you. "I can find out when Mrs. Strong has a break today or tonight," he says. "But I need you for the doctor part. You're great at that."

Tyndall halts them in front of a decaying house that used to be the Tarascos', but now it has gone rental. Her mouth bunches to one side. Within the house, a pack of dogs moans and barks at them. You can hear their nails skittering and scraping the windows, doors, walls, and floors. She holds her ears and shuts her eyes tight until he pulls her along and around the corner onto Utica.

They stop again. She's breathing heavily. She's suppressed a fit. "Even then, with all of us trying... the problem is this: the only person who can save her... is her."

30

Driving them to St. Louis for a fill-in gig at Masher's, Patrick grouses about money and cancellations and how no one pays for songs from The Bitter Sweet Art Gallery on Bandcamp. People just watch the set on The Jillions or view YouTube clips from it over and over. Those watches aren't downloads and don't count for anything with festival planners, bar owners, and venue promoters now that this virus offers the perfect excuse to say no.

"So we make nothing. But The Jillions are making all the money in the world!"

"Like they need any," Casey adds.

She presses her cheek against the Peugeot's cold window. The gray concrete nightmare of I-44 at Rolla feels more comforting than this discussion. Her foot hurts. Moving anywhere with the boot and crutches makes her hip ache, her calf throb, her armpits sore, and her spine and shoulders cockeyed. The pills aren't getting it done anymore, even when she takes two at once. She's read online where you can crush them, dissolve them in water and inject them. But then there were also gruesome pictures of abscesses that came from people too eager or too stressed to wait for the powdered Roxie to fully dissolve. A chunk of it lodged in a vein, then blew up into an infection, and, if that didn't kill them, it pitted their arms or legs forever. Roxicodone: So much glamor in so little time.

Patrick rages while her heart careens down a concrete ditch into a blackened sewer grate. She jolts awake when he says: "And who the hell do we know who's ever had this virus? It's not even as bad as the flu, and that kills hundreds of thousands! Thank God for St. Louis and Masher's. Moira's got guts. Nobody's gonna put a mask on that crazy bitch!"

"Look at it this way," she says. "It's cool we can do this, with Spring Break extended. Right? I mean who would think that a virus would land us a fill-in gig? And, bonus, it's in the Lou and on the Landing. And I bet they're on extended Spring Break. So crowd size." She rips a hunter's whistle and points up at the saggy headliner. Doesn't lift him. Once he's determined to grump, it rains all day.

Traffic slows to a crawl through grimy orange cones and battered barrels. Mist dots the windshield. Cold silvers its glass even though the defroster's on with such force it lifts her bangs. The blower's air smells like wet gym socks. On four successive concrete construction barricades, someone has sprayed graffiti TRUMP PENSE JESUS REPENT. Rainwater and headlights make the red, white, and blue paint on the barricades shimmer.

"How'd they spray that with traffic always going?" Casey asks. "That's super heroic."

Patrick flashes a look at it, and his eyebrows snarl. "Not how you spell Pence."

"Maybe it's a conjugation of *Pensar*? Like, All Y'all Think. Maybe one of the Latino Conservatives of Rolla painted this? I mean, that's a beautiful job."

A horse trailer lurches up. No working taillights, no license plate, and the trailer is jammed high with household junk, all getting doused in the rain and grimed with exhaust. Patrick barely gets the Peugeot stopped.

"Trump and Pence?" he sneers. "Nothing makes that beautiful."

From the stanchions of the trailer, a huge stuffed bear throws its arms out and rocks drunkenly. The bear looks so blissed, she kind of wants to be him, heedless and goofy with a head full of stuffing, happy and along for the ride.

171

"This could be a song," she says. She motions to the bear and the barricades, but her hand looks so thin and gray, it's like someone sketched her in pencil. She buries her fingers in her jacket, where she squeezes the cylinder of the pill bottle. Maybe two at Eureka?

"Tink, quit saying that and make it happen. Why aren't you working in your SWURNL? We need a song with a video of you that blows up like DJ Guetta meets Kelly Rowland. $75 million that French douche is worth."

"Wait... is Masher's now a gay dance music place?"

He glares at her. "Or Maren Morris. 23 million streams. Not watches: Paying streams! You're short and loud and fun to look at. Get to work, Ruthie with a Guitar."

She whacks his arm and is about to swing again when her phone buzzes. She digs it out of her jacket. Her text blooms with messages. All the hick towns they've passed through must have bled them out of service for miles. Everybody's in a panic about some email. She opens her email, and here's the one from Glendale High everybody's freaking about. It takes her several minutes to understand it.

"What?" he asks.

She sniffs. "The governor issued some kind of stay-at-home order. Till April 26!"

Patrick's phone rings. She snags it out of his jacket like she's supposed to and reads him the caller ID. It's Moira. On speaker phone, Moira, owner of Masher's at the Landing, tells them she's canceling the gig. All live music is canceled till April 26. Moira goes off about the Pike County sheriff who became governor and how he doesn't know squat and has caved to Bill Gates's plandemic to stick chips in us all and take over the economy and spoil the President's reelection. On and on: Chinese labs, doctors claiming every death is the virus to make money. This lady wakes up every day and drives her own car in St. Louis traffic to open a club she owns and operates, with big-time success, and she gets to vote and own a gun. Yet this stuff is what fills her head? All Y'all Think Jesus and Repent for real.

Patrick interrupts her. "Moira, Moira! We're almost to Cuba. Casey got out of school just for this. Can we at least get some gas money from you?"

Casey crushes the Kleenex in her fist. This sucks. All of it.

"Nobody's in school, you asshole," Moira says. Then the speaker phone goes dead.

The bear dangles so far out the back of the horse trailer now, his fat arms toss blackened rainwater along the Peugeot's hood each time traffic jerks forward then halts.

"She's right," Casey says. "About me not being in school." She wipes her nose and drops her phone on the console where he can read it if he wants. "Glendale says I'm graduated. That's it. Senior year's over."

She taps two blue pills into her palm.

Slowly he cups her hand and closes her fist on the Roxies. Slowly to show he's choosing not to hurt her.

"Before you do that, Tink, get on your phone. Find us an exit. Please."

31

She texts Devon and Tyndall and sends Patrick away. She can't work with him right now, can't take any more of his raging. Devon's on some jobsite—it's spring and suddenly everybody's got a stimulus check coming and wants a lawn miracle. Tyndall's at the hospital. There. She can get outside of her head and stress about some things that are not the songs she can't write and not the songs they can't sell. Why not worry about Tyndall getting exposed to this virus, or Mom? How does Tyndall fight something invisible? It could lurk anywhere. At least Mom wears latex gloves and has cleaning supplies on her hands all day. Mom with her orange caddy spiked with brushes, draped with rags, studded with cylinders of abrasives, spray bottles of bleach, hooked ready on her arm. She's been so awful to her mom lately. And here Mom is a warrior in grief. That hospital ER uses Tyndall up. She's just a kid. Will they even protect her if she gets sick since they don't pay her? Here they were seniors, she and Tyndall and Devon. Just minutes ago, the best year of their lives blasted away because of a virus that has yet to sicken anybody she knows.

Whammo! Right back in her own head, throwing her own pity party. She picks up her guitar and strums the chords to that new song by Luckbox. She heard it in the Peugeot, an album Patrick made them listen to all the way through. She doodles in a C major lead pattern and soon picks out the minimalist hook Luckbox deployed. Wait, there's something familiar. Oh, they mangled a George Harrison riff. It's like

Luckbox was trying to learn a Beatles song, got it wrong, and then this shiny thing tumbles out.

How many of Patrick's arrangements work that way? His songs sound like some hooch-sick band in a Gold Rush saloon wants to cover a Janis Joplin song they heard, but they only heard it once from a time-traveling space alien. Worse, they teach each other by ear since no one can read music. A game of telephone, never playing a song precisely, always adding new music when you have to fill in chords and notes you don't know or can't yet make. And then, oops, here's this new music, not like before, but with the color and smell of before. What if she could write a song by stopping all this craziness in her head, craziness that the song has to be new, that it has to be self-expression, and that it has to be solely from her, the song she alone could write? Like any song ever was entirely from one person to begin with. Maybe what Eve sang to her first kid out of too much love and worry—that was the only original song ever to exist. Eve doesn't know it's a lullaby, let alone a thing called a song. Ever since the Apple, Adam gets to name everything. This wavering heartsickness rises from Eve's lungs and neck and mouth. It's not speech but more, a sound that is not the river and not the wren and is not the wind teetering in the mulberry leaves, but just her fear and love and joy and hope set to rhythm. Each part she repeats grows richer, like seeing a bush blossom out new every spring. The baby stills. Then Adam yells at her to stop all the crazy wailing. But that little baby, he looks up at Mother and wonders, touching her lips, *How can I do what she just did?*

She quits playing and stares at the pill bottle. Patrick hasn't loaded her up in a while. His forgetting is willful. He parts with pills like a miser. This new music she hears in her head, will it be there if she never touches a Roxie again? That's too scary to think twice.

Her hands, even in the warm yellow light of Dad's basement, they seem thinner, smaller, and gray. That guitar teacher at Paladino's, when she had to quit because Mom and Dad said $94 a lesson was just too much, he was from Nashville. The day she quit, she was too embarrassed to tell him the real reason why, and what she said came out wrong. He got huffy and told her that her hands were too small, she was too small to play guitars anyway. Not every girl can grow up to be Lilly Hiatt, he spit. In her fury, she learned to play a bass—I'll show you what small hands can do—and that got her in New Wave Vultures.

When she swipes her phone, Twitter burns with people howling about liberty and who is lying (apparently everybody), and fear. *How am I going to make any money if people can't eat inside the restaurant?* Who knew liberty meant all this about going to Pilates and eating chili-cheese fries and drinking beer with strangers?

After a long while it frustrates her that she flipped the phone over and swiped it awake intending to check if Devon or Tyndall had texted any updates. Instead, what has she done? Scrolly Numb Numbs. Forty-five minutes devoured drifting through a vomitorium of fear and fringe and freak outs. She feels zombified, and not just because the Roxie is fading. When she was a kid playing hide-and-seek one summer break, she fell asleep under the crawlspace of the house for hours. She woke up to sirens and dragged herself out of the crawlspace hatch. All the kids—Devon and Tyndall and the Brodbeck twins and those Correy girls—and her mom and dad raged and cried and laughed. But she was as numb as a worm, cold, dusty with lime, and dimpled with gravel. An EMT with big, soft arms foamed her skin with hydrogen peroxide, then cradled her, while more sirens howled in. A cop's daughter lost—every agency in the city with a siren on a vehicle sent help. That's how she feels now, crawling out of Twitter. She's cradled in the folds of the smoky sofa, stupefied despite the sirens and the yelling and crying. Like a drug, the screen pulls you under. Getting a grip, she texts Tyndall and Devon that the garage door is open and the backdoor unlocked.

Liberty. She bangs around on the guitar again. All at once a melody occurs to her, the whole thread of it, angry, forceful, simple, all in barre chords, A to G to D, then fly up to the tenth fret with two short attacks D to G, like... No, who cares what it's like? Then the G and D on the tenth fret and a whip back to A at the fifth solves the chorus.

She's thumping away at it joyfully when Tyndall appears and sits down on the sofa. She meant to put the pill bottle away. But crud, now Tyndall has it in her hand, and she reads the label. Hard to tell what she thinks with that mask on. Casey keeps the song going, hesitant to fall out of the moment, but she mutes it down to just power chords, which sound deep and throbby on the Martin. Maybe there should be a diminuendo part like this?

Tyndall sets the pill bottle back on the glass coffee table. Puffy skin ripples blue under Tyndall's eyes like when she was little and first put on medication. She's in scrubs, but they smell freshly washed, and her hair is darkened from a shower. The hospital must be terrible. "You don't have to play more quietly." Her mask crackles when she talks. "I can think and read despite the majestic expression of your genius."

Casey laughs. "Amazon Bitch, I've so missed you." She puts the guitar aside and steadies its neck between cushions. "Your hands, Tyndall. They look like Mom's."

Tyndall holds up her hands. "So much hand hygiene we have to do."

Tyndall grabs her hand tight, but her gaze steadies on the pill bottle. To Casey's amazement, her friend holds something back, edits herself. You can see it in her gray eyes. She's swallowed something she wants to say. Maybe Devon taught her that? Tyndall leans back, tries a slouch, and pulls Casey's hand onto her soft stomach and squeezes the back of Casey's hand against her.

After a long while, both of them slouched back, feet on the glass table, Casey speaks. "Senior year: Gone! Did you even think they could do that?"

"Your voice is rough. Roxicodone is destroying your vocal cords. They won't care anymore to work, even though your heart tells them to. And when it's done, you'll forever sound like a kazoo is stuck in your trachea."

She frees herself from Tyndall's grip. Tyndall's hair, darkened with water and braided tight on both sides of her head, makes her look even more like a giant Viking warrior queen.

"I'm going to tell you the truth because I love you. Even when I hate what you do to yourself, God wills me to love you."

Oh, My God, no one in the world can be as sincere as Tyndall Hastings. Casey drags the boot across the glass table, then presses her face into Tyndall's soft arm, throws an arm over her stomach, and curls up against her as best she can. Poor Tyndall. She's plumped up so fast, just like Casey worried she would. But, oh, she's soft and warm. Casey burrows into her.

After resting that way for a long while, she asks, "Why do I *so* not want to be told what to do? Could I be any more Ozarks?"

"When the Roxicodone wears off, you feel rotten, don't you? And not just your foot. That substance makes you want more of it to the exclusion of all other benefits of the substance. And to the exclusion of all life around you: Your Lord. Your mother. Your friends." Tyndall's wide eyes scour the ceiling as if she is reading a medical book up there in the graying acoustic dots. "You need to get back to what the Lord wants from Casey Strong, and not what the drug, which is a Demon, wants of you. Roxicodone wants you to consume it until you die. What does Casey Strong want? Let's listen to what the Lord is saying."

Casey swallows. "I want to write a song that gets 23 million streams."

Tyndall rummages in her scrubs. Does she wear scrubs all the time now? They're not flattering, and they make her thighs look porky. Her skin smells of lavender soap and the chalky hint of powdered deodorant. She drags out her phone. "Simplify. Why not just 'I want to write a song'?" She shifts Casey off of her so she can fiddle with the phone. "I learned of this child in an article in the *Quill Magazine*."

Tyndall is the only person Casey knows who reads high school journalism cover to cover, even the advertisements.

"There's a TikToker named TeeGo. An eighth grader who will be a freshman at Glendale next year. He plays HexNite. You know, the MMORPG where you buy the avatars and fight zombies across the globe."

Casey shrugs. She doesn't game.

"So he records songs set to clips of what his fish-faced avatar does running around in HexNite, and then he posts these video-songs." Tyndall finds what she wants and sets it up, then hands the phone to Casey. "Play that."

In the TikTok, a fish-faced humanoid stands upright on two skinny legs and flexes two gangly, lobster-red arms. It wears tan cargo shorts and a medieval-looking tunic. It runs, somersaults, leaps, and climbs rickety structures. For the audio, a voice sings through a filter. That's TeeGo singing, Tyndall tells her. The filter makes TeeGo sound like a breathless three-year-old. The music in the background reminds Casey of the backing tracks to an Akon song. The vocals are not keyed to anything the fish-faced creature does. Its lips hang like a carp's mouth. Pee, tea, knee, me—the rhymes are as baby-like as TeeGo's auto-tuned voice.

"83 million streams," Tyndall says.

"Are you trying to bum me out?"

Tyndall takes the phone back from her. "There are dozens more he's made. He's still in Pershing Middle School. He's made hundreds of thousands of dollars from ads that run alongside the clips."

"You want me to go all hopeless? What the hell, Tyndall?!"

"No," Tyndall says. She grunts when she's frustrated about not communicating. "Simplify. Just make the good song first. Quit it with the shares and views and streams to something you haven't even created yet. This," she shakes the phone at her. "This is what 83 million streams gets you. A toddler squeaking about fish pee and a music-thingy that only matters to role players vegged out and gaming in mom's basement."

"We're in mom's basement. Right now. And I'm worried I'll never get back out."

Tyndall's eyes look like she's about to go blank. "I just want you to focus on something you want, something worth making, worthy of the talent the Lord birthed in you. But I don't want you to focus on the world's value of it."

"Look. Stop," Casey says. Even when she is with her old friend, she thinks about the pills and taking one. "Okay. At the most basic level I want to write a song."

Tyndall nods. "Good. That's God's purpose for you. Don't let go of that." They are quiet for such a long time, the comfort begins to wane as the want for a Roxie begins to rise.

"I saw someone intubated yesterday," Tyndall says. "Remember Mrs. Kelso?"

"That heavyset civics teacher?"

Tyndall nods. "They jammed a tube down her throat, with a laryngoscope and blade and suction." She purses her lips and makes a slurping sound. "Then we flipped her on her belly, like she was a big, fat, dead fish. So she could breathe better." The light fixture above the couch makes a prison window shine on the wide, gray pools of Tyndall's eyes.

32

Devon pulls the ProMaster into the gravel lot at the hangar office. In the twilight, he squints. Some kind of metal shackle he's never seen mars the front door. Someone's duct-taped a printed notice below the door's grungy steel-barred window. He leaves the van running and trudges to the concrete pad at the entrance. He's parched, and his Merritt polo clings sopping to his gritty skin. Caked with soil, his fingernails ache, and a hoop of fire whirls in the muscles of his shoulders and back. Bold black letters on the duct-taped sign read "GREENE COUNTY SHERIFF" and "Execution in Landlord's Action for Possession of Premises for Non-Payment of Rent."

He didn't have to deal with the weeks of Canvas and school from home. Glendale declared him graduated. Stimulus checks spawned more work requests to Merritt Organics than ten guys could have tackled, but Dad did no hiring. "We only have one damn van!" Dad insisted. Dad threw himself instead into some kind of lawsuit about the lake, him and Lawyer Turin. They were even interviewed in what's left of the *News-Leader* by the Pokin Around guy. Dad was so amped about that, Devon asked him if the publicity was his only goal. Bad move—for a month they haven't been able to stand in the same room and be civil much less discuss a problem. Dad is supposed to be the office manager. Rent's on him.

All the work brings Devon a great relief, considering what his classmates rage about on social media. He wears a mask when speaking with clients, but for most of his day, he works alone, outside trying to improve lawns. With the stimmy excitement, though, new prospects want big one-and-done fixes—correct this French drain, which is now under a pond; we killed the whole backyard with lawn spray from Wal-Mart; the builders covertly buried a waste fire that has collapsed into a slough. Recurring fees from application visits, that's the lifeblood for Merritt Organics, not these disasters. He can help maybe one in four new clients. Sadly "consultations" are free, and regular clients, slapped with furloughs or trapped working from home, cancel right and left.

At the backdoor to the hangar, same Sheriff's sign and a matching metal shackle block him. A sparkling new padlock bolts the Duraflex door to the loading dock. He longs for the bottled water in the office fridge. At the back of the ProMaster, he wavers, trying to get the heat sludge out of his head so he can plan tomorrow's applications without resupplying the van. Why's he the one standing here, broiling? A prop plane throttling up for takeoff at the airfield grinds his anger to an edge. All of Dad's generation, they hop in their Bonanzas and fly off into the blue, or race around with Lawyer Turin in his Maserati Levante fighting environmental crusades. Yeah, that's right. The lawyer powering the Save the Lakes of Southern Hollow campaign (SLOSH, the lawyer branded it) drives a new Maserati SUV. And here's Devon staring at the eviction notice and who knows what kind of debt.

At home, Sherry Jean's Focus is not in the garage. He finds Dad asleep in the basement recliner, a bottle of Jack in one hand, his other hand on his stomach. He has a stomach now. The house is quiet, save for concerned yammering from TV/E, the environmental channel, on the television. No sounds of Sister upstairs.

He could head straight to a shower, and then see what's in the fridge. But, staring at Dad, he's stopped by a mix of fury and pity. Rather than blissed and passed out, his dad grimaces, eyes shut tight, as if even managing this escape is a struggle.

Dad jolts, blinks, then rubs his face. He sets the Jack bottle away from him with great care. Then Dad fumbles through junk on the end table, finds his glasses, and puts them on. They magnify his battered eyes and make them seem even more puffy.

"She left," Dad croaks. "Took the baby and left. She's been moving all her shit out for weeks. I just... I didn't even notice. It was all yoga pants, mostly, right?"

Devon swallows several things he wants to say about Sherry Jean Plumly. "There's a sheriff's note on the hangar. Front and back, and even the Duraflex is padlocked. Non-payment of rent."

Dad bobs his eyebrows. "Well, get this." White spittle clings to his bottom lip like a paste. "Lawyer Turin is gone."

"Like dead?"

"No. Absconded. Vamoosed. House for sale. No le respondé." Dad stops and smolders, face and neck purple.

War erupts in Devon's heart. Here their landlord has trapped the family business behind a padlock and yet Dad's worried about Lawyer Turin. He can see Tyndall stamping her foot and threatening violence if he doesn't show mercy. He draws his Dad a glass of water from the basement sink.

"So what about Lawyer Turin. Who cares?" He sets the glass down.

"Absconded with money, Son. Tons of it. My money, Shelton's money, Wortham's money. He convinced half the lake we should sue the Hammons estate. Turns out..." Shaking, he drinks from the water. "The Lakes are not even part of Southern Hollow Subdivision. They're titled in some worthless shell company. We couldn't have sued them anyway. Nothing to sue."

"So's that where the rent money went, Turin and SLOSH and his Maserati?"

"That's where *all* the money went, Wise Ass."

Rage fills him—he's filthy, exhausted, fed up with clients, lungs choked with dust and pollen. He bunches his fist, but a vision of Tyndall comes to him. How her gray eyes above her face mask have become intensely expressive. Sunday, she wore a Merritt Organics ballcap, and they walked all the way past the Old Morkan Quarry and back. In just that strip above her mask and below her cap you could see so many emotions and efforts. She listens, flirts, warns, exults, even wrestles her own gusts of anger, and all in that exquisite band of eyes and brows. She insists on the mask even outdoors. A healthcare worker, she's a savior in the hospital, but a vector out in public. Because she hates how the mask throws her breath up her nose, she rarely speaks when wearing one. This makes her eyes work even harder. He wants her hand in his right now, and the yearning almost floors him in his exhaustion.

"Sell me the company for a dollar, then," Devon says.

Dad blinks at him.

"If Sherry Jean's car won't be in the garage, I know what will be. Tell me where you keep the bolt cutters."

33

Mom scores a shower chair from some old lady who died already. Rich clients sometimes push things they no longer need on her. With the virus fear growing, Mom only cleans a few big homes. Lots of cancellations, mask or not. Who needs an office cleaned when most of the employees get furloughed, and the upper-ups can work from home?

Mom bleaches the chair out in the garage where Dad's Mustang used to be parked. Mom then positions the chair in the downstairs shower stall, and teams it with the stool Dad used to sit on when cleaning the cat box. Casey's been showering in the garage sink—hair, pits, and cracks. But Mom complains she's sporting rest home smell, Eau de Coot.

Dad built the downstairs bathroom and shower like emergency showers he witnessed in St. Louis factories. Speckled brown tile to the ceiling and across the floor, then a step down into a smooth, concrete pit with a drain recessed in its middle. Mom insisted on adding a tension rod with a curtain.

"Alright, so boot off, and then we back you in, plop you on the chair, and you rest your bad foot on that little guy." She points at the cat box stool.

Casey's foot and shin shine copper and dark blue. Her ankle has disappeared in a puffy bruising. Just one look at it takes the wind out of both of them. Poor Mom. She's been up half the night watching all the riots from Minneapolis and Louisville. Her eyes look like someone pounded them into her face with a rubber mallet. Casey has warned her a thousand times, if the news involves the police, turn the TV off.

Mom bites the side of her thumb. "When's he going to pay for this? I don't think we should wait any longer."

"Not now." She just Roxie'd up good before starting this shower adventure, and she doesn't want anything getting in the way of a smooth plunge.

Mom runs the shower long enough to get hot water then cuts it off. The shower is just a steely head looming above the drain and now the shower chair and cat box stool. Once Mom dumps her in, it's a commitment. Mom grips her under the armpits and lifts her from the toilet seat. Maybe Mom has seen this kind of care done in all those nursing homes she cleans, nurses lifting elderly people? "Manager at Shady Rest said Cox and Saint Martin's may start canceling surgeries." Mom grunts as she talks so she sounds extra frustrated. "If we keep screwing around with this, Casey..."

From the shower seat, naked with her foot up on Dad's cat box stool, she feels crushed and tiny. She clings to Mom's fingers to keep from yelling. She cannot show anger; she cannot lose Mom's help now. Patrick hasn't answered texts or calls in almost two weeks. She has twelve Roxies left. That might get her through three days if she naps a lot.

It hits her that Patrick said the surgery and pins would mean more Roxies. Instantly, her gut and groin ache. She wants the surgery, but does she want it so she can get better?

Mom has one hand on the tap, but stops. Looking down at her daughter, she takes a deep breath. "I'll shut up. I get it."

"No, no," Casey says. "I'm just real tired of this."

Mom straightens up, squares her shoulders, and nods. "We need to just do this surgery. I don't care how it gets paid for. I can dodge a big hospital bill a long time. And I sure won't be the first in Southern Hollow to declare bankruptcy because of a doctor."

Maybe it's Mom's voice echoing on the tile, but Casey feels like she's looking up from the bottom of a crypt. Where the hell is Patrick? Why won't he answer?

Mom's face is like a mirror, and she's trying so hard to

smile that her skin rumples around her eyes and the tears flash but won't fall. "Get your soap, Little Bitch. Get ready."

"Wait. Would you mind getting my cell phone and set it on record, set it right there on the toilet lid? And don't close the curtain. Please?"

Mom blows a raspberry. "I'm not pulling the curtain, kiddo. You fall off that chair, and we're even more screwed." Mom wipes her eyes on the bath towel. When she gets the phone, Casey shows her how to set record, what to punch. Mom steadies the phone on the potty lid, then touches the shower tap. "Ready Freddy?"

Casey holds the soap to her mouth like the bar is a microphone. "Go!"

With the water blasting down, she starts, from the bottom of her crypt, partly to make her mother laugh, but mostly she sings to keep from screaming.

Liberty's that easy lie they sell
When you don't have a dick or a car.

Mom cackles, and Casey's heart blooms like a sponge drinking water. Oh, thank God for the sound of her mother laughing.

Liberty's that creepy eww you smell
When Boomer gets your tab at the bar.

Liberty, liberty for all!
Liberty, liberty, you're on call!

After the shower, she's listening to the melody on her phone in a loop, and waiting for her fingers to unpucker, shivering with the Martin in her lap. She stops the recording, calls him, and tells his voicemail he needs to get over here. She has a song. For reals.

34

The Chief Medical Officer, the Head of Respiratory Therapy, the Chief of Emergency Medicine (Dr. Correy), the Chief of Supply, the Head of Human Resources, and the Chief of Nurses gather staff in the auditorium and broadcast on Teams to anyone quarantined or on leave. All departments will divide so that the hospital can erect distinct virus wards with containment and donning and doffing rooms for sterile entrance and mitigated exit. In addition to Personal Protective Equipment doffing, teams will construct a separate doffing room for providers involved in aerosol-generating procedures to avoid self-contamination and facility spread.

When the Chief Medical Officer delivers that news, the whole auditorium takes a breath. Tyndall hears it even though they are all masked up.

"Oh, my God," the ER Nurse next to her says. "This shit must be terrible. And here we been wallowing in it."

Tyndall has no facial expression to react and share feelings with her. The mask covers most of her face anyway. Carol is her name. She has complex pupils—green, brown, yellow, riddled with black specks. Before this, Carol has been indifferent to Tyndall, even aloof sometimes. She's busy. She's an ER nurse. She saves lives, even of morons and wastrels.

Head of Respiratory rises and runs through slides and videos about a fascinating device—a Powered Air Purifying Respirator. They call it a pâ-purr, PAPR. $1,000+ a crack. Saint Martin's is buying two dozen. In the video there's a provider called "a buddy" who works in the doffing room and helps

Respiratory Care nurses get this PAPR space-suit off without self-contaminating.

"I think I want to be that buddy person," Tyndall says.

Carol gives Tyndall a long look. Carol's black hair grows as kinky as steel wool, so she draws it back in a severe pony. "Sweetie, them suits are gonna be dripping gooey with deadly boogers." She watches the video some more. "You are a bossy fussbudget, though. You might could do what she's doing."

After the presentations, everyone has to stay. Supervisors meet providers in coveys. The chic lady from Communications calls names through the lectern's mic and directs you to a supervisor. Once you've talked with a supervisor, then it looks like you can leave. Eventually Dr. Correy and the Chief of Supply call for her and Frank Spanner, who is Supply Supervisor I. She's worked with him before. Dr. Correy and the Chief of Supply want her and Frank to design, organize, and implement the main donning room.

Frank, who slumps a lot, straightens up through all this, but he watches Tyndall instead of Dr. Correy and the Chief of Supply. "I thought we sent all the ILEs home."

"This one we retained," Dr. Correy says. Tyndall wishes not to be the subject.

Frank asks that the Head of Human Resources please join them, right now.

Tyndall smooths her scrubs and straightens her badge. Cheryl, Head of Human Resources, rose in the hospital from nursing. Like Casey, she's tiny but prettier, and she rock climbs. Her blonde hair is much more under control than Casey's ever is. It's like a sparkling yellow helmet. Her silky blue mask matches her dress.

Now that Cheryl's with them, it's a lot of people standing close together. Tyndall digs her nails into her palm but keeps her fists behind her back. She starts the 4-7-8 breathing exercise. But that makes her chest stick out way too far—why is there no good way to stand when people get so close? And aren't we supposed to remain two arm lengths apart?

"Frank?" Cheryl asks.

"I will not work with a volatile, Asperger's child on something this critical."

Everyone backs up and stiffens. They all then look at the Chief of Supply.

He's a red-bearded man, from Arkansas originally, and his accent can be difficult to understand. "Frank, we don't got time nor manpower for your BS. Tuck it in."

"This poor child," Frank starts, "I will not babysit. I have no training in special needs care. And you all just tasked me with something critical. She's an unstable, spoiled, privileged zealot. I cannot." He puts his blue palms up. He's one of those who still wears sterile gloves all the time.

There are so many things Tyndall wants to say. From the glances these three adults flash at her, she can tell her eyes must be wide and dull, the abandoned mannequin expression Devon scolds her about. Like meeting a ghost, he says. At least Frank doesn't look at her. She might strangle him if he did.

"No one is asking you to care for anyone," Dr. Correy says.

The red-bearded Chief of Supply, his forehead and neck, even his arms turn the color of poached salmon. "Remember who reconciled all that inventory when NetMed collapsed?"

"We sent her into the storeroom cage. Alone with a clipboard." Frank Spanner's forehead vibrates like Ben's used to when he would fight with Father and Mother. "Alone. Where she could throw all the fits she wanted to. I will not supervise a child on the spectrum while transforming a donning room for something this dangerous."

Hold your breath for a count of 7.

Cheryl lowers her chin, and her eyes glow the way briquettes do down in Marion's grill. With that yellow helmet of hair, she might batter Frank Spanner to death.

Make a whoosh sound on the count of 8. Everyone but Dr. Correy glances at her. Her mask, dewy and hot, clasps her chin. She's afraid her nose will poke free. *Inhale quietly through your nose to the count of 4.* Her chest swells. Feels like it's in everyone's way. Frank points and swallows, a signal he is about to talk more.

Cheryl cuts him off. "Frank, we don't always have choices about whom we work with. And those choices are about to narrow significantly. Across all departments."

"Have you ever worked with one of them?"

"Seems to me…" Tyndall steps forward. She's tall enough, broad enough to blot out the whole of Frank Spanner, to erase him from the group with her strong body. She steps right in front of him, and her shoulders tingle with the power of it. "Seems to me that Mr. Spanner is not prepared to work with others. Please reassign me away from him. I want to learn to be the Buddy in the sequestered doffing room where providers doff the PAPRs after aerosol-generating procedures." At her back, she can feel Frank broiling. If the Chief of Supply had lasers in his eyes, Frank Spanner would sizzle down to a crispy kibble. "The one who assures that self-contamination is avoided. As seen on the video."

Cheryl looks up at her, and her mouth drops open—you can see because her silken mask caves in and darkens.

"Tyndall," Cheryl begins. "You understand… do you fully comprehend what you are volunteering to do?"

Dr. Correy touches Cheryl's arm. "She does."

The computer tablet Tyndall has mounted to the wall in the doffing room glows with data points from Frank Spanner's donning room. It's useful data, though she would rearrange all of its display. Most critical, the provider who is about to emerge from the virus ICU, Misty, Respiratory Care nurse, checked out an iPad. That likely means a death call to family if no chaplain is available to assist. These small things carried in that travel without protocol, they frustrate her, but they also tell her the emotional freight the attending provider may bear.

Tyndall scrolls down and spends some time recalling Misty via her photograph, a heavy, short young woman with glowing, olive skin, and beautiful black eyebrows. Identifies Catholic. In the photograph Misty smiles, and she wishes Misty were her friend, Misty's face is so inviting and caring. She wishes they could talk over Java Chip Frappuccinos. Tyndall has doffed her too many times today. Misty will enter from the ICU doorway here in just a few minutes. Her battery pack on the PAPR won't last much longer. Scrolling down, yes, it's clear, Misty has endured a long shift. This needs to be her last procedure.

The door to the anteroom from the hallway buzzes, so not Misty. Cheryl and Dr. Correy busy themselves with hand hygiene. Finished in the anteroom they enter the doffing room and take the two chairs Tyndall rarely uses. Why are Cheryl and Dr. Correy here? She can't conceive of a greeting, so she doesn't bother and turns to the ward door. She holds her gloved hands up, palms facing her, and waits for Misty. She can sense Cheryl shifting in her chair, and Tyndall reflects that without any adipose, those hateful chairs would be even more punishing. Cheryl starts to say something, but Dr. Correy touches her shoulder.

The ward door buzzes and Misty enters in her bunny suit. When she sees Tyndall, those big, brown eyes melt behind her face shield. She's instantly a wet wreck. The PAPR whirs and that numbing hum is the only sound in the room.

"iPad?" Tyndall asks. Thank God, Misty holds it up. "Place the iPad face down on that counter. Departing or returning?" Tyndall speaks loudly but only with authority and not with any emotion. The question is critical. The doffing routine changes if you have to send the provider back in to care for more ventilated patients.

"Departing," Misty says, her small voice lost in all that equipment and in her struggle.

Tyndall takes over. The voice she uses reminds her of Nora's—direct, loud, but with no hint of anger. Urgent love in the face of danger. If Misty makes one mistake, she can deliver a viral load to her eyes, nose, or mouth, a contamination that will at minimum drop her from the Saint Martin's workforce for ten days, and at the worst land her on her belly with an intubation tube ram-jacked down her throat.

"Back to me. I'm going to unfasten your gown. Nod when ready."

Misty's hood crinkles and her bonnet dips then rises in a nod. Tyndall pauses at the name handwritten in black permanent marker on the back of the gown. The I in Misty is dotted with a miniature heart. Name lettering is usually childlike and rugged on these gowns, but hers is pristine and feminine. Misty, and below that boldly: RCN. She unties and pulls the fasts on the gown open, careful not to touch any part of Misty's back.

"Grab the gown at your chest. Don't bunch it. Slide it forward. Down your arms. Down. Now into the waste container."

When Misty finishes, the nurse pauses. Her shoulders shake; her back rises then falls.

"Turn to me." Misty's face bunches in a shining red fist of sorrow or anger, Tyndall can't tell. She has thanked the Lord every hour in this doffing room for her inability to grasp facial expressions as completely as neurotypicals claim they can. "Remove your gloves. Glove to glove. Back of the fingers now, skin to skin. Waste container. Hand hygiene."

Misty is so distraught that Tyndall chooses to initiate and mime the proper washing motions so that the nurse can lose herself in imitation. Freed of the gown, the hood and face shield can make providers seem like balloon-headed sufferers of acromegaly, but Misty is stout, and this balances her appearance. Her tears are still flowing, but her breathing seems settled. She has that shattered look of Nora's after a terrible fight and a long cry.

"New gloves."

Misty jerks as if awakened and pulls on new gloves.

"Face me. Come close." Tyndall unties the shroud.

"Show me your back." When Misty complies, Tyndall

grips the blower assembly on its belt. It's like a giant, heavy fanny pack. It hums against her fingers and makes her sterile gloves sputter against her palms. "Unbuckle your blower belt." When Misty complies, Tyndall has the full weight of the blower assembly and belt in her two hands. "Lean forward. Grip the loop on the top of your hood. There, you have it. Lift. Lift." Misty's not getting it to move correctly. "Lean forward more, Misty. Now lift." Misty is so tired that her arms are not delivering the strength she needs. "Close your eyes tight. Tight. Lift up and away from your head. Up and away. Eyes tight." This is awkward because the hose must remain attached to the shroud and belt, and Tyndall has to raise the belt to give Misty slack. Misty must not open her eyes, because the face shield and shroud are teeming with virus. "Now out and away." The back of Misty's arm trembles. "Use both hands. You're tired, I know. I'm right here. Eyes tight. Okay. Hand me the headcover shroud and face shield. Eyes tight. There you go." Misty's head is bowed, eyes closed. She totters. Then, with her wet eyes still puckered, she moves her hands toward her mask which has come undone in all this effort.

"Stop! Don't!" Tyndall barks. Her heart slams in her chest. Misty freezes. "Do not touch your mask or face. You're fine, Misty. Do not fix your mask."

Misty nods, but her forehead reddens. The tears start again. Tyndall has noticed that sometimes one tiny miscue in this process brings all of the danger and horror back to the nurses she helps. Especially if the nurse makes the misstep, then all composure can dissolve, and suddenly you're dealing with a real crisis.

"I'm right here. We're both safe. Open your eyes. Doff those gloves. Glove to glove. Then that one skin to skin. Waste container. Let's do hand hygiene." She pins the shroud, hose, and humming blower under her elbow. Then she imitates what Misty needs to do washing with the hand sanitizer. "New gloves." By the time Misty finishes, her mask is dangling. "Now, waste container that mask. Here. Take a new one. Do not touch the front, or your eyes or nose. Just the loops. That's it. Mask up, Buttercup." Misty snorts, and her crying eyes pinch at their corners, so she might be smiling. Tyndall might have gained her a laugh.

Free and safe, Misty stands there for a moment, unsteady. Then Misty bows her head, and Tyndall extends her right hand. That's the rule: You must bow your head for Tyndall to pray over you. When Misty's eyes shut, they're so bruised with fatigue it appears she's been in a fistfight. "Lord God," Tyndall says so loudly Cheryl jumps in her chair. "Thank You for granting this warrior the strength to do Your Will and the courage to deliver Your Mercy."

Misty whispers an Amen. Then, blinking, the RCN nurse gives a weary glance to Cheryl and Dr. Correy. "Dr. Correy? Ms. Gebhart?"

Tyndall pulls the three wipes she'll need next and hangs them from her scrub pocket. What could these two administrators want with poor Misty? Jesus, help her.

"Misty, go home and rest," Cheryl says. Her voice sounds rough.

So it's her they came to see, not Misty. This might not be so good.

Once Misty has left through the anteroom door, Cheryl stands and so does Dr. Correy. "Tyndall," Cheryl begins. But she stops for a long while.

If this is about the praying, she may not be able to keep her cool. It all started with that RCN nurse, Rodrigo, the one everybody calls Fabio. He bowed his head, and in his sex-drenched accent asked, "Teen Dull, pray for me?" And so she does, and then he tells everybody on his shift. Soon two-thirds of the nurses bow their heads at shift's end. Still, even in a Catholic-run hospital, vicious secular humanists run rampant.

"Tyndall," Cheryl begins, "I don't think I could've done what you just did. Not the way you did it. There's some grant money we've secured. We need to put you on full-time."

With one of the wipes, Tyndall mashes the button that turns off the PAPR's blower, and the PAPR makes its long goodbye sound: WEEP. It's like a command that Tyndall cannot comply with, not in this setting where there is so much help the nurses need.

When Tyndall doesn't answer, Cheryl looks up at Dr. Correy. Though they are many arm-lengths apart, Dr. Correy reaches out. From across the room, both she and Tyndall mimic squeezing hands.

Lately to get to the parking lot, you have to walk through most of the hospital, all the way from the virus ICU ward to what used to be a service hallway alongside Emergency. Though in daylight you encounter grumpy, confused patients masked up and scurrying to their specialists' appointments or EKGs, phlebotomy, endoscopy, or MRIs, Tyndall doesn't mind it. That is until end of shift at night when the last hall before the exit crowds with a mix of patients and visitors who ought to be sequestered in the ER lobby. Instead they're seated in misery on the floor, or pacing around yakking into their phones with their masks on their chins. Tyndall can't understand how these aren't all suspected virus cases, even the maskless guy lying there elevating his arm, which ends in a bloody wad of a towel bound with baling wire to his wrist. She keeps her head down. She can't turn for breathing space toward either wall. Patients mill on both sides of the hallway.

She's almost free and into the back parking lot, when two swinging doors, which are supposed to be floor bolted, fly open. A woman with visible biceps, triceps, long hair, and no mask is howling and struggling with a masked EMT and the ER nurse, Carol. The woman is likely so loaded with virus she's shedding it even from her bulging eyeballs. Her skin is the gray-brown hue of cream of mushroom soup. The woman shrieks that Carol is lying. That she doesn't have the virus, nobody does, it's all a giant conspiracy from Demonic, liberal, global-health bureaucrats.

Then Tyndall recognizes her. It's the Girls' Sunday School Teacher from Victory Faith Triumphant Church, the woman who barred her from Sunday school class and tried to ban her from worship. This crazy virus! Just from her skin color, her oxygen level is probably low 70s at best, and yet she's fighting and yelling like some raging ISIL terrorist.

Misty weaving with exhaustion comes to her mind. Tyndall relives again the vision of the respiratory care nurse so fatigued she can't even command her arms to raise her shroud, her eyes tight, tears streaming. The unmasked Sunday School teacher flings Carol backwards, and somehow, she's snagged Carol's mask in her fist. Red rage floods Tyndall's vision.

Just as she is about to pounce and destroy, someone grabs the back of her scrubs at the elastic of her waist and at the cuff of her neck. With a male bellow, he hauls her upward and rushes forward with her, bashing through the doors and out the exit into the blast of fresh air in the back parking lot.

She rips loose and whirls. It's Frank Spanner, bent over and gasping. She stops herself from smashing him across the back and kneeing him in the balls.

"You can't," he huffs for breath. He sticks out a gloved hand to keep her away. "We can't." He shakes his head. "We can't lose you. Not right now. That in there. Not your job." His mask bulges out and crackles in.

Tyndall's breathing heavily, too. With one hand behind her neck and another at the small of her back, she's all twisted like a pretzel. "Why'd you do that?" Her skin itches where he touched her.

Frank straightens his back. The mask hides almost every-thing about his expression. His eyes shine, meaningless as glass beads. "Nurses talk, Tyndall." He huffs. "Saint Martin's can't lose you. Not like that. To a fool."

Still pretzelled around touching her back and neck, she

stares at him. When she doesn't say anything for a long while, Frank snorts and shakes his head. "Tyndall, you are so strange. Go home. Get some rest. We have to do this all over again tomorrow. For the good ones and for the lunatics and for the liars." He shuffles away into the dark parking lot.

When Tyndall sees Mother's face lit up in the Lincoln's dome light, Nora with her pretty yellow mask on, she wonders if this is when you cry.

35

So she has a song. That somehow gets him right away. Mom hasn't been gone ninety minutes, and the basement door to the garage pops open. He strides in wearing navy tech shorts that look like they're from Brooks Bros., shining, backless black leather slippers, and a spotless, retro Clash T-shirt. Good thing he's got that pill-toting backpack over his shoulder. He's wearing a mask that matches his shorts. Mom wears a mask all the time at work. But Casey hasn't been anywhere. Why wear one here? He keeps his stolen sunglasses on.

Even though she's clean, she feels raggedy and lost wearing the old jade-green kimono Devon gave her. She doesn't have a bra on and wears just a maroon pair of Pershing Middle School gym shorts. Real easy to get down and back up.

He stands for so long saying nothing, she wonders what he's on? Is he angry? He's hard to read even without the mask. At last he sits on the couch. "If you have a song, play it."

Asshole. That smug, coked-up, Glendale rich kid tone zings her right back to the song's mood. She chops into it. Maybe the Roxies have roughened her voice like Tyndall says, but she uses that. She wants to slice him with her music.

Is Liberty that girl in mask and gloves,
Or the fascist in the hoody breaking glass?
Do flaming bottles crash to earth like doves?
Blue Lives Matter, or you can kiss my ass?

Liberty, liberty, what's the cost?
Liberty, liberty, we're all lost.

The whole time she plays, Patrick sits there behind his sunglasses and mask, unmoving, like he's too cool to breathe the basement air. She doesn't care. For once, the audience is just herself. The only success is getting it right, chord by chord, line by line, verse by verse, chorus by chorus. If it's a song she can play to make her mother laugh and make Patrick Turin seethe, well, then that saw has got a whole range of blades. A, G, D. She pulls the song together with the diminuendo ending and fades off with that.

Patrick is still a long time. Then he removes his glasses, very slowly. God, there are no cameras here to behold your glory, Buddy.

"That's real Angry Bitch. But that's okay. That's a whole thing. Like Gayle."

He pauses a long time with his head cocked. Masks are creepy, but then she recalls he never smiled much anyway. Flat, thin lips almost always frowning. She can picture them easily under that navy fabric, how some of the freckles along his lips look like purple sores.

His songs swirl all over the place with bats and Varna Man and doomed hearts and black lakes, and mountains on fire. Her song is to the point, direct, right now.

"Why not have parts of it in French?" he says. "If a song has French in it, you get all the man-buns with trust funds *and* all the college-bound VSCO girls who are so concerned, they're learning a second language." He hooks his sunglasses on the collar of his shirt. "Add French, and, hey, you mystify the MAGA head but win his girlfriend who secretly wants to rock to it and has had it with all his pistols and Viagra."

She sets the Martin aside, finds her phone down in the cushions, and on Google Translate she pushes "Liberty for all" through the translator.

She's fixing to lay into him about everything. Where's the

money for my foot? Where's my Roxies? What's your deal with all this French crap? But wait. *"Liberté, liberté pour vous tous!"* Liberty certainly tastes better in French. When the robot translator reads out *vous tous*, it sounds like voodoos. Huh, more than one voodoo? We are for sure plagued by that. We can't even talk about wearing a mask without two voodoos fighting. *Pour* sounds like poor to her. She says it a few times, poor voodoos. How fun!

He starts to correct her French, but she shoots him a palm and a snarl.

Sure, then, Liberty, Liberty, Poor Voodoos. That'll show 'em she's worse than Ruthie with a Guitar. She plays it all through again, and by the first chorus in French he's patting percussion on his knees. He closes his eyes at the big open chords of her bridge.

LIBERTY, LIBERTY, POOR VOODOOS

Liberty's that easy lie they sell
When you don't have a dick or a car.
Liberty's that creepy eww you smell
When Boomer gets your tab at the bar.

Liberté, liberté pour vous tous!
Liberty, liberty, poor voodoos!

Go to college, rack up all that debt.
Boomer's in his lake house safe, you bet.
Take that third job to pay it off.
Make that check out to Lady DeVoss.

Liberty, liberty for all!
Liberty, liberty, you're on call!
Liberty, liberty, what's the cost?
Liberty, liberty, we're all lost.

Liberty, I've watched this dodge too long to believe in
your slick song.
When you sing, it's not for us. It's for all your fear inside.

Is Liberty that girl in mask and gloves,
Or the fascist in the hoodie breaking glass?
Do flaming bottles crash to earth like doves?
Blue Lives Matter, or you can kiss my ass?

Liberté, liberté pour vous tous!
Liberty, liberty, poor voodoos!

Poor voodoos, why stay so upset?
Your two views, is that all we can get?
Fight like hell, so that's my only choice?
I'd be chill if you cancel your voice.

Liberté, liberté pour vous tous!
Got it from a meme, must be true!
Liberty, liberty, poor voodoos!
Whatever he says, it must be for you.

Liberté, liberté pour vous tous!
Liberté, liberté pour vous tous!

She repeats the French part for four bars and dials it down
from bouncy to diminuendo, then done.

He nods. "Fire up SoundBlitz. Where's your laptop?"

She points. He uncovers it from her spent SWURNL sheets,
scoots it next to her on the glass coffee table, then opens it.
He's all industry, out to the car and back—cables, sticks and
his Alesis SamplePad Pro drum machine, headphones, mic
on a table stand with a shock mount and pop cover. This feels
like most of the gear from his apartment.

Arms crossed at her chest, she watches and tries to keep

the kimono closed. "So... why's all this recording stuff in your car, Chief?"

He's dashing around, setting up his JBL PA, adjusting its camera, clipping a mic on it to pick up her Martin, plugging in the cables to the laptop. He's kneeling at the laptop, and moving the levels on SoundBlitz. She asks again.

He wags a finger. "Don't get out of the zone," he says. "Pick up the guitar and here's the mic. Level check. Where's the thermostat?"

She points, and he hurries over and bumps the temp way up so the AC won't throb.

"So you don't answer any texts or calls, no DMs. But I tell you I have a song, and Curly saddles right on up."

He sits with his freckled legs crossed under the glass table and patters away with his sticks on the drum pad machine, watching the levels. His mask is high-end with a nose wire and such firm fabric, she can't see him breathe. She has a flashback to that high school night backstage, the premiere of Glendale's "Oklahoma," when he strutted in last minute wearing his red bandana, leather fringe, and chaps, stinking of clove cigarettes and weed.

"Listen! Laurey wants her love potion, Bitch." She knocks her pill bottle flat with the neck of the Martin. "Or you lay the money down for my foot. This is killing my mom."

He sets the sticks flat beside the pad, steadies them with his palm. "Casey, let's get this down. This is really important. This is your moment. You have a song." He sticks a thumb drive into the USB port of the laptop.

"Plenty of memory on my laptop."

"Tink, focus." He's unwound his legs and wormed out from under the table and now he's adjusting the GoPro on the JBL.

"Asshole, we're not filming anything unless you get me a bra or a T-shirt."

He stops. The mask bulges then draws back. He's got his face mostly behind the GoPro, and its viewscreen changes the color of his forehead to greenish blue. "Tink, you look fantastic. That kimono, and your hair. Like angry Greta Garbo in deshabille."

"Get in your backpack and fill that pill bottle with Roxies, or I'm not lifting a finger."

His greenish blue skin purples. "You're on the edge of making some great art here. I don't get why you have to be so transactional."

"Puts me in the mood. Get them pills."

He makes some last adjustment to the camera, and she senses that he's drawing every action out to show he's the one in control. And, hell, he is. The only thing she can withhold right now is her music and her voice.

He surveys the JBL, all the cables, his Alesis, the laptop, and camera. Finally, he stoops to his pack. It's an odd size, not much bigger than a bowling bag, but square. Its black leather matches his shoes. A silver clasp on its front pocket flap has a French word stamped on it, like Meter. She recalls the inside was crimson when she unzipped it so long ago when Ralphie thought Turin carried ecstasy. She had never seen a leather pack with a flocked interior like that.

He kneels behind the couch, and she can hear him unzip it. The feelings inside her—relief, excitement, exquisite fulfillment—God, this is awful. She shivers when she hears the Roxies shifting in the big bottle. He sets the bottle on the glass table. Three quarters of them are gone. There had been enough Roxicodone in there to last like a year.

"Level check," he says.

She snorts. "Exactly. Pour all the rest of them level into my pill bottle. Then hand me mine and get that big one off the table and out of the camera shot."

He nods. "So you're into this. Let's play this thing." He opens her pill bottle. When he fills it, each blue wonder clatters down. There's a rush and an ache, like he's dropping diamonds one by one into her heart. Her eyes are wet. Her nose drips.

"Gimme." She snatches the bottle, taps out two Roxies, then tucks the bottle behind her. He holds her set of headphones while she swallows the pills. He's arrayed a black, multi-socket adapter on the glass table, and it has so many cables sprouting from it, it's like it's growing hair. She unrolls a pack of tissues from the kimono sleeve, wipes her eyes and blows her nose, while he tucks his legs again under the glass table and pulls on headphones. They check and set levels. His fingers hover over the laptop, waiting for her.

"So, no percussion till after the second verse," she says. "Once I say DeVoss, get busy clicking rims, then brushes, and build."

He fiddles with the Alesis and its dashboard until he has only snare sounds, and the rim clicks he's isolated on one sample pad. Then he wrenches out from under the table and checks the camera on the JBL. For a guy whose music sounds like Zachary Taylor's playlist, he sure wizards this technology. She realizes he's rewinding the video on the cam to make sure he looks good in the shot. He always looks great in profile, from a distance.

"Mask on or off?" he asks.

"Off, Doofus."

He drapes it along the table's edge so it's in the shot. He picks up the sticks.

She lights into the song. It's like they've practiced it for years when he clicks in. They truck right through it, A G D G D. She feels that blessed lift that making music delivers, when she is not herself, not the dead cop's daughter with a broken foot stuck in Mom's basement and jacked on Roxies. Out of body, she is Casey Strong, the girl who sings, the girl who wrote the song, "Liberty, Liberty, Poor Voodoos." Even the French tastes right, and on the last four lines with the thumping strings deadened, she delivers Liberté, liberté, pour vous tous with that spritz of the French voice on Google Translate. His clicking the rims follows her instinct to quieten down. Then, though she didn't plan it, she thrums an open A minor and lets it waver. Somehow in sync, he picked up on the ending. As the Martin rings, he muffles the sticks against his thigh, bows his head, and closes his eyes.

She bites the warm, waxy pick to keep from squealing. He touches Save Tracks on SoundBlitz. The USB flickers as it swallows the session. He plucks it from the port and pockets it. Then he twists from under the table, slides over to the JBL, and its camera.

"Keep the headphones on," he says. "Give it a listen before you celebrate."

"But don't you think?" She curses then swings her booted foot up from the floor to the couch so that she's laid back and relieving its throb. Gingerly, balancing on her elbows, she gets herself situated in as much comfort as she can find. The cold cylinder of the pill bottle chills her back. She'll not let him see that stash again now that he's finally done what's right. "I mean, how the hell? It's like we knew that song for ten years or something."

"Chill, Tink. Listen first."

He runs the playback through SoundBlitz from the working copy on the laptop. If he nabbed the USB, he must think they're done, right? They did it? It's hard to keep up with his wack habits. He's more superstitious than a stoned Tarot reader. Though she listens with her eyes closed, she can feel him watching her and not the levels on the laptop screen. She opens her eyes, and, like a hawk on a wire, he stares at her. Thug. Weirdo. She closes her eyes again—the levels register just right. Her voice rages and twangs. His sticks nail down the rhythm. The guitar leads but never overwhelms. She drifts deep into the song. They got it in one take. You could fight in the studio for days and never master it like this. One take!

"Again," she says. "I can't believe this. Play it again."

She squeezes her eyes shut—she doesn't want to lose even one second of this feeling. He starts the song for her again. Then she can sense him moving around, stowing stuff, heading to the car and returning. That satisfies her, too. Proves he knows they nailed it. They don't need anything more, a perfect song in one take. She jams her palms to the headset. He must have set SoundBlitz to loop the project. The song starts again. She can feel her left leg trembling—her heart swims in ecstasy through a metallic lagoon dazzled with floating blue flowers of starlight. She will never feel a greater high than this.

When his hands grip her hip bones, it's like an electric shock thrums up her spine to her skull. He has his mask back on, and the sunglasses. He's got her by the hips. He's crawling on top of her. Before she can knee him in the balls, he presses her Glock, icy cold, against her forehead. All the cables, all the equipment, gone. Just the headphones she is wearing, and her laptop.

His knee pins her thigh. Pain rips through her foot. He yanks her shorts down, and the elastic stings across her bottom and entraps her at the knees. The boot freezes and weighs her right leg down. She claws her nails into his ribs and back. She rolls her eyes. Is the clip in the pistol? Oh, shit. It is. The crown of the barrel slicks an oily circle on her temple. She can't glimpse the safety, but his finger is on the trigger. If she kicks, if she tries to tuck and roll on him, hell, if he slips, that's it. She's dead. She wants to scream. But even if she started screaming, his finger could nick the trigger. He's bracing himself with a hand dug into her left shoulder.

When he violates her, it's like a rake handle stabbing and tearing. A groan escapes before she can square her jaw again. The boot, her shattered foot, his weight on her, and the pistol, she can't twist away from him.

"You've earned it," he says. "Say it's what you've always wanted."

"No," she yells. "Get off me."

One padded earpiece mashes her left eyeball, and the other earpiece broils against her cheek. She nabs the cable from the headphones in her fist, then jerks down. But he's too fast and lifts the muzzle to avoid the headband knocking the gun free. He jams the Glock harder against her temple.

He grinds into her more forcefully. It hurts like hell. "Now you're a songwriter. Say it's what you always wanted."

If she could jam the heel of her palm into his Adam's apple, but he's got his head bowed. Stiff, patchouli-smelling curls rake her face.

Showtime. She starts to cry—he'll want some of that. "Yes. Always wanted," she gasps. "Thank you. Owe you everything. Everything I am. Deserve this."

That does it for him. He starts to quiver and buck. When he arches his back, his head rears up. She smashes her palm upward as hard as she can into his Adam's apple. She cringes away from the gun barrel. He gags. But he's still in her. Trying to twist away, she grips his hip bones. He cracks the butt of the pistol against her head.

36

Fluorescent light chills her. She blinks. Tan metal rails rise at her sides. Yellowy tape straps a wicked needle into her wrist. A rush of nausea pins her flat, followed by a lurch of grinding pain down her legs. Her foot feels caked in cement. Something's beeping. What's swimming up there? Ceiling tiles. There's a pitcher on a cheap bedside table. On it glows the same logo from Tyndall's security badge: Saint Martin's Hospital.

Her scalp itches. With a trembling hand she feels around her noggin. Some smartass has parked a pussy hat on her head. No, a bandage. A nurse enters wearing a shimmering face shield that gives her a jolt.

"Oh, My God, look at you awake! Sweetie, it's okay." The nurse strokes her arm. "I'll page your friend, Tyndall. She sure has made you her special case. Just rest."

Big gray eyes, two windows to a rainy day in the mountains— she has dreamed these for so long, when she sees them again now, she's unsure... dream or life?

The warm pressure clasping her hand sure feels real. The sturdy figure in the face shield, mask, gown and bonnet... above the mask, thick eyebrows shine in a Nordic orange she's never seen on anyone else. Yep, this is Viking Warrior Princess Tyndall Hastings. But in a space suit. Jesus, am I contagious? Do I have the virus along with all this other mess?

"Oh, Lord, how I have prayed, and now You have answered." The mask and face shield make Tyndall sound far away.

Tyndall fetches her a cup and straw. If ever there were ever living water, this is it.

"Good," Tyndall says. "That's great, Casey."

"Help her rest," says another voice. There's another nurse in the room.

Casey grips Tyndall's wrist and holds it to her.

"It's okay, Casey. We won't take Tyndall away right now. But you need to rest and get strong. So many people want to talk with you."

The cop rustles in the chair, and when she reaches up toward her mask, Tyndall snaps at her.

"Sorry, okay. This is a lot." The cop waves a hand around her headdress and shield.

"Tyndall is always a lot." Casey croaks.

Those gray eyes lock on her. At last, she's relieved when Tyndall gives her two thumbs up. With all this masking and shielding, it is so hard to read anybody and get how they feel. Maybe this is how Tyndall has always felt, unable to sense what a glance, a smile, an eyeroll means? Tyndall's all she's got. They will not let Mom visit—the virus is that bad now. She stares at Tyndall, and the nausea and pain fades into a warm backwash of love.

"Okay if I record this?" the cop asks. She waggles a handheld audio recorder. "The docs say your memory seems really good, which is a miracle."

Casey snorts.

"We're going to move fast, then." The cop settles her handheld recorder on her knee. "So... did you take the fentanyl before he hit you on the head?"

And that quick, it's about what Casey did and not about him. "Have you tried France? He was really into French stuff."

Long pause for everybody.

"Never done fentanyl," Casey adds. "Least ways not knowingly."

"You almost died from it."

Tyndall doesn't budge. So this must be true. He smashed her head with her own gun, and then gave her fentanyl. She remembers Dad saying fentanyl only took a flake to kill.

She shrugs, and this hurts, but she forces the gesture. "Maybe he wanted me dead?"

"You had Roxicodone in your system, too."

She points at her foot in its cast. "How about some Roxie in my system right now?"

Tyndall shakes her head.

"You know, Officer Stahley, I'm feeling this is all of a sudden about me. But I'm the one who got raped. So..."

Officer Stahley does the sit and watch pretty well, too. Finally she says, "Take me through that morning, everything you remember."

Casey narrates that morning, the inspiration, the cameras, the equipment, playing and recording the song. The ice chips in her pitcher rattle as they melt and settle. Sounds like someone crunching across a hard snow. Someone unwelcome and awful.

She tells the cop about the rape and what he said and what she did. And that the Glock was hers. He must have got it when she had her eyes closed listening to her first song.

She stops for a minute. Suddenly it's hard to breathe. Tyndall's eyes are locked on her hands in her lap. She can't tell if Tyndall's restraining herself or praying. She just said all that, out loud, to her best friend, but also to this stranger, a cop. A cop like Dad was. Thank God they sent a woman.

The cop is quiet. Even with the recorder on her knee, she's writing in an old-fashioned notebook. Probably hard to do with latex gloves on, but she's managing.

"What happened to the song?" Casey asks.

The cop's eyes widen. Casey looks at Tyndall, still in prayer mode.

Officer Stahley resumes. "So your mom reported a laptop stolen, and the Glock." She points at her forehead where Casey is wounded. "He didn't take your guitars," she offers.

"Send him a medal," she croaks.

"Someone, we believe it was him, loaded a song called 'Liberty, Liberty, Poor Voodoos' onto the platform Bandcamp that afternoon, from your laptop," the cop said. "The song has become kind of a sensation. Ton of folklore around it. Neighbors saw you were taken in an ambulance. Someone posted cell video. Most of Southern Hollow was locked down at home. People are pretty outraged that we can't find him." The cop's mask shifts around. "With the pandemic trapping everyone, the song has become, well, almost like a snuff film. A snuff song, I guess. Super viral. Some on social media insist you're dead. Some claim you're on the lam with him and having a lark at the world. One Substack says you'll come back from the dead as an Ozark angel and wreak voodoo vengeance." The cop shakes her head and blinks. "You're not connected with President Trump's campaign, right? There's a big thread about that. #Casey of Ozarks=Joan of Arc, or something. How you'll return from the dead to assure his reelection."

"I'm not with any political thing."

After a moment taking notes, the cop shrugs. "Well, here we are. People will believe anything that gets them through the night. If you could, please, stay off social media. Don't make things any more confusing for yourself or misleading for us. All our tips right now, they're from nuts. Lonely madmen. Cooped up crazies. We think it will be better for our pursuit if you just heal and lay low. There's no getting ahead of all these wild stories. And the media. No help there. All they want is death and rage and blame and jizz." The officer pops a hand to her mask. Tyndall doesn't stop her. "Sorry. I get so frustrated. These are crazy days."

Tyndall sits forward. "Casey, you were in a coma, and we didn't know what you would want about a lot of decisions.

So many. Whether you wanted the song turned off or what. Marion has been helping, lawyering for your mom. He says Bandcamp has terms of service rules. He'll help you do whatever you want. Whatever you need." She pauses. "But Officer Stahley is right. The song. 'Liberty, Poor Voodoos.' It's its own giant thing. Giant."

"Show me." Another violation—he stole her phone.

The cop closes her notebook. Tyndall pulls her own phone from her scrubs, goes through an elaborate process of removing her gloves, using hand sanitizer, then a hand wipe on the phone.

"Jesus. Tyndall. I'm already in the hospital."

Tyndall swipes at the phone a bit, and then hands it over to her.

On Bandcamp, the photograph accompanying the song stops her cold. It's her face in closeup with the headphones on, both hands tight to the earpieces, eyes closed in listening ecstasy. Her hair settles in waves—Mom made her condition it three times. Casey Strong is glowing, freckled, like some tiny, adorable farm girl who has just achieved her first peak. He must have taken this from above, when she drifted deep into listening to the song, just before he assaulted her. He took this from her. Those were her last seconds.

"The picture," she says. The cop approaches. Casey tilts the phone to her. "That was just before he raped me."

"Oh… Casey, I'm so sorry," the cop says. She makes a note.

Casey scrolls down. 18 million streams and counting.

"Where's all the money from this going?"

Tyndall pulls on new gloves. She reaches for the phone, Casey thinks, but instead Tyndall touches Casey's hand, gingerly, the hand stuck with the needle. "Marion is eager to help. But that's all encrypted, the money. We can't see it."

"Before, he had my part of everything we made ACH'd into Mom's checking. Bandcamp let him do that. There should be my money there. Somebody's going to have to pay for all this hospital time." God, she sounds like a rusted hinge on a shack door. The screech of her voice upsets her as much as what she's saying.

The cop nods. "Sorry. That's not happening, Casey. As far as we can tell, the funds are all just sitting there in suspense at Bandcamp."

Her shaking causes the phone and its picture of Bandcamp and her satisfied face to blur. "Oh, God. It's like I got everything I ever wanted and instantly it's all stolen."

The cop grips the bedrail. "Casey, for your dad, for you, we're going to catch him and charge him with everything we can. Larceny. Rape. Two counts attempted murder."

"He tried to kill Mom?"

The cop looks up at Tyndall. A nurse, who must have been hovering in the alcove by the door, steps in.

Tyndall watches the nurse, or maybe it's a doctor, or a supervisor? She's wearing a lab coat. Tyndall's head is bowed, her chin averted, but Casey can see her mask moving. It's the Tyndall-mutter, when her strange friend has a frantic, even vicious conversation with the universe. Doctor scrolls through something on a tablet while Tyndall eyes her. At last Tyndall emits an exasperated roar—her teeth must be clenched. Her face shield fogs. "Casey, you're pregnant. So if he tried to kill you by giving you fentanyl after hitting you on the head... then some at this hospital would argue he tried to kill two people."

Outside, a cloud blocks the sunlight. The hospital room swims. The gray in Tyndall's eyes blows in a gale over everything. Casey tries to focus on the picture, her flying with her first song perfected in her ears. But she can't. 18 million streams. She sticks the phone back at Tyndall. "Tyndall, for just a second, that was me."

37

With no vaccine yet, Tyndall notes that some colleagues at Saint Martin's even less exposed than she stay in hotels or in separate wings of their homes to protect their families. Marion refuses to have the conduct of his household dictated by global healthcare bureaucrats. So Tyndall wears a mask at home—Mother and Father refuse. She demands that Nora leave her meals at her bedroom door. With her usual, weaponized patience for yet another of her daughter's obsessive whims, Nora accommodates, but Mother takes this adjustment as an opportunity. Nora enforces portion control. Tyndall drops fifteen pounds.

She knocks on Father's study door. Marion waves her in and motions to a chair. His laptop glows; his reading glasses cling to the ledge of his nose. Papers, books, and envelopes teeter on his desk in towers of clutter, like it used to be in the old days up at his law office. On top of one stack is an opened letter from Magg & Vireo, the dreaded law firm that represents Bandcamp. She pulls the chair an extra two feet away from the desk.

He smiles watching her. "I thought the rule was two armlengths apart?"

"Mother and I have much longer arms than you."

He raises an index finger and parries it like a tiny sword.

She sits but lets out more of a sigh than she wishes. She catches herself about to grip the chair's studded leather arms. These and the desk came from his old law office in Plaza Towers. The office looked out over a sorry restaurant, and always smelled of what was frying below. Behind the desk hangs a Gothic-themed lithograph elaborately framed to make it look ancient. In the print, a heavyset, bearded old man, surrounded by clutter and curios, unloads boxes of drooping papers. Her father, in his sport coat, silver hair, and new gray beard, is calcifying into "The Philosopher" of the print hanging above him.

"I want to thank you, Father, for helping Casey and her mom."

Marion's expression changes, and she puzzles at it.

"I'm afraid I have more to ask of you, please." She folds her hands in her lap where they won't contaminate anything. "All this death. I see it, see what it's doing to people."

He removes his readers.

"I feel The Lord has not only granted me a critical purpose," she continues. "I feel He is also showing me how fragile this all is. How we need to say the words we mean to and do the things we intend for the people we love. Right now."

Marion remains still. In wellness sessions online, Dr. Shanna Halston instructs her to make "quick lists" of what a neurotypical's gesture may mean. She hates this—it pollutes and confuses interactions even more. But while quick listing Marion's pause, it occurs to her, with her record of violence, that every day Marion Hastings braves her presence. She could say something like she just did, and any behavior imaginable might follow if he objectively examines their history. Her fits, her rages put Ben, Nora, Marion, and Tyndall herself in the emergency room on multiple occasions. The Hastings family should have its own wing at Saint Martin's, Ben used to joke. Yet God Almighty wove a fiber into Marion Hastings to marvel at. This man has loved her, despite what good sense and self-preservation dictate.

He nods. "I want to say, Daughter." He licks his bottom lip. His lips dry and chap just like hers. Here all along Devon has claimed it's all this medicine Tyndall has to take. Marion's lips chap, and he's not on any regimen stronger than baby aspirin. "I am deeply proud of what you do up there at that hospital." His voice roughens like he's choking. "It astounds me that people used to line up for a block and pay money to watch a movie about some post-apocalypse dystopia. Hunger Champions, or whatever that was. When here and now we're living it. You're a hero for saving fools from this mess."

"Heroine. But that is not what this is about," she says.

He smiles. "With you, My Dear, it never is about what I imagine it to be."

"I want you to please show Devon Merritt how to obtain one of those Paycheck Protection Program loans." She begins. "His father has…"

He raises a palm. "I know. The Lakes. Lawyer Turin. All in the *News-Leader*."

"Also that kneeboarder, Sherry Jean Plumly from Blue Eye, has left him."

Marion's eyebrows rise.

"Devon thinks he has bought Merritt Organics for the sum of $1. He knows how to do the work, but he doesn't know how to do the lawyer and money parts of owning a business." Now comes the big thing she wanted to say first. She breaks down and grips the arms of the chair. With just a squeeze, the leather emits the odors of a dirty grill and endless frying. "I want you to understand that I am going to make him ask me to marry him."

Marion rubs his face with his palms. "As ever, above a solid foundation of practicality and right Christian feeling, you erect whole and eccentric cities of insanity."

"You will not help him then?"

"Tyndall, he is as strange as a gleaner from Moab. His gods are not our God." Marion burns for a moment and makes a fist atop a tower of papers. "But I most certainly will help him. You're my daughter, and I love you."

"Will you be a bombastic jerk and make him uncomfortable when he is here?"

"It is God's critical purpose for me that I make him as uncomfortable as possible. Show me the son whom the father chastiseth not."

"I don't understand. Chastity is not a strength with his father."

"Isn't David Merritt aptly named, then? A certain King David..."

"Father, focus!"

Marion sits up straighter. His jaw tightens.

"Please don't ruin my chances. They are already pretty slim. I am not easy to be with, let alone to live with..."

"You don't say."

"... and..." she counts to stop herself from getting any louder and wilder. This is her father, and Oh, God, she needs him. "Father, I cannot correct that. That is terminal."

38

On the tablet screen, Mom looks small in her Zoom square. Her eyes seem bruised. Her roots have grown out so there's a base of gray and then the bleachy sear of a bad color job. She wears a fuchsia polo shirt with a logo that Casey's never seen. Weak light leaks from a high up window, so it looks like Mom's waiting, grumpy and anxious, on a stool in some dark alley. From her culottes, her calf bulges—such leg muscles she has—and you can just make out the fading gray of the Republican elephant tat. Above her a truck rumbles, and then, when the light it blocked bolts down, you can see a huge, filthy sink next to Mom and metal shelves stacked with cleaning supplies. This must be at her new job in Branson. She's probably on break or hiding out from her cleaning foreman.

The only progressive nurse in the whole hospital insisted this consultation was Casey's right and set up this Zoom call through an intern from Planned Parenthood in St. Louis. Shanna Somebody, Tyndall's counselor, is here in the room with Casey, along with the progressive nurse, who claims she's from Rhode Island. They're all waiting on the doctor at Planned Parenthood. Counselor Shanna says she doesn't need a screen. She's there only for Casey, but it's clear from her tone she's not in favor of this. The nurse from Rhode Island has her part of the Zoom on her phone somehow.

"See, I told you," Rhode Island says to someone in St. Louis. Her accent is outrageous, like a drunken version of a Puerto Rican movie star whose name Casey can't recall. "She's the Poor Voodoos girl, right?" Rhode Island winces at Casey. "Sorry, kiddo. Only way to get this all set up." You have to concentrate super hard to understand people behind their masks.

Shanna smacks a clipboard against the steel of her chair.

The nurse from Rhode Island, she has straight hair dyed like a magenta metal. She gives Shanna a scalding look. "Try me. You know how short-staffed this place is? They're paying me more to be here than you'll make this whole year, Jesus Freak."

Whoa, Casey loves her now. This counselor, Shanna, is the whitest human Casey has ever seen, porcelain white. Even her eyebrows are peach-blonde, and now she's humming with rage like Rhode Island ran voltage through her. If this weren't so terrible, it would be kind of fun.

The intern at Planned Parenthood puts her mask on, mutes herself, then rises and speaks to someone out of the picture. A gray-haired man with thick glasses and a blue-gray lab coat like a shop teacher's sits down. He removes his mask. From his eyes, he's listening to the intern off screen. He pushes his glasses up and asks something. As he gets an answer, his jaw buckles. Then his chest heaves, and his shoulders slump.

With agonizing care, he reaches forward. His index finger blooms gigantically as it nears then passes the camera to press unmute. Now even the skin of his face is gray as the camera struggles with focus and lighting. "I'm Doctor Bailey with Planned Parenthood. Who is the adult parent or guardian on this call, please?"

Mom answers with her full name and also her date of birth without his asking for it.

"Who are the caregivers present, please? This is Saint Martin's Hospital? In Springfield?" he asks and does not hide his surprise.

Shanna Halston identifies herself as counselor—when

did she start counseling Casey, like two minutes ago? The nurse identifies herself as Nurse-Prac Viola DeSanctis from Rhode Island Hospital.

The gray doctor stares at the screen. "And our patient is...?"

"I'm Casey Strong. And my birthday is January 6, 2003."

Doctor Bailey nods, "Hi, Casey. So, you're still seventeen."

He mutes and leans to his left where the intern stands. He listens awhile, then unmutes. "A famous songwriter, too. Well..." He pats at the pocket of his coat. Maybe he used to smoke, and he kept cigarettes there? Are we all always jonesing for some lost, sweet thing? "Famous or not, everything we are about to share is governed by HIPAA and, unfortunately, by Missouri state law. This is all confidential. Why are you in the hospital?"

To say this out loud, she carves a dead space around her heart. Imagine this is a cover song. A cover song you've got to sing, with depressing, bleak-ass lyrics. But the country fans love it. So here we go, key of C. "I was raped and then smashed on the head with my own Glock, then raped some more, and then given fentanyl in an attempt to kill me."

Shanna turns wide but cold eyes on Casey.

You knew the lyrics, Pumpkin. I'm just here to sing 'em.

"Oh, and my foot had been shattered for months, but me and Mom couldn't afford to fix it. And the monster who shattered it is the same who raped me. He was supposed to pay for the foot." Everybody's quiet. Time for the turn. Flip that script in the last verses so the final chorus delivers its wallop. "But, you see, he shattered my foot way before he raped me. And I was fighting him. So I kind of started it. With the foot, I mean."

Shanna's eyes above her silky mask run all over Casey's face, examining. Nurse DeSanctis nods at her and says, "Doing good, Casey." You can't mouth or whisper with a mask on. You just got to blurt it.

"It's like the most awful country song ever, huh, Doc?"

Casey lets up, because in the Heavenly light shining down in Branson, she can see glowing streams running down Mom's face.

Dr. Bailey touches his glasses, and holds so still, Casey and Nurse DeSanctis both say, "Oh no, he's frozen. We lost him." But then he looks up with a frown. "Don't stop the Zoom. It's okay. We're here. Casey, when did the rape occur? What was the date?"

"July 7."

"Dr. Bailey," Nurse DeSanctis steps forward when she speaks into her phone. "Patient presented nonresponsive with TBI. Patient was in a coma for five weeks, but her DOCS numbers were really strong, and in no time her Glasgow got up real high. She's been conscious here two weeks in observation, and we're just starting PT with the foot."

Long pause. At least Dr. Bailey is taking notes. That's hopeful.

"Her obstetrician is not on this call?"

"The virus, Dr. Bailey," Nurse DeSanctis says. "Nonattending. We're... I mean, bedside Caesareans, Doctor. We got caregivers in here from... well, Rhode Island."

Dr. Bailey nods. "When was her last menstruation?"

Everyone is quiet. Shanna peels back some documents on her clipboard. She leans toward Casey. "Dr. Bailey, Dr. Shanna Halston." Her voice is extra loud to get around the mask and over to the tablet. Casey extends it toward her. It's a joy to have that IV needle out of her hand and be able to hold and lift things. She wants her Martin. "We don't have a date on that, so we can only assume that date of injury/incidence is same as last menstruation."

Casey draws the tablet back to her stomach. What if a baby inside her now can hear all this? That flaps across her mind, like some vicious bat in one of Turin's songs. The nurse that Nurse-Prac DeSanctis replaced told Casey that since Casey was a selfish, Godless drug user, her baby was going to be too small to live. Casey raised hell and got her demoted to the virus ward. Casey tries to smile at Shanna with her eyes and a wrinkle of what nose you can see above a mask. Shanna's eyes, blank as the glass eyes of a doll, watch her.

"Casey." Dr. Bailey clears his throat. "I'm sorry to say we lost our case, *Planned Parenthood of St. Louis v. Parson*. An abortion in Missouri is a right that is offered to you, but not after eight weeks."

"Eight weeks?" Nurse DeSanctis blurts.

"In your case, and during this pandemic, I see obstacles." What Dr. Bailey says next sounds like he's reading from a card, but it's clear he's memorized it and has had to say it again and again. "In Missouri, a patient must receive state-directed counseling that includes information designed to discourage the patient from having the abortion, and then must wait 72 hours before the procedure is provided. Counseling must be provided in person and must take place before the 72-hour waiting period begins, and that counseling must be given by the doctor who will perform the abortion. You would have to be ambulanced up here. Hospitalized somewhere in St. Louis throughout those three days and nights."

"Where the Jesus are we? Mississippi?" Nurse DeSanctis says. "Oh, My God, Casey!"

Shanna rises from the chair. "Nurse DeSanctis, I warned you this was a huge mistake." Once Nurse DeSanctis has herself under control, Shanna leans toward the screen. Casey tilts the tablet so its mic catches Shanna better. "Dr. Bailey, I can't see moving her until late next week at the earliest. I'll get with neurology to make sure, but..."

Dr. Bailey removes his glasses and rubs his eyes. Casey imagines Tyndall scolding him for touching his face. "That puts all this well past eight weeks. From what Nurse DeSanctis said, your health is no longer threatened. The law is fetal heartbeat, no exception for rape."

"So... I would've been better off if I'd stayed in that coma?"

Everyone is silent. What crushes Casey is how Mom looks slumped on her stool, hid out in some cleaning closet in Branson, eyes dripping and wide, face pale, blasted, and drenched like at Dad's funeral.

"You know, Doc," Casey says. "I used to really love me a good country song."

39

"Amen. This all reads End Times to me," Marion says. Father has managed to do what Tyndall refused to teach him—cast the Victory Faith Triumphant Sunday broadcast from his phone to the big screen television. "I sense the thief in the night, Mother."

"Oh? Like that one on the TV with both fists in our checking account?"

Neither parent wears a mask, so Tyndall sits double-masked in a camp chair at an eight-foot remove from the sofa and her parents. The Reverend Jack Sprague from Australia has beamed in today. He's tallying up all the plagues and earthquakes and wars in an accent that Tyndall associates with steakhouses and diving cages plunged in the ocean to torment great white sharks. Despite counting all the plagues, Reverend Sprague has spent six minutes and twenty-seven seconds discounting the current virus and venting about elites, the United Nations, Liberty, Plandemics, and why the Faithful must gather in person this Christmas. How clear it is that global health bureaucrats target the Faithful, he says. Why else would the World Health Organization be so focused on the effects of singing? Reverend Sprague shuts his eyes in an ecstasy of defiance and motions to a substantial choir stacked in risers, hardly an inch between them. They burst into song. Tyndall notes aloud her concern that many of the women, mouths wide, lungs bellowing, are just like she is, plump-armed and heavy-breasted, likely long trapped gorging their fears at home. Now they've emerged bulging, ripely fattened for the virus and its devouring ventilators. There's a conspiracy.

Nora frowns at her. "Just now this revelation, Daughter?" She glares back at Marion. On the screen, the Facebook Live worship broadcast ends, and the next video promises a nearly naked nubile about to sing some hit. "A little news, please?" Nora begs.

After his fiddling, on comes the clip that's been running all weekend, America's Mayor in front of a landscaping company delivering a press conference about The Big Steal. Tyndall wonders what an appearance of the President's legal team might do for the profile of Merritt Organics, but then Devon and his father would lose their minds.

Marion lifts the remote and presses pause. "Mother, Daughter, I must speak with you. I have this morning read *DONALD J. TRUMP FOR PRESIDENT, INC. v. BROCKVAR, et al.*, that Pennsylvania filing that Giuliani's addressing." He's quiet for a bit. "I'm afraid it's a sham. Not a whisper of hard evidence. They are lying. They have lost the election. Watching the conduct of this, his lead counsel especially, I am further convinced. If this is perpetrated in courtrooms across the country, I will have to speak out."

Nora goes pale. Uproar followed Marion's resignation from the Missouri Supreme Court when he "spoke out" to expose a smoldering Gehenna of waste and corruption. Reporters camped with video cameras and bazooka-like zoom lenses in the cul-de-sac. Ben, bedraggled and spiraling, became a news item when he took the trash to the curb. The scandal of a crusading conservative evangelical Christian judge and his partying son fueled the Twitter rage-o-sphere and nearly took all the heat off the justices Marion was shaming. At last, the state auditor's hearings vindicated Marion. Everyone forgot Ben.

Mother bunches her fists on her knees. She's wearing a tennis skirt and polo—it's 75 outside. In mid-November. An ache blooms in Tyndall's heart. She never thought this way about how fouled up the weather has become, not until Devon. It's like she holds something of him inside her now. To her delight and distraction, she can think like him. Raw want bubbles up her neck and fires her cheeks. Thank Heaven for the masks.

"Really, Marion?" Mother asks. "Must we always be relevant?"

"Thou Shalt Not Bear False Witness," Marion says. "Mother, I gave my life to the Rule of Law and the Sanctity of the Courts."

"And we merely gave our lives to Our Lord Jesus Christ and to you, Marion Hastings."

Off they go.

Tyndall rises, goes to her bedroom, and fetches her day bag. At the alcove to the garage, she waits until they pause in their fighting to look at her.

She unlatches her mask. "I'm going with Devon to Branson to check on Casey." They have yet to deny her these trips. Casey Strong is a charitable work, and although Charity is not a Moral Duty at Victory Faith Triumphant, strangely Faith without Works is still dead.

"You know," she adds, "among my friends, among most of my classmates, I am one of the very few God has blessed with both a Mother and a Father still cohabitating. Yet yelling is how you two choose to spend your Sabbath. How neurotypical!"

Devon whirls the Charger down a cul-de-sac in a new subdivision southwest of town. Despite construction and roofers pounding on a Sunday, the two of them scramble to the backseat. Masks have the unintended benefit of eliminating the kissing, which she finds slobbery, nauseating, and unhygienic anyway. They paw fervently until he's spent, and she's flush and dizzy. They speed to Yummy King Donuts, defiantly open despite the raging pandemic. While he cleans up and changes underwear in the bathroom, she sits alone outside at a chilly, concrete table and inhales a chocolate cake donut and a Krissi Cold Foam. Nora would scream. When she returns to the car, she loosens the drawstrings on her scrubs, then thrills at fighting him off. Who knew just a flash of her flesh could have so much power? With his mask on, he's like a sex-crazed cicada.

"Is this love?" she asks. Hills thrust upward, and brown, furry valleys plunge. "Is this how this is supposed to be, Dip-Dip?"

"Nothing is how it's supposed to be right now." They enter a bridge that makes her feel they've launched off a ramp into the wild blue.

He glances at her, then grabs her thigh. She places her hand over his and traps it deep.

"I'm terrified," she says.

"Of what?"

"Sometimes of everything. I'm terrified the President lost, even though he's the worst liar about the virus ever. And now about the election, lying. I'm terrified of what I see at the hospital. I'm terrified we'll never get a vaccine, and I'll make you sick or Marion or Nora, or Casey. We're going to meet outside, right, in that crappy courtyard?"

"Yep, all masked up in that crappy courtyard in the metal chairs you hate."

"I'm terrified that we're not supposed to be together, because you're a Godless, tree-humping, communist socialist. And yet you let me do everything I want and say anything I want and be exactly who I want to be." She lets go of his hand and begins to punch his shoulder. "And you let me eat anything I want, and you hardly ever tell me to stop. If we were together all the time, we would need a tractor trailer to haul me to Branson."

"Stop. Hard to drive. Stop hitting."

She quits, and then tries a session of 4-7-8 breathing. His hand is still sunk deeply in her thigh, and that's steadying. On the sevens, the hold after the big inhale, his eyes are not on the road but on her chest. Somehow, that's also steadying. What's not steadying is that her belly brushes the back of his hand when she inhales. That's a surprise and infuriating. On the exhale, her mind fills with the taste and smell of the kettle chips they bought last time in Branson. She's instantly famished and even more upset. But she cannot take any more Quietarol—that will erase the upset but redouble the hunger.

"It's all a Satanic Conspiracy!" she shrieks.

His eyes move from her chest to her face, and then to the road. She can truly say anything, throw any kind of fit, and he'll still be right there. Inhaling four beats, she wants to pin him down and romp all over him—another conspiracy! Oh, why can't The Lord just leave her alone to do what she wants as much as she wants?

"Is this what it's supposed to be? Am I supposed to be terrified all the time?"

"Well, I am. So… we're together like that."

"Are we just together because we need each other?"

"How is that such a bad reason to be together?" he asks. "Especially if we admit it. I need you *and* I want you. I'm so grateful to you. And to your dad. It's like nothing in the whole world makes sense right now but you, Tyndall."

She runs her gaze up and down his wiry, compact body. His mask is an especially aggressive green. Ben used to paint that color on models of dive bombers. Outdoor work makes Devon muscular, even wizened. The sun and wind will hurt him soon—you can see that in the way the ravaged corners of his eyes pucker. But, oh, right now… she mutters so that she can see and taste the name of every single muscle along his exquisite shoulders.

Casey's not alone. Out in the gravel courtyard, there's a girl with her at the same wooden picnic table, both of them masks off, and they're singing. Casey has her Martin up against her pregnant belly, and her toothpick legs stretched out on a bench. This new girl, she's sitting in a tattered lawn chair that looks like it's been salvaged from Lake Taneycomo. She appears older, but maybe she's not. Her skin color Tyndall recognizes instantly. It's Ben's. Her shoulder bears a tattoo of the American flag but with black, blue, and no red, the Blue Lives cops flag. On her calf, a tat of a muscled arm and above it is tattooed OZARKS M–something in old-timey script. They're singing that slow song of Casey's about Spokane.

Devon and Tyndall hang back. Against Marion's advice, Casey's mom sold the house, her only asset, to pay off what hospital bills she could. Then she moved down here to these failed timeshares. They're arranged like a 1950s motor court, with cottages in a square. Casey's mom cleans them for rent and then works for the company that owns these cottages and tons of other timeshares plus motels and hotels, where people who labor in Branson for next to nothing are staying instead of the fancy vacationers who were supposed to fill them.

The girls don't stop singing, and they're good together. This new girl has a deep, heroin-scraped voice. Casey's voice flies an octave above it. Their duet transforms the Spokane song—it's now two women singing that they can't love. Tyndall grabs Devon by the waist and plants her mask against his ear. "If you clap when they stop, I'll knock you out."

Finally Casey plays the last part, then sets the guitar aside. She digs and finds her mask in the pocket of her sweats. Tyndall's heart sinks. The mask is the blue disposable kind, and it should've been disposed of long ago. The tattooed girl does not pull on a mask.

"Tyndall! Devon!" Casey exclaims. "This is Starlette Yarberry."

Starlette waves, and Tyndall notices a recent track in the crook of her freckled arm. Her hair is a blonde-orange mess like Casey's and her eyes are nearly the same blue. Eerily they could be twins, except that Casey is tiny. "Casey talks all the time about you two."

Tyndall slips her backpack off her shoulder. She extracts a box of disposable masks and extends the box to Starlette, who peers at it with half-lidded eyes. "Oh, no thank you, Babe. I don't need nothing like that. I can't go nowhere." She sticks her left leg out and points at a bulky, black bracelet above her Crocs. MODOC is stamped in white on the bracelet. She puts on a cowboy hat she kept hooked on the chair back. "I don't see nobody but Casey. Well mostly. Santy Claus better take this virus away with him, 'cause I only got one more month with this ankle anchor. Come January, you look out. I'm a'goin' wild."

She closes her eyes, raises both fists in the air, and sways to some slow music that no one else hears.

Casey snorts. "You hick. Put a mask on so they can sit down with us."

"Really?"

"Yes, please," Tyndall says, extending the box again.

Starlette pouts, then at last shrugs. Tyndall pulls one out of the box for her. Starlette thanks her. After she's looped it on, she looks Tyndall up and down.

"You're right, Casey, she is like a big ole Viking Princess. You know when I was at community college, taking history, Professor Hernando said one problem them Vikings suffered back then was they would fight like hell all summer, and then hole up and feast and guzzle all through the winter, and then come back out so fat." Starlette stares at Tyndall. There might be a smirk under her mask. Her exposed nose and her eyes wrinkle. "They'd have to just kill themselves to get back in any shape to fight again. Now that'll wear a body out. Ain't that right, Nurse Tyndall?"

Tyndall extends a new mask to Casey, who crumples the old and puts on the fresh one. But the mask sags—Casey's face is abnormally small like all the rest of her. Tyndall straddles the bench and sits behind her pal. She twists a knot into each loop to pull in slack. When Tyndall is finished, she pats Casey's shoulders. Casey sighs and collapses back against Tyndall as if her friend were a bean bag chair. Tyndall swoops her arms around Casey to steady her pregnant pal.

Starlette watches the two of them with her head cocked and a strange look in her eyes that Tyndall cannot parse. OZARKS MUSIC, that's what her calf tattoo says.

"Did Professor Hernando teach your class the leading cause of death during the times of the Vikings?" Tyndall asks.

"Swords and hexes I'm guessing," Starlette says. She's shielding her eyes and squinting up at Devon who has the sun bright behind him. His green mask bears the Merritt Organics logo and fits snugly. It must be almost eighty, and he's in shorts and a tee. Tyndall examines his quadriceps, biceps, and pectorals. She fears Starlette soaks in the same.

"The leading cause of death when the Vikings were active was intoxication. Becoming lost and dying of exposure while intoxicated. Attempting to befriend wolves and/or bears while intoxicated. Falling headfirst off the back of an ass while intoxicated," Tyndall says. "Addiction has long been our downfall."

Starlette's face and eyes disappear under the cowboy hat.

"Warned you," Casey says.

"Tell them what we're going to do once you have the baby," Starlette says.

"Starlette and I are going to start performing and take all my music back like Taylor Swift did."

"Especially Liberty Voodoos. That whole thing is crazy," Starlette adds. "When they find that asshole, I hope they Tase him till he sizzles."

"So, Starlette, are you related to a law enforcement officer, like Casey?" Devon asks. He touches his shoulder to indicate her Blue Lives tat.

She glances at her shoulder with drowsy eyes, as if she wants to make sure the ink is still there. "No. Dated a motorcycle cop. Cops are real sexy till you try and live with one."

Tyndall's jaw squirms as Casey's warm, sweaty hair digs into her chin and neck.

Casey pushes away. "Damn, it's hot out here," Casey says. "Let's all go in, yeah?"

"You know, you all go on and catch up," Starlette says. "I'm just going to smoke and enjoy this out here. I grew up in Fort Smith. So this ain't even started on hot."

"Stay where I can see you," Casey says. "No being alone till Meemaw gets home."

Devon helps Tyndall up, then they both help Casey up and Devon gets her guitar. The timeshare cabins have sliding glass back doors, and Tyndall wants this wide open even though the Strongs' cabin has lost its screen. Devon opens the front door, the few windows that will open, and all the doors in between while Tyndall explains airflow in vast detail, especially the case data of the South Korean woman in a restaurant. Devon catches her eye and makes a pistol shape with his index finger and thumb and blasts the pistol against his temple. That's their signal—change the subject or just hush.

Casey lowers herself to the threadbare couch, which was maybe blue once. She props her swollen feet on the coffee table and mashes a snowdrift of bills, even some letters between Marion and Bandcamp. The cottage is otherwise spotless from manic cleaning. Casey waves the Martin away when Devon offers it. She's focused on the courtyard where Starlette smokes, slouched in the lawn chair, cowboy hat pulled low.

Tyndall follows Casey's gaze. "Starlette is an abuser of opioids."

"Yeah? Well, so was I, Princess."

"You don't want her to be alone because she has heroin in her possession now, and you don't want her to use it alone in case it kills her." Tyndall watches her friend very closely. Going on five months pregnant. She glances at Devon. His hands are bunched at his waist, and his eyes bulge above the mask.

"Casey, don't you have enough to worry about?" Devon asks.

Casey's forehead turns scarlet. "I thought these visits were supposed to be a distraction from this shitstorm Mom and me are in?" Her bellybutton has already pooched outie now—she's so small, there's no space for a big baby to grow. "I have to have something next." She strokes her stomach. "This cannot be my only next. I'll die."

It suddenly turns oppressively hot and humid, and Tyndall regrets her insistence on airflow. This pandemic— every solution unleashes a new disaster! "You are doing the right thing for your new friend to watch her," she says. "But you are the wrong person to do it."

"Judge me? That's just great, Pal-O," Casey says. "Do you know how hard this is? I can't get free of this." She points at her swollen belly. "For wound-up crazy Jesus stuff that made it a state law that even a raped girl can't have a second chance. Batshit-crazy Jesus stuff like you and Nora and Marion have barfed at me all my life. Well, here I am like the Virgin Mary, stuck in a dump about to pop from a kid. And I didn't get to say, Yes, thanks, let me be the Handmaid of the Lord."

Devon grips Tyndall's shoulder, an escalation among their signals. "Easy now. I think we're all kind of hot and tired. When's your mom back, Casey?"

Casey mutters something.

"That's not so long off," Devon says. "Tyndall, why don't we..."

"Yes," Tyndall says. "But..." She swings her backpack onto her lap and unzips a pocket. She removes a dose of Narcan nasal spray. She clears a space among the bills and places the box on the coffee table. Then she takes hold of Devon's hand.

Casey lifts the box. "Why do you have this? Why'd you bring this?"

She stares at her friend. It's like a trick question—no answer will make anything better. And the truth may not help you at all, so Devon claims. In her mind she can see Devon's fingers shaped like a pistol. "I love you," Tyndall says. "You are my friend."

They are all quiet for a long while.

"I've hidden it from her sometimes. The smack. I can't take one more sad thing in my life." Casey rubs the heel of her palm against the bottoms of her eyes, one then the other. But then she stops and looks up at Tyndall. Casey holds her palms out as if they're filthy.

"You'll be okay," she says. "We've learned the virus is almost entirely airborne. You can wipe your eyes and mash your fingers in them all you want."

Casey rolls her eyes. "I want a hug, not a diagnosis, you big weirdo." When Tyndall reddens and shakes her head, Casey snorts.

"Bring me my headphones, please, before you go. Plug them in to that."

After Devon obliges, he leans into Casey and whispers something, a long something. Casey nods. Then she grips his arm and begins to weep again. With effort, Tyndall excuses herself for the bathroom and lets them be together.

Driving back through the darkening hills, they're quiet. At a long light, Tyndall strokes his hand. "You don't need to… we don't need to pull over and roll around, do we?"

"Too worried."

She nods. "You should be."

"Tyndall, you know she's right. She's stuck in that dingy place and forced to have a baby when she was raped." He takes a deep breath, his mask collapsing in shadowy hollows. "What you and your parents prayed for and voted for and wanted, well that's Casey now. She gets to live that. None of that is her fault, but now she will have a child to remind her every day that she was raped. A child she has to scrounge a sitter for if she's ever going to work, let alone pursue her dream and play music. A child who's going to need her love and doesn't deserve how hard that's going to be to give."

Tyndall makes the shape of a pistol with her thumb and index finger. "So, you wish she could've had an abortion instead?" When he nods, she presses her index finger tight against his temple. "Okay, give this a try. Imagine now that you're her little baby." She drops the hammer of her thumb.

40

Returning from Washington after storming the Capitol, the Sharpe brothers—two narrow-faced men who bankrupted the chain of rural convenience stores they inherited—smash in the windows of the Hastings home and hold Marion and Nora at gunpoint. Since the Sharpes failed to capture and hang the Vice President and Speaker of the House on January 6, this judge, neighbor, and locally prominent traitor to President Trump, Marion Hastings, will do. Marion convinces them to adjudicate their trial on the back porch. After all the sun is booming, and it's almost seventy degrees in mid-January in the Ozarks. Besides, his cul-de-sac property on South Eureka Terrace backs up to the wetland of God's Cove. After scouting and arguing, and then some posing with their captives and posting with their cell phones, the Sharpe brothers agree. The Sharpes gag Marion and Nora and, once outside, zip-tie them to their iron patio chairs. Pleased to giddy with themselves that the zip-ties have at last come in handy, the Brothers Sharpe commence to pontificate about The Storm, The Steal, and 1776 but pause when both brothers find their chins and necks bedazzled by red beads from range-finding laser scopes. A camouflaged FBI agent rises from the sluice of God's Cove, a stinking bog that mars the Hastings' backyard and is the origin of First Lake. The agent hand-signals to comrades. At first Marion doesn't see this sage and brushy nightmare rising. Nora does, though, and suffers a stroke. Mother arrives via ambulance with an FBI retinue of shining black SUVs at St. Martin's emergency room, which is still reeling from its December viral peak. She gains healthcare only through the interventions of both the Doctors Correy.

Frank Spanner yanks Tyndall from her shift in the doffing room, tells her to shed all her PPE and scrub out. In an administrative office on the top floor, Dr. Shanna Halston and a woman in a dark suit who claims she's with the FBI inform Tyndall of her family's role in American history, and of the unfortunate outcome for Nora. The Brothers Sharpe advocated violence for weeks on Bunker Hill—a far right, darkweb chat room. There these two brothers posted not only their journey as neo-revolutionaries, but also their intent to return home and deal "Jesse James-style" with Marion Hastings, the retired Missouri judge who had been on local television and talk radio eviscerating President Trump's narrative of a stolen election. The day after the Capitol Insurrection, the FBI contacted Marion, and he agreed to become a "silent target." Father could not inform Mother or Daughter of his patriotic choice.

Tyndall imagines she must appear fully unplugged, despite the mask hiding her dropped jaw. If ever there were a string of facts, a narration worthy of an open-mouthed zombie/mannequin stare, this is it.

"We need you to stay off social media. Do not speak with any reporters," the FBI agent says. Even indoors, she wears dark sunglasses, and Tyndall can see her own round, masked face and blonde hair in their giant lenses. "We'll handle this story."

In her head, Devon's voice says hush. But she cannot. The walls crawl with red, the walnut paneling pulsing like exposed muscle tissue. "You don't want me on social media for a reason. You don't have this under control."

The FBI agent remains as still and mum as a ventilated patient.

Shanna hasn't kept her flat therapist's face very well through this encounter. Four times, above her mask her pale eyebrows arch, and her eyes bulge as the agent speaks. "Tyndall, Saint Martin's Hospital doesn't know anything about all of that," she says. "But do understand what the hospital *is* doing. Your mother is receiving the best care possible."

"That is not true under prevailing conditions at this facility."

The FBI agent glances at Shanna. She then faces Tyndall. "Ms. Hastings, do you have any further questions of me at this time?"

"Yes. How long has it been since anyone has told me the truth about anything?"

Shanna's eyes pucker. "Agent, I believe we're finished here."

"We are not at all finished," Tyndall says. She stands. The agent reaches to touch something hidden beneath her coat and at her hip. "Agent is going to escort me to ICU, show me Mother, and then let me speak with Father. No debate."

The PPE required to enter ICU in the hastily sequestered stroke ward now feels extensive and at the same time flimsy. In short order Tyndall is hairnetted, gowned, bootied, and gloved. Nora blinks when a nurse tells her Tyndall has arrived. Wired and tubed in the ICU bed, Mother seems a sliver of herself. Her skin is so exposed and tender, its contours ripple like browned grass in a winter yard. She gropes for Tyndall's hand.

She whispers. "I couldn't stand. Even when those men dressed like our shrubs cut us free, I couldn't stand from my chair."

In the waiting room, a hunched Marion grips his head. His thick, silver hair is spiked and wild. When he looks up, there's no mistaking the sorrow and panic in his eyes. Tyndall marvels at how loud and readable her father's face is. When she approaches, Marion does not flinch. She sits beside him.

"I'll be lost without her," Marion cries, and then he melts into a sobbing wreck. When he's finished, he straightens up his shoulders and rubs his eyes with his thumbs. "I couldn't

tell her," he says. "I had no idea this would happen. Tyndall,
I believed the Sharpes and all of them to be buffoons. Rabble.
When the FBI said it wanted my help catching local knot-
heads..." He gives Tyndall a probing look. "What must you
think of me?"

"I was thinking of me," Tyndall says. "I hope one day
I love Devon Merritt as much as you love Nora right now.
I pray the Lord I'm able to show it, but in a much timelier
fashion than you have managed. The time you two have
wasted fighting rather than loving appalls me." She takes her
father's hand and squeezes it in both of hers. "Mother recog-
nized me, exhibited a controlled grip, and related significant
details of the adverse event. All positive signs post-infarc-
tion. We have a long road ahead. But the Lord loves you,
Marion Hastings. I know of no other way to explain how this
family survives you."

Holding hands, she and Devon watch the sunset over First
Lake, how the whole surface of its befouled four acres suddenly lights up rippling with orange, pink, and crimson, as
if an ember has come alight beneath the bare oaks. At just
the right moment in January the fire of sunset pours down
the filthy stream and advances like glowing lava on God's
Cove and the Hastings' house. Tyndall has finished telling
him the whole story of her day. The last news truck gurgles
up Lamonta. Something far more sensational and enraging
is happening elsewhere, and they must go film that since the
Sharpe Brothers are locked up for the night.

"So Casey wants me to come tomorrow to Branson, but
alone," Devon says.

"Why?"

"I don't know." He toggles around on his phone and hands
it to her. It plays a dark, chaotic TikTok with sound made terrible because a cell phone recorded it and now a cell phone
plays it. After a bit, she recognizes Casey's song, "Liberty

Voodoos." That's not Casey singing, but it sure looks like her, though taller. "That's Starlette. Remember her?" Devon asks. "It's in some bar on Lake of the Ozarks. Casey sent me this. She's furious."

"I'm sure she is." In the video, maskless revelers bounce and sway, packed indoors.

Devon takes his phone back, holds it like a mic, and imitates an announcer. "Coming to a ventilator near you: Kharma Bob and the Vectors with Starlette Yarberry, featuring their killer hit, 'Ivermectin Love Potion'."

"You're not funny. Focus! Why does Casey want you to come alone?"

He shakes his head. "I don't think I should."

On the drive, January hills bristle. Valleys sparkle with blue-white remnants of a snow that fell south of Springfield, but not north. The Earth lashes out—so many signs of its dying. And here he drives a Dodge Charger to Branson. His only other choice for this trip, the Dodge ProMaster, makes an even worse carbon offender. Up a long rising curve, a Tesla flies past them. He's run a business now just long enough to calculate the monthly obligation that slick, red, electric car represents. Probably leased, he tells himself.

Next to him, Tyndall rummages in her medical bag, a substantial fanny pack, double and triple checking. Casey can't afford prenatal care. So of course, Tyndall throws herself into a new role—obstetrics care nurse. She assumes a fresh identity and direction with obsessive passion but without attention to the results or the actual work required. It seems to him as if adopting the gear, the language, and the behaviors, that's enough for Tyndall.

"Am I just equipment in a role you're playing?"

She looks up at him, gray eyes placid above the blue mask. Impossible to read. "Tell me with your words what you mean."

"Did you say to yourself last fall, before the virus, 'Now I wish to become Girl with Boyfriend?' Was that a new role you chose, and I was just part of it, like scrubs or a mask?"

She sighs. "Dum-Dum." She resumes her rummaging in the medical bag. "Some time, way before September 2019, I said, Lord, look at Devon Merritt. Look at all of him that You, My God, made. From his heels to his cute bottom to the angel whorl at the crown of his dim head. And the Lord said, 'I have made you want him all for yourself.' But then I wondered, What must I do to deserve God's gift?" She holds a digital thermometer up to the winter sunlight, mashes its buttons, and squints at its display. "I have become convinced, though, that while there is nothing I can do to deserve God's gifts, there is so much I can do to squander them." She straightens her arms out and clenches her fists. It's an anxiety relieving exercise. "I wish sometimes that God made me worry less. He does that for some people. But for me, He makes me worry more. Or… the people who tell me what He is doing or will do, they make me worry more."

"That," he says, nodding. He waits on her through the fourth and final clench of her gesture. Since childhood he has known this habit and the relief it brings her. The depth of that knowledge floods his heart with a tenderness he did not believe possible. "You know, I think I no longer worry about what a life with you might be like. Loving you. I can imagine it more clearly after all this than anything in the future that I've ever tried thinking about."

She looks at him, then at the road ahead. She's quiet for so long, he becomes anxious. "Impressive in one so neurotypical." Did she mean to mutter that? "So… why does Casey want you to come alone?"

He shrugs.

"Nora suffered a stroke. She is, Praise God, stable and responsive. But my mother and father need me. Yet here I am hurrying to Branson. Because of Casey. It is always her show."

They make a plan. They'll park out of sight—the parking

lot to the timeshares is usually a litter of vehicles. He'll walk into the chalet alone. If at any point things go wrong, or when he gets Casey settled, he'll text Tyndall the word IN.

How can she ever get any of it back?

Casey strokes the impossible, tight globe of her stomach. The child raises a ripple across her gut, the motion like the fin of some shark devouring her insides.

In the laundry cabinet of the one bathroom, in the toy bank safe Dad gave her when she turned eight, a sandwich baggie frosts from the Chinese Roxies Starlette's cousin brought her. The blue-fogged plastic overwhelms the good talismans secreted in the safe—the bat nut seed pod; the Irish Rosary she stole in St. Louis; the necklace of bass picks from The Debs.

Through the sputter and fog of winter light, cars on 76 whisper sad conspiracies. Tourists have departed, so it's just the dregs like her and Mom out there, running errands on precious gas. How Mom hung on to the cleaning job she doesn't want to know, but a certain male supervisor has kept Mom out a lot lately. She comes home smelling of hotel liquor and stale cigarette smoke.

Some evenings Casey can weave a ballad of blame. It's all Turin's fault—he did this to me. It's the doctors and the drugs—how could they prescribe this poison? It's Starlette, who learned my songs and then took money to sing them the instant she ditched that ankle bracelet. But those verses paint her into a vicious Ozarks cliché, the ballad every washout sings. This mean old world done this to me. Rich, smart people far away have set the whole universe against me. Everybody's fault but mine. Her Martin stares at her, its astonished mouth wide open. Yesterday after she played it, her fingers smarted, it had been so long. From her seat on the floor, the battered gray walls of the chalet pitch and tilt. Maybe this is the bottom of the chute she first felt that night Turin busted into the Vulture's dressing room above the

Cedar Shake? But then every time in life she thinks she has reached bottom, the floor crumbles again. Please, God, there has to be a something next.

A car crunches in the gravel lot. Pretty soon, Devon's blond head changes the gray outside. His hair has grown and bounces like a helmet that's too big. He looks for a second like young Brian Jones before all the bad drugs and booze. A beautiful tough. She tries to tell herself that this feeling deep in her gut is the right one, the one she ignored, the one she put away, the one she was wrong about. He is the only something God has left for her.

The chalet always smells like bleach when you first open the door. Casey looks up at him from a blanket on the floor, her scrawny legs stuck out in a V, arms resting on her big belly. She's wearing a giant aqua blue Glendale tank top Tyndall gave her and bright red gym shorts in January when there's snow in the valleys. She extends both hands to him, wriggles her fingers. She doesn't have a mask on. He's not going to push that.

"Help me up?"

Her sandy hair is longer. In those sapphire eyes, pleading but happy to see him, in those merry freckles, he feels the old ache, and even the heartbreak again. He stoops, takes both her hands. She's such a weight and so stiff now, that when he finally gets her stood up, her momentum carries her into a sudden embrace with him.

She melts, draping her arms around his neck, hanging from him. She pushes herself against him awkwardly, her hard round middle crammed against his groin.

"Not going to cry," she says into his chest. "I promise."

When she backs away, her eyes are sopping.

"What's happened? Mom okay?"

"Mom's fine. Help me."

Helping her to the couch, he gets a flash of lifting his

mother, of piloting her wrecked body to the hospital bed they kept at home. Casey, though, is filled with a new life. But it's crushing and draining her, like a cancer. He can see that in the puffy skin around her eyes, the sorry hue of her cheeks. Her freckles seem the only healthy color, and they stand out against her sallow forearms. By March or April, she'll have to labor to deliver this baby, and it already seems too much.

She mashes a palm under both her eyes. He kneels to keep eye contact with her. The carpet against his knuckles is cold and greasy, yet it smells so powerfully of carpet cleaner, the scent almost vibrates. He's thinking and sensing like Tyndall—a smell that pulses. This amazes him, and he suddenly wants to share that with Casey. But he edits himself.

Casey grips the tattered seam on the sofa cushion and rocks a little. With her lips pursed, she lets out a tense breath. "Devon, everything is falling apart. I'm out of options."

"Hey, it may look crummy and dark right now, but…"

"Don't," she says. "Listen to me." She reaches out but can't touch him, her arms are too short. Things like that had always turned him on—anything that showed off how different, how compact and petite she is. He loved helping her reach things, lifting her, raising her to ride on his shoulders at rallies, football games. There was a local band she was so into—SALT, that was it—with the girl bassist who sang. He remembers Casey singing their songs, her abs pasted to the back of his head that summer, and the raw, beautiful force of her pipes in song against his neck and skull, his whole head throbbing with her power.

He edges forward on his knees, and she touches his cheek.

"This feels crazy. It sounds crazy. But maybe not?" she asks. Her breath silvers the frigid room.

He touches the back of her hand.

"Marry me. Marry me and get me the hell out of this. I was wrong. I was all wrong back then. I didn't realize what I had, what I could've had. Until you're out of Southern Hollow, you don't understand how hard the real world lives. Devon, this is terrible. It's taken everything." Her face reddens. Her eyes grow wet. "And now, in this shithole, I have to have a child. And I don't have anything to give it. And you know how I got it."

He's holding her hand tight to his face, gripping it. Imagine: she could be his again. For a second, he's frozen there. Could they be together once more, forever? But this way, her begging with everything lost, feels all wrong. "Casey, this is a rough patch. Bad luck. But you're way too talented to be stopped. Remember you dreamed…"

"Don't! There's no dreams. There's no music. There's this nightmare, and there's not this nightmare." She's yelling. She gets herself quiet. "And you're my savior out of it. You always were."

He could just say yes, I am. And I'll take you. I will make you mine.

But outside, in the icy Charger, Tyndall Hastings stares desperately at the phone, one hand gripping the medical bag, her heart pounding, ready to serve, ready to save, ready to love them both.

He removes her hand from his cheek. His shoulders slump with the weight of this. "Casey, I love Tyndall. She loves me. It's all different now."

"You can have Tyndall. We can be married, but you can have Tyndall." She's talking super fast, stretching an arm out as he backs away. "You can have me, you can have Tyndall, you can have anyone you want, as much as you want. Just get me out of this."

He stands up. The browned carpet melds with the raggedy couch and whirls into one soiled color. Casey's face pinches, desperate.

"I can't do it," he says at last. "I can't do that to Tyndall."

She bows her head, rocks a little. Her ears blaze fire red. Finally, she says, "Help me up. I have to go to the bathroom." She shambles like she's an eighty-year-old. At the bathroom door she pauses for a second. "I want you gone when I come out of here."

"There are so many other ways we can help, Casey."

"We?"

"Me and Tyndall."

She flips him the bird.

He starts to say more but stops himself.

She shuts the door and slams on a faucet at full force.

He's blinking at tears. The carpet and couch still tilt and roll under him. He pulls out his phone, imagines Tyndall waiting, staring at her phone.

—She's so upset.

—about what

—She asked me to marry her.

—i'll kill her you said no right

—She's in the bathroom. She wants me gone.

From the bathroom, there's a tremendous thud as if something heavy just hammered the vanity. Then there's a thump on the floor and against the door.

—IN IN IN

He's yanking the bathroom doorknob back and forth. Of all the sorry fixtures in this chalet, this damn knob and lock work great. Tyndall shoves him aside, then rears back. In three kicks the door cracks, splits, then buckles. Two more, and she has it open.

The faucet roars and steams. Casey is crumpled on the floor with her back to them. Tiny diamond shaped blue pills scatter all over the dark linoleum.

Here's her forever friend dying in her arms. Casey's lips and fingers turn blue just like Ben's did. Her Casey—who betrayed her and tried to take this amazing boy and steal this love she and Devon have built—her Casey showered with splinters and pills and overdosing in her arms. Oh, My Lord, how dare You force such a choice on me?

246

Time slips. She unzips the medical bag. In her haste, the Narcan flies out and rolls. She's yelling, but Devon has it, hands it to her.

Tried to take him away from her. Pupils vanish. Eyes all sapphire starlight now. If you want to leave so badly, why not just let you?

This is when I become who I am supposed to be.

From the foldaway bassinet Marion and Nora bought her, April Strong, four months old, red-haired, sapphire-eyed, concentrates on her mother's face. Casey strums the Martin and sings a Lucinda song about secrets. April arches her back and sticks her tongue out in that way that worries the doctors.

But right after the tremor, the baby's smile returns. April makes an O with her mouth and tiny lips, raises her chin, and follows Casey's lips with her eyes. Another O, a rocking of the chin in time, almost. Then a quarter note escapes, C. A real C, no mistaking it.

Staggered, Casey shifts into the first A-minor of the chorus. This is where she needs Starlette, that lower harmony. Dead Starlette, thief and witch. April tracks her mother's mouth and song with bulging eyes and devouring delight.

Outside the bedroom there's a thud against the wall— Tyndall wrestling with Devon. Both mother and baby jolt. "Just do it already," Casey shouts at them. Still strumming, she stares nose to nose with April and her wide eyes. April makes the O shape with her mouth, her fingers nipping Casey's lips and teeth. C comes out again, not in time, but still C. Her counselor insists that April may be difficult to love, a terrible reminder. But every hour, this little one helps her push aside the hollow ache and keep on. The tongue pokes out; the back arches. She exposed this poor baby to an opioid, and now to music.

"Oh, baby, I'm so sorry," Casey says.

A knock at the door jamb. Devon enters. He's pulling his shirt back on. "Some lady in a suit pulled up in this crazy SUV. There's two of them. One SUV behind her."

"Well, there's no drugs in here. They can kiss my teeny butt."

"Not black SUVs. Funky blue and funky orange. Never seen any like them before." Devon says. "Look, you do not want Tyndall answering your door."

She hands him the Martin just as the knock at the door comes. The peephole frames this young woman in a navy pantsuit with killer flared ankles. With her face and dampish brown hair, though, she looks a lot like Julien Baker, small, pale, and powerful. That would be a kick. These SUVs behind her are designed crazily, like weird cars in foreign films Turin forced her to watch. Springfield cops still have her Glock tagged somewhere in evidence. Sure would feel good right now to lift that in her hand.

She parts the door.

The woman smiles. "Hello. You are Casey Strong, please?" Her accent is French. She clutches a laptop against her slim waist, and then lifts the cuff of her suit coat to show Casey a KN95 mask strapped to her wrist. Casey waves it off, tells her we're all vaxxed, and asks her in. Relentless Tyndall made her get the vaccine.

In the other SUV, the metallic-blue one, a black-suited driver waits, sunglasses drilled on the grubby, dilapidated chalet next door. He's a meaty guy with a blue-stubbled chin. Probably not a cop. He and Julien Baker's twin share a nod as Casey lets her in the chalet.

"Merci." She makes a fist, and, after hesitating, Casey reciprocates and gives her a bump. "My name is Antoinette Guisson. I represent Grande Routière Automotive of France. We can sit somewhere, please?"

Casey leads her to the sparkling but cheap Formica and chrome table that separates the kitchen appliances and patch of linoleum from the exhausted carpet of the living room.

Antoinette takes the offered chair. "You have been some kind of a chore to locate," she says.

"Why you looking for me?"

Tyndall walks in with April clutched at her shoulder. Tyndall starts to say something, but Devon makes the pistol with his fingers and points at his temple.

Antoinette opens the laptop and jabs in a thumb drive. On the screen, a golden sand beach unfurls before a purling, iron ocean. An enormous shark's fin-shaped rock looms in the frothing water. A voice says something in French—noose ah von ah ten do. From the speakers erupt the thumping chords of Casey's Martin, then her voice, *Liberté, Liberté!* Two sparkling red SUVs, like the weird ones outside, plow across the beach. As the vehicles bound over the sand, gorgeous kids in the cabs glance at each other in ecstasy. Their supple, honey-colored skin is perfectly tight. The SUVs spin to face the camera with the rock and ocean behind them. A voice Casey recognizes from a movie trailer says, "The Annunciation, the new, hybrid-electric SUV from Grande Routière Automotive of France." Her Martin bangs to crescendo, and her voice rises to Liberty for all!

Antoinette closes the laptop. "So, that is your song, 'Liberty Poor Voodoos'?" she asks. She crosses her legs and cocks her head. It's like Julien Baker has a professional clone who goes to the office for her. "This music was offered to Grande Routière Automotive by a musician of your acquaintance."

"Yeah? Kind of a story behind that."

Antoinette nods. "That was our concern. Who owns what, who did what, who played what?" She rolls her small hand in the air. "As Brits say, Smells fishy. But the song. It captivates us. It speaks to the roadmap of our global brand."

"Her voice," Tyndall exclaims. "Fountain of Hollandaise sauce!"

Casey smacks Tyndall's hip. "Well, that's great. But it's all screwed up with him, and I can't even go out and perform it, 'cause..." She hooks a thumb over her shoulder at April blinking at them from Tyndall's arms.

"Well, as for him and his rights," Antoinette says. Reaching in her lapel pocket, she draws out a photo and hands it to Casey.

It's Patrick Turin, eyes shut, bloodied, bruised, head to one side, his Troubadour Molly shirt ripped and crimsoned. She squeezes the photograph so tightly, her thumb smarts.

"He slipped himself into Alsace somehow during the virus. In addition to trying to sell your song to our company, he double-crossed some Bulgarians. Sûreté says *heroine*." Antoinette watches her. "He cannot assert rights to your music anymore. Dead."

Tyndall leans over with April. Trembling, Casey sticks the picture up at them. "Oh, April," Tyndall says. "That's your awful daddy."

April lifts a fistful of Tyndall's blonde hair and waves goodbye with it.

Antoinette looks at the baby and then at Casey. She touches Casey's wrist. They all stay quiet, even April. Here's where just one pill would be grand to help a girl not care at all.

"So... there are papers for you to examine about what Grande Routière Automotive Company wishes to do with your song," she begins. "I leave them." Antoinette smooths a thick document flat to the tabletop. She pokes her prim finger at her phone number on the cover page. "Outside, I have a choice for you."

She shuffles out the door behind Antoinette, and Devon follows, and Tyndall with the baby. Shafts of yellow sun sear the gravel lot. Antoinette hands the laptop over to the blue-chinned driver. A few blinds and curtains across the court-yard pop open. Casey fidgets. In her bare feet and wearing her Daisy Dukes and jade kimono, she feels Tres Bransón.

"A gesture of good will to open," Antoinette says. "An aperitif. Grande Routière hopes you will choose Monaco Sunset Orange or Boutrouilles Surf Blue. Quickly, please. Jasper there, he is dying for a smoke, and I will not let him soil your options."

The blue-chinned driver snarls at Antoinette.

"You're giving me an SUV? An electric SUV?"

"Hybrid-electric." Antoinette waits a moment, then shrugs. "Darling. It is what we make. We want what you make as part of our brand narrative. You are under no obligation. Well, no written obligation." Antoinette winks. She opens her left hand, and in her palm are two key fobs. "Orange?" She dangles the blue key in her right hand. "Or blue?"

"So the one thing I ever wrote becomes a jingle to sell cars?"

"The first thing you ever wrote," Tyndall says.

"It's already been a lot of things to a lot of people, Casey. For free," Devon adds.

April blinks in the summer sunlight, and this makes her plump face seem serious.

Casey takes the orange key from Antoinette.

"Ah, good. It will match your hair. And Baby's." Antoinette climbs in the passenger seat with Jasper in the blue vehicle. "Title will be in the glove compartment," she hollers. Jasper backs up the humming blue car, and they crackle away across the gravel.

She holds the key fob for a bit and looks at her dazed pals. She presses the lock on the fob, and the Orange Annunciation makes an annoyed toot. Very French. April grins.

"Come here," Casey says, reaching out to Tyndall for the baby. She sways with April, makes the car toot again until the baby starts laughing and tapping her little ears.

Devon and Tyndall hold hands and ease closer. Devon admires the car. Tyndall watches the baby.

"So... is this a sellout?" Casey asks. She toots the lock, and April wriggles with joy.

Devon shrugs. "It's French and hybrid-electric, so how could it be?"

Tyndall groans. "The poot that comes from your mouth!" Tyndall's gray eyes scan the car, then look Casey up and down. "God filled you with songs. You can write them."

Casey takes her hand, the hand that saved her. That didn't have to, that maybe shouldn't have. The hand that saved April. Now, there's a song. "Yes." She joins their circle. "Yes, I can."

Acknowledgments

Thanks to Phillip Howerton and the staff at *Elder Mountain: A Journal of Ozarks Studies*, which published an excerpt, "Casey Strong," adapted from this work.

Thanks to Andy Havens, for letting me in the studio and tolerating all my watching and questions. Thanks to Larry Cataldo for reading this, and for agreeing to be Mitch's Dad.

Thanks to all those musicians in all our bands: Brian Hoover, Ben Asher, Derek Gover, Chris Lages, and especially to Erin Mayfield (sorry about the Fostex), Jeffrey Sweet, Jeff McNabb, Tony Nimmo, Peter Bender, Eric Robbins, Steve Rich, and my best man, Michael Fitzwater.

Thanks to all those musicians who taught me: Andy, Dan Palen, Robby Gilkerson, Bradley Rowe, Randolph Thomas, Sean Chapman, Gary Gebhart, and above all Dave Painter.

Thanks to Miranda Myrick for her time and counsel about the opioid crisis and its impact on Springfield.

Thanks to Andy, Justine Lines, Brad Barkley, Susan Perabo, and Randolph for reading and critiquing.

And, as ever, thanks to James Whitehead for the pistol to the temple.

About the Author

Born and reared in Springfield, Missouri, Steve Yates authored *The Legend of the Albino Farm: A Novel* (Unbridled Books), *Some Kinds of Love: Stories* (University of Massachusetts Press / Juniper Prize Winner), *Morkan's Quarry: A Novel* (Moon City Press), and its sequel *The Teeth of the Souls: A Novel* (Moon City Press). His novella, *Sandy and Wayne*, was chosen by New York Times-bestselling author Lauren Groff as the inaugural winner of the Knickerbocker Prize, published in a letter press edition by *Big Fiction* and later published as a standalone book by Dane Bahr at Dock Street Press, and continues in print from Southern Hollow Press. His fiction has been anthologized in such volumes as *The Literature of the Ozarks, Yonder Mountain: An Ozarks Anthology, These Storied Hills*, and lauded in *Best American Short Stories*. He is associate director / marketing director of University Press of Mississippi, a founding member of the Mississippi Book Festival, and was the founding book editor for the *Clarion-Ledger / Hattiesburg American* Mississippi Books Page. He lives in Flowood with his wife, Tammy.